RED SKY

RED SKY

A RAISA JORDAN THRILLER

CHRIS GOFF

CROOKED
LANE

NEW YORK

Published in the United States by Crooked Lane Books, an imprint of The Quick Brown Fox & Company LLC.

Crooked Lane Books and its logo are trademarks of The Quick Brown Fox & Company LLC.

Library of Congress Catalog-in-Publication data available upon request.

ISBN (hardcover): 978-1-68331-126-3
ISBN (ePub): 978-1-68331-127-0
ISBN (Kindle): 978-1-68331-128-7
ISBN (ePDF): 978-1-68331-129-4

Cover design by Craig Polizzotto
Book design by Jennifer Canzone

Printed in the United States.

www.crookedlanebooks.com

Crooked Lane Books
34 West 27th St., 10th Floor
New York, NY 10001

First edition: June 2017

10 9 8 7 6 5 4 3 2 1

FOR MARDEE, WHO INSPIRED ME TO
KEEP REACHING FOR THE BRASS RING,
AND FOR ADDIE, WHO WAS BOOTS ON
THE GROUND FOR RESEARCH

Chapter 1

Raisa Jordan stared out across the smoking debris, her gauze mask ineffective against the smell of burning flesh and jet fuel. Small fires still flared in the rubble of People's Republic Airline Flight 91, and the stench and devastation were overwhelming. Bodies littered the wreckage—some still strapped into seats, others scattered like rag dolls on the scorched earth, some in pieces. Fragments of the plane's fuselage along with luggage, computers, phones, books, blankets, pillows, and clothing were strewn across the ground for miles.

She shifted her gaze. The midsummer sun hung low on the horizon, partially obscured by clouds and smoke. Occasional rays of sunlight danced across the lush Ukrainian farm fields, touching the wreckage and highlighting colors in the otherwise scorched remains. Near the shell of the aircraft, a yellow handbag waited on the ground to be retrieved. Looking down, her gaze lit on an orange teddy bear propped against a tangle of twisted metal, as if set there by the hands of the child who had carried it on board.

Jordan's vision blurred. Her tears streamed unchecked.

"*Shcho ty tut robysh?*"

The sound of the voice jarred her, the words foreign. Getting a hold of herself, she wiped away her tears and turned to find a Ukrainian soldier standing behind her, a captain by his insignia.

"I'm sorry, I don't speak the language," she said. "English?"

"*Ni. Presa tut ne dopuskayet'sya.*"

1

Jordan got the gist. He didn't speak English, and he thought she was a member of the press. She pulled down her mask, then lifting the card and lanyard hanging around her neck showed him her credentials. "*Vy govorite po-russki?*" Do you speak Russian? "*Ya ne iz pressy. Ya zdes' po gosudarstvennym delam.*" I'm not press. I'm here on government business.

"*Da*," he said, switching languages. He gestured with his rifle for her to move closer and squinted at the badge. "What business does the U.S. Diplomatic Security Service have out here?"

"We had a DSS agent on board this flight, escorting a fugitive from Guangzhou back to the U.S. I've been sent here to help identify and recover the bodies."

While the captain spoke with his supervisor, Jordan contemplated the debris field. It reminded her of pictures of the crash of Malaysia Air Flight 17, with one obvious difference. That had been mayhem. This was organized chaos.

She knew it was bad when David Lory, the DSS regional security officer in Ukraine, sent a Marine contingent to intercept her at Kyiv Boryspil International Airport. She had escorted Mrs. Linwood, the Israeli Ambassador's wife, from Tel Aviv to participate in a week-long International Women's Leadership Alliance. Why the Alliance had chosen to host their annual July meeting in a country at war was anyone's guess, but the plan had suited Jordan. She was to accompany Mrs. Linwood to the Intercontinental Hotel, where the Ukrainians would take over security. Jordan was responsible to be present at night, but during the day, her hours were her own.

That is until Lory had thrown a wrench into the works. Five hours ago, he'd sent the Marines to the airport, along with orders for Jordan to rent a car and set off immediately for Hoholeve.

In route, she'd managed to wrangle a few more details on the assignment. There'd been a plane crash. PR Flight 91 had departed just after 7:00 AM from Guangzhou, China, headed for Krakow. Halfway through the flight, without so much as a mayday, the plane had gone down. Wreckage was strewn across six miles outside a small farming community roughly halfway between Kharkiv and Kyiv.

Within an hour of the crash, the Ukraine head of air accidents and incidents investigation had taken control, declaring himself the international investigation commander, or IIC. His job was to over-see the hundreds of people swarming the scene—everyone from avia-tion specialists and first responders to the military and media. On his watch, there would be no indelible photographs of dead bodies plastered on the Internet, no looting, and no destruction of evidence.

Growing impatient at being kept waiting so long, Jordan looked at the captain, who was still on comm. "Does he need me to go over there?"

The soldier turned his back to her.

Jordan gazed back at the wreckage, her agitation and impatience growing with the impending twilight. Her time in Kyiv was already limited, and Jordan could little afford the wait. Her original plan had been to head straight for the Kyiv Medical Institute of the Ukrai-nian Association of Folk Medicine that afternoon. More commonly known as UAFM, it was the school where Alena Petrenko insisted that she'd studied bioenergy healing under the tutelage of Jordan's father. If it turned out to be true, it was a part of his past Jordan knew nothing about, one that didn't jibe with what little she knew about her dad.

She didn't want to believe any of what she'd been told, but if she ever hoped to reconcile the image of her father with the man Alena Petrenko had known, she needed to verify facts. And she needed to do it quietly. Because—if what Alena Petrenko had told her was true—the revelation not only would bring down an icon but would likely end Jordan's career.

"What was the agent's name?" the captain asked, jarring her from her reverie.

"George McClasky."

The sixty-year-old man and forty-year veteran of the service was a DSS legend. Forced to retire from active duty at age fifty-seven, he still contracted part-time with the agency, helping with highly classified missions. Lory had texted her McClasky's most recent photo. Tall and beefy, with thinning gray hair, he was more than twice her age and left behind a wife and four kids. Jordan admired both his dedication and his tenacity. Theirs was a profession where the average agent was more like her—someone in their late twenties to early thirties and for the most part unattached. McClasky had not only maxed out his years of service but held onto a thirty-five-year marriage in a profession where relationships were often the first casualty of work.

"And the fugitive he accompanied?"

"Kia Zhen." A twenty-year-old Chinese American from San Francesco, suspected of gang affiliation and charged with espionage. No photos were currently available. No more specifics forthcoming.

"*Tak*." Signing off the radio, the captain waved her forward and nodded toward her credentials. "DSS Special Agent Raisa Jordan, it says you are an assistant regional security officer-I. What does the *I* stand for?"

"Investigations." Though mostly on paper and more often routine.

"Well, this one must wait until tomorrow." He gestured toward the road. "We are closing this area for the night. It will be open again at dawn. Check in with the IIC command center as you leave. Tell them I sent you. Tomorrow you must have an official sticker for your credentials or you won't be allowed back inside the barricade."

"I'm sorry, I didn't catch your last name."

"Melnyk."

"Thank you, Captain Melnyk." Jordan nodded at him, then turned back. Making a mental note to give the IIC a picture of McClasky for ID purposes, she cut south, walking along the backside of the fuselage as she made her way toward the car. She figured she might as well cover as much territory as she could while she was here.

Overhead the setting sun colored the clouds a deep red but provided little light on the ground. Heat from the smoldering wreckage kept the chill of the night air at bay. The fires made walking treacherous and slow. She wished now that she'd remembered to put on her duty belt with its flashlight.

Studying the mangled remains, it was hard to imagine what'd happened. While the Malaysia Air flight had been shot down by pro-Russian rebels, Hoholeve was hundreds of kilometers north and west of the war zone. The only logical conclusion to draw was that PR Flight 91 had experienced some type of equipment failure, causing the plane to break apart midair.

Near the skeleton of the plane's midsection, she nearly stumbled over the bodies of a man and woman, their arms entangled as if holding tightly to each other as they fell from the sky. Near them lay the body of a young woman wearing an oxygen mask.

Jordan fought back another onslaught of tears. The idea that there had been time for passengers and crew to contemplate their fate horrified her. She remembered being in a car accident at the age of sixteen and the fear that gripped her in the moments before the sedan had flipped. She could attest to the fact that in what you perceive to be your final moments, your life flashes before your eyes.

She paid more attention to the wreckage as she neared the end of the mangled piece of fuselage. According to the airline, McClasky and Zhen had been seated in row 30, seats A and C. The seating chart placed them aft of the wings in a two-seat configuration. Based on her assessment of the aircraft, she should be nearing their section of the plane. Still, the odds of finding either man in the gathering darkness were slim.

When the end of the burned-out hull came into view, Jordan picked up her pace. All she wanted right now was to be clear of the devastation. In a few more yards, she would reach a path to the left, leading to the road. Then for the second time that day, her plans were derailed. Near the end of the fuselage, in a row of seats that had landed upright on the ground, sat George McClasky and Kia Zhen. McClasky's neck was twisted at an unnatural angle, but otherwise he appeared unscathed. She would have recognized him anywhere. His eyes were open, and he seemed watchful of the prisoner shackled into the seat beside him.

Zhen's corpse was mangled, his face unrecognizable, the features sheared away, leaving a bloody pulp, and his body canted sharply to one side. One of his legs twisted behind the chair at an odd angle, and his right arm dangled from tendons, his fingers brushing earth darkened by his own blood.

"I found them," she blurted out, her shout triggering an echo that traveled downline from person to person and back again. A flashlight flared at the edge of the road near the press barricade, and Jordan immediately wished she'd stayed quiet. If she wanted to ensure the protection of any classified materials McClasky might be holding, the best thing to do was take them off his body. If she'd kept quiet, she would have had more time to search. Now all she had were seconds.

She knew he would carry documents allowing for Zhen's transport to the United States, along with his and Zhen's passports. But Lory had alluded to the fact that McClasky possessed some critical intel pertaining to national security—information he had refused to share with his boots on the ground in mainland China. From what she knew, he'd told his supervisor he couldn't trust the secured phones and Internet at the station or his contacts in Guangzhou. With the recent security breaches of U.S. corporations and government data by the Chinese, Jordan didn't blame him. All anyone could hope for now was that he'd written down what he'd heard rather than entrust it to memory.

Jordan did a quick glance around. The closest people to her were several Ukrainian soldiers and the pack of journalists they held at bay near the edge of the road. The nearest soldier was three, maybe four hundred yards away. She estimated she had sixty to seventy seconds before he could reach her.

Flipping open the agent's jacket, she checked McClasky's left inside chest pocket first and found two U.S. passports and the travel documents authorizing Zhen's extradition to the United States. In McClasky's right inside pocket, she discovered a small top security envelope addressed to the director of the Diplomatic Security Service.

"*Shcho ty robysh?*" the soldier yelled, running toward her from the road. He spoke in Ukrainian, but taken in context, his meaning was clear. He wanted to know what she was doing.

Holding up her left hand, she shook the passports and travel documents, while using her right hand to stuff the envelope under her waistband at the small of her back.

"I can identify these men," she explained in Russian.

The soldier started to reach for the papers when the captain she'd spoken to earlier pushed him aside and snatched the documents out of her hand. "What are you yelling about? I thought I told you to leave."

"These are the men I was searching for." She pointed to McClasky. "He's a diplomatic agent in possible possession of sensitive materials."

The envelope burned against her spine.

"I don't care. This area is closed," Captain Melnyk said. "You must come back tomorrow."

Jordan shook her head. "I can't leave this man's body unguarded."

A bit of an exaggeration given the area was under the protection of the IIC and Ukrainian military, but she preferred to arrange immediate transport if possible.

"There is no other alternative," the captain insisted.

Jordan stood her ground. "According to the Vienna Convention on Diplomatic Relations, the Ukraine may not detain a U.S. citizen protected by diplomatic immunity. Nor may it ever seize U.S. documents or property."

Captain Melnyk looked incredulous. "Your man is not being detained. He's dead."

"It doesn't matter. Let me make a call, and I can have a Marine detail here in one hour to transport him back to the U.S. embassy in Kyiv."

She doubted she would win the battle, but she had to try. She hadn't been able to check more than McClasky's jacket pockets.

Crossing her arms, Jordan waited for Melnyk to determine the next course of action. Night had closed in around them, and she was struck by how dark and chilly it had grown. A half-moon hung low in the western sky, its light weak behind heavy cloud cover. In the distance, warm light shone from the windows of a few farmhouses. There were no streetlamps or perimeter lights to illuminate the crash scene, only the glow from the fires burning in the wreckage.

The soldier who had first arrived leaned over and spoke to Melnyk. He in turn shook the paperwork in her face.

"Sergeant Hycha says when he arrived you were searching this man's pockets. What were you looking for?"

"As I explained, he's a DSS agent accompanying a fugitive. Any items in his possession are the property of the U.S. government."

An argument could also be made that the envelope tucked in her waistband should have been turned over to the Ukrainian soldiers, to be delivered to the U.S. State Department through official channels. Six months ago, it was protocol she would have followed, but a lot had happened since then.

Melnyk looked at the paperwork in his hands and then barked something to the sergeant in Ukrainian. As the NCO, or noncommissioned officer, trotted away, the captain turned back to Jordan. "I need to report to the IIC before we proceed further. Before I can do that, I need to find someone skilled in reading English."

Jordan was quick to volunteer. "I can read English, and I'd be happy to tell you what the paperwork says. It identifies *that* man as a fugitive of the United States." She pointed at Zhen. "He was being returned to the United States for prosecution of crimes against the country."

Melnyk stared at her for a moment, looked at the Chinese American's broken body, then stepped away and spoke into his radio. After what sounded like a heated discussion, he turned and barked orders to the soldiers still standing around. The men jumped into action, spreading two body bags on the ground.

"What's going on?" she asked. It looked like Melnyk might be preparing to release the bodies, which surprised her. Unless he was simply preparing to take them away.

Chapter 2

Vasyl Kozachenko listened to the rustling of leaves in the dense overhead tree canopy and considered what he'd just heard.

"You're joking," he finally said, balling a fist. "How is it possible for this to happen?" The bodies should have been destroyed. It should have taken weeks to identify them.

"I found it hard to believe myself," said Stas, the man on the other end of the phone. "What am I supposed to do now?"

"Intervene!" *Was it too much to ask*? Kozachenko paced the length of the truck. "You must prevent a transfer of the bodies to the Americans, at any cost. We have no way of knowing how much he knows and if he wrote it down. We can't afford to take chances."

"It's impossible, sir. They've sent someone here to investigate. A woman. She was caught rooting through the pockets of the dead agent, and now she insists on staying with the bodies until the transfer comes through."

"Did she find anything?"

"Only identification papers. But she insists McClasky could be carrying classified information."

"Use your authority, Stas. Pull this woman aside and question her. Find out what she knows."

"My hands are tied, sir. There is nothing I can do. Captain Melnyk has taken charge."

Kozachenko turned and continued pacing in the weak moonlight. He felt uneasy about this turn of events. In most cases, it would have taken weeks to locate and identify the crash victims. By then it wouldn't have mattered. Now if they couldn't prevent the Americans from repatriating the bodies, they would have no choice but to destroy the transport. "Who is this woman?"

"All I know is she's some DSS agent they sent out looking for the agent on board."

Kozachenko stopped walking and stared down at his boots. He expected the law enforcement arm of the U.S. government to send an agent, but this one had arrived too quickly. "Did you get her name?"

"*Nyet.*"

"What does she look like?"

"Tall, skinny, with dark eyes and dark-red hair. She looks like trouble to me."

"Well, find out who she is and how much she knows." Kozachenko lifted his head and found his men watching. He must have raised his voice.

Stas hesitated. "What should I do if they leave with the bodies?"

Kozachenko refused to consider failure a viable option. He hadn't worked his way up in the ranks by being a nice guy. Instead, one by one, he had crushed his adversaries. *It was as easy as killing bugs*, he thought, swatting a mosquito that had landed on his sleeve. He flicked it away. "Do your job, Stas. Call me back when you have more information."

"Da."

Kozachenko clicked off and cursed their luck. The plan required their convoy to travel at night and be in strike position one week from today. The way things were going, they might still be bivouacked in the Dykanka Regional Landscape Park for the next seven days.

Last night had gone flawlessly. During the Soviet era, the city of Kharkiv, Ukraine, had been the USSR's third-largest scientific and industrial city. More than half the people who lived there were pro-Russia, including the border guard. When they'd crossed into

Ukraine at Belgorod, they'd only needed to pay him seven thousand *hryvnias*, less than three hundred fifty dollars. Double the guard's average monthly salary, but half of what Kozachenko had expected to pay.

Once across the border, he and his men had made excellent time. Traveling the M roads, they had arrived outside of Dykanka before sunrise, found a secluded spot, and set up camp undetected. But that morning, everything went sour.

At 7:00 AM, the *pakhan*, his boss, had called to say the Chinese American had been arrested and was headed home on board People's Republic Flight 91. The pakhan's orders were clear. Kozachenko and his men were to shoot down the plane.

Firing the weapon had elevated his anxiety, but it'd also brought a sliver of satisfaction. At first, he feared detection. If they were caught, it would have derailed a plan that was years in the making. But given no other choice, he'd opted to look upon it as a test run—both the gun and his men had performed with precision. Afterward, with the weapon buttoned down under the tarp, he'd slept well. The likelihood of anyone ever realizing the plane had been blown out of the sky was slim. Even if they did, by the time they came looking, the gun would be well on its way to serving its true purpose.

"Is everything okay, Vasyl?"

Kozachenko looked up and watched as Anatoliy Barkov, his second-in-command, approached.

"Nyet," he replied, resting his elbows on the front fender of the truck. He explained what was happening on the ground in Hoholeve. "If they begin to transport the bodies to the morgue, we may be forced to fire the weapon again."

A look of concern crossed Barkov's face. "We can't do that."

Kozachenko frowned. He did not like being told what he could or couldn't do. He understood not wanting to fire the gun. The whole reason behind shooting down the aircraft was to keep the weapon secret. They'd taken a big risk firing it the first time. To shoot it a second time was tantamount to waving a red flag in front of a bull.

It only increased their chances of being discovered. But allowing the transfer of the two bodies to the U.S. authorities posed a much more immediate threat.

"It's better to act than do nothing," Kozachenko said.

"Of course, you're right, Vasyl. But physically, we cannot fire the gun."

"What are you saying?" Kozachenko stared at Barkov, who to his credit did not look away.

"When we fired the weapon, we discharged the compulsator. It must be recharged."

"Then do it, now!" Kozachenko knew the weapon required a specific level of electricity to operate, but he thought it had been handled.

"It's not that simple, Vasyl. Recharging the unit requires us to run the truck's engine. Our plan was to recharge it tonight while we drove."

Kozachenko looked around the small clearing. Allowing the truck to sit here and idle would make too much noise and use too much fuel. He felt a sharp pain in his belly and reached in his pocket for an antacid. "Then let's hope Stas can handle things on the ground."

"And if he can't?"

Kozachenko broke a chalky pill between his teeth and swallowed, following it up with a swig of water from his canteen. "Then we'll have to find another way to take care of the situation. Make no mistake, the Americans must not be allowed to claim those bodies."

Chapter 3

Jordan's legs ached from standing. According to Captain Melnyk, they were still waiting for word from the IIC on where to transport the bodies. It had now been over an hour, with nowhere to sit.

To stay warm and ease the tension in her muscles, she walked the crash site near McClasky and Zhen. In the light cast by the waning moon and the glow from the fires, she took a closer look at the fuselage. There was one section near the wing where it appeared something had punched inward, tearing the metal.

A missile?

Moving in for a closer look, she discovered pitting along the fuselage. In a number of places, she could see small metal fragments embedded in the body of the plane.

Shrapnel?

It seemed an unlikely placement for a hole caused by an engine explosion. Maybe the plane had struck something upon hitting the ground?

She called Melnyk over and pointed out what she'd found. He scoffed at her discovery.

"We might be a country at war, but we are four hundred kilometers away from the fighting. The crash was most likely caused by a mechanical failure, an engine exploding."

"Except this spot on the body of the aircraft would have been protected. Do you see how the metal breaks right here above the wing? I think it's possible this plane was shot down."

Melnyk dismissed her theory with a shake of his head. "Don't let your imagination run wild, Agent Jordan. We don't need you spreading rumors. This was a terrible accident, some sort of catastrophic failure, nothing more."

Jordan hoped he was right. It was up to the IIC and the aviation experts to determine the cause of the crash. A task that would likely take weeks—if not months—of investigation. Still, as she watched him walk away, she found it hard to shake the feeling that something was off.

Turning back to the hull, she snapped several pictures of the damage with her cell phone. Then, after making sure no one was watching, she pried a quarter-sized metal fragment from the fuselage and stuck it into her pocket. One fragment wasn't going to change the course of the investigation. She would run it past the lab rats at the embassy and see what they had to say.

A flash from the road caused her to snap her head up. Scanning the crowd, her gaze stopped on a tall, dark-haired man pressed up against the press barricade and snapping photos in her direction. Had he seen her take the fragment or was he just photographing the scene?

For the most part, she viewed journalists like hyenas—offensive and sneaky predators feasting on the sensationalism of a moment. Distanced by pen and lens, they inhabited a world of sound bites and photographs, capturing impressions that highlighted the most dramatic elements, which they manipulated for effect. Too many times the real story was lost or ignored, usurped by moments taken out of context and distorted by the reporter's own bias.

Squinting, she tried getting a better look at the man—an impossible task at this distance and in this light. Then, leaving Jordan with a sense of unease, he stepped back into the crush of reporters and vanished.

Jordan decided to look on the bright side. If it was hard for her to make out features in this light, even with a telephoto lens, the reverse should be true. The likelihood he captured a clear image of her from that distance was practically nil.

Walking back toward the bodies of McClasky and Zhen, Jordan stamped her feet against the night chill. In spite of the fires, a dampness permeated her bones. An aerosol can burst in the wreckage and she flinched, the explosion tweaking her already fried nerves. Her head pounded from breathing the fumes of the burning jet. All she wanted was for Sergeant Hycha to return so she could get out of here.

A few minutes more and she spotted the sergeant picking his way back through the crash site. Now maybe someone would tell her the plan.

The captain, who stood off to one side conferring with his team of soldiers, sauntered over when the sergeant drew near. "*Ya dumav, vy nikoly ne buly povertatysya.*"

"In Russian, please," Jordan reminded him.

"I said I thought he would never return." Melnyk snatched an 8½ x 11 manila sleeve out of the sergeant's hand. Opening the flap, he stuffed the transit paper and passports inside.

"The IIC had questions," Sergeant Hycha said in halting Russian. "He requests that someone accompany the woman to the morgue."

"The agent," Jordan corrected him. Her gaze ping-ponged between the two men. "I take it this means you're not releasing the bodies." They'd been waiting over forty minutes, and this wasn't what she wanted to hear, though admittedly it was what she expected.

Melnyk ignored her. "What else did the IIC say?"

"He thinks your solution for securing the documents is good."

Melnyk nodded and then handed the manila sleeve to Jordan. "Seal it and sign your name across the flap."

"Why is this necessary?" Jordan asked. "Why not just let me take the papers?"

This was exactly why she'd remained quiet about the envelope secured in her waistband. The sooner the director knew the contents of the communications, the faster the U.S. State Department could counter any potential security threats. Following protocol, it could take weeks.

Melnyk handed her a pen.

She chafed at the lack of verbal response but licked the manila sleeve, pressed it shut, and scrawled her name across the closure. "Now what?"

"Put it in the body bag," he said. "When it's zipped shut, I will secure the bag with a tie and sticker, which you will also initial, and then we'll transport the bodies to the police station morgue in Reshetylivka, where they'll be kept under guard until you submit the proper repatriation documentation."

"Why not save us all some work?" Jordan asked, again challenging the need for the extra steps. "Let me call in the Marines and have them transport the bodies back to the U.S. embassy in Kyiv. I promise, we'll fax you the paperwork in the morning."

"*Zarozumilyy amerykans'ka divchyna, vy povynni dumaty, shcho my idioty,*" Hycha said, posturing and stepping toward her.

Melnyk raised his hand and silenced his NCO. "The sergeant says the IIC requires proper documentation be on file in order to release the American bodies."

With the sentence construction similar to Russian and many of the words the same, Jordan was fairly certain the translation was more along the lines of "Arrogant American girl, you must think we are idiots."

"That's what I thought," she said, squatting down and placing the envelope on McClasky's chest. "I need to make a phone call and inform my boss of the plan."

The captain nodded. "Make it quick."

Jordan had held off calling Lory until she had a clear picture of how things would go. Now she stepped aside and dialed from her cell. Lory answered on the second ring, and she gave him the recap.

"Just go with it. They have their procedures, and this ensures any information McClasky has on him remains with the body."

"But sir—"

"Let's not make any waves. Accompany the bodies to the morgue, and then find a place to sleep. We'll deal with the rest tomorrow." He paused. "By the way, good job on finding our boy."

"Thank you, sir." She refrained from mentioning the envelope she had secured at her back. There were too many ears, too many people who might understand enough English to put two and two together.

By the time she hung up, the bodies were tagged and bagged, and the captain was ready for her to initial the seals. She'd barely finished scribbling the letters when the soldiers started hauling the bags toward a waiting military ambulance.

"Captain, I am to stay with McClasky. I'll need to leave my car here tonight and ride along."

"That's out of the question," he said. "Only authorized personnel are allowed in the ambulance."

"I have my orders."

He studied her a moment, then jerked his head toward the road. "You'll come with me."

Not exactly the outcome she'd been looking for.

"In that case, Captain, how about I just follow you in my own car?" It made more sense than coming back out here in the morning. She'd already found McClasky and Zhen. With any luck, the morgue would be closer to Kyiv.

"Nyet. I have my orders, too. The IIC wants you accompanied. You'll ride with me, and Sergeant Hycha will follow us with your car." Melnyk extended his hand. "Your keys."

"That really isn't necessary."

He flashed a thin smile. "The IIC wants to ensure your satisfaction in the treatment of your diplomatic immunity."

Captain Melnyk clearly had his orders, just as she had hers. Jordan looked toward the ambulance and watched the soldiers securing the back doors. It was time to concede the point.

"Fine," she said, digging the keys to the rental car out of her pants pocket and handing them to the captain. He tossed them to Sergeant Hycha and then gestured for her to go ahead of him toward the road. She started to move past him when Melnyk placed his hand on the small of her back.

Jordan tensed.

"What is this?" he demanded, moving his hand up. The envelope crackled against the flat of her spine.

"What's what?" she said, moving away.

Melnyk caught her arm. "Don't play with me."

Knowing she'd been caught, Jordan reached back and pulled out the envelope. "It's a letter."

"I told you she stole something off of the body." Hycha jabbed a finger into her face. "We should be arresting you."

"On what charges? This envelope is addressed to the director of the Diplomatic Security Service."

"You took it off your dead agent's body."

"Prove it. I just pulled it free of my belt." She didn't feel the least bit guilty about lying. Her job was to secure any papers McClasky carried, not to appease the Ukrainians. If she'd learned one thing from her experience in Israel, it was that sometimes, in order to achieve your goals, you had to be willing to scuff the lines.

Hycha's eyes narrowed. "It doesn't matter what you say. The letter is now in our custody and a matter for the IIC. Give it to me, Captain, and I will take it up to the command center."

"No!" Melnyk said, taking the envelope out of Jordan's hand. "We'll handle it like the other papers."

Jordan weighed the pros and cons of arguing. Sometimes it came down to knowing which battles to choose.

"But, sir." By the whine in his voice, Jordan could tell Melnyk's response wasn't to the sergeant's liking. "At least let me search her to see what else she has taken."

The fragment weighed heavily in Jordan's pocket. No doubt a search would unearth it, and then they'd be accusing her of tampering with the crime scene. Now seemed a good time to mount a defense.

"I have diplomatic immunity," she asserted. "Taking the letter and searching me are both in direct violation of the Vienna Convention."

"Move back, Sergeant Hycha." Melnyk stepped between the two of them, facing Jordan. "I admire your spunk, Agent, but I believe the sergeant is right. You're lying about this." He held the letter near her face. "I think this envelope holds the secrets of a dead man."

If only she could open it and find out. Jordan planted her hands on her hips. "It seems we've hit an impasse."

"Not really," he said, pointing her toward the makeshift parking area. "I'm going to allow you to add this to your courier's packet. After that, we'll follow the ambulance to the police station as planned."

She was relieved he wasn't going to make an international case of it and pull the IIC into the mix. Of course, there was no telling what the sergeant might do.

Climbing the embankment to the parking lot, she waited beside the ambulance while the soldiers unloaded McClasky's body. Melnyk broke the seal on the body bag and extracted the manila envelope, giving it to her along with a pen. Once the papers were secured and the body bag restowed, Jordan handed him back his pen.

"What now?" she asked.

"We take a ride in my *kozlik*." He gestured to an old UAZ-469—an older model, Soviet-style, light utility vehicle affectionately referred to as a "goat." "Courtesy of our former government."

Jordan hesitated. "Mind if I grab a few things out of my car?"

"It depends. Are you retrieving your luggage or a weapon?"

"Both." Her 9-mil and duty belt were locked in the glove box, and her bag was in the trunk. "I'd rather not leave them in someone else's possession. Is that a problem?" She waited for his reaction.

Melnyk shook his head and flashed a thin smile. "But make it quick."

"I'll need my keys."

"Sergeant Hycha, go with her."

The walk to her car was done in silence. Hycha mumbled under his breath, but there was no direct communication. Jordan was okay with that. Retrieving her duty belt and 9-mil from the glovebox, she picked up her go-bag and slung it over her shoulder.

"Any idea how far it is to the police station?" she asked, hoping he'd understand her Russian.

"104 kilometers."

She ran the calculations in her head. Well over an hour's drive.

"Any chance of finding a toilet before we leave?" She figured she had nothing to lose by asking. She'd already earned herself a military escort.

Hycha pointed to the ditch.

"One with some privacy?"

Hycha pointed to a lone oak several yards down the road.

"Of course, why didn't I think of that?" Jordan muttered, striking out for the tree. She swept her flashlight from side to side as she walked, avoiding the ruts and washboard and staring out at the fields on either side of the gravel road. On one side was total devastation. The land burned, scarred and littered with bodies. On the other side, the fields remained unscathed, covered with sunflowers waiting to greet the day.

It brought to mind other disaster stories—a fire roaring through a subdivision taking out some of the houses yet sparing others, or a tornado hopscotching through a neighborhood. Insurance agents dubbed them "natural disasters" or "acts of God," which begged the question, if there was a God, how did he choose who lived and who died? Why destroy some lives and leave others to continue on? With her flashlight beam lapping at the charred edges of the wreckage, Jordan found it hard to believe there was a master plan in all this.

Stepping off into the ditch to climb the small embankment, she could see the ambulance, the captain's UAZ, and Hycha leaning against the trunk of her rental, talking on the phone and watching her.

Once she ducked behind the tree, Jordan called Lory again. This time she told him about the envelope.

"Not much we can do now. I'll get the repatriation paperwork started. You stick with the bodies." He waited a beat, then added, "Nice try."

"It failed."

"No harm, no foul. We'll sort it all out tomorrow." He clicked off, and Jordan tucked her phone back into her jacket pocket, her hand brushing against metal.

The fragment. She needed to protect it somehow. Pulling a small plastic baggie out of her go-bag, she put the fragment inside, marked the outside of the sleeve, and tucked it into her toiletries pouch.

"What's taking so long?" Captain Melnyk yelled. "Let's go."

"Almost finished," Jordan shouted. Then dropping her pants, she squatted and peed.

Chapter 4

Lying prone on his sleep sack, fully dressed with his boots on, Kozachenko listened to an owl hooting in the distance. Animals rustled the underbrush. The murmur of the men talking around the campfire lulled him toward sleep.

He startled when his phone rang. It was Stas calling from Hoholeve. Kozachenko sat up. "Da."

"I have bad news. An envelope was found, but I could not get my hands on it." Stas relayed what had happened. "It will now go with the bodies by ambulance to the nearest police morgue, the one in Reshetylivka."

"When?"

"As soon as the DSS agent is finished relieving herself."

"Can you find a way to destroy it?"

"Nyet. There are too many soldiers around."

Kozachenko jumped to his feet, sprinted for the truck, and pulled a map out of the glove compartment. "What is the route the ambulance will take?"

"They'll drive through Myrhorod and south from there."

"And the DSS agent?" Kozachenko asked.

"The captain is escorting her to the morgue. Once the American embassy file the correct paperwork, the bodies and documents will be transferred to her. I've been ordered to follow behind them with her car."

23

"Did you find out who she is?" Not that it really mattered, but Kozachenko had a feeling about her.

"According to the rental agreement in the glovebox, her name is Raisa Jordan."

Apprehension stirred in Kozachenko's gut. He'd been right to worry.

"That's the name of the agent Ilya ran up against in Israel six months ago," he said. "Not only did she thwart his plans, but they pinned the bitch with a medal for her efforts. What the *fuck* is she doing here?"

"Are you sure it's the same person?"

Kozachenko found the man's ineptitude hard to stomach. At some point, Stas needed to step up and do something more than deliver bad news. "I doubt there are two DSS agents with her same name. The woman is dangerous. Don't underestimate her. Find out everything you can about her. If she knows what Zhen told McClasky, she's a liability."

"Do you want me to eliminate the problem?"

Kozachenko scoffed. "Are you telling me you can dispense with a U.S. government agent when you can't lay your hands on a simple envelope?"

Silence.

"It's as I thought." An Old Russian saying popped into Kozachenko's head: *God save us from our friends; from our enemies, we shall save ourselves.* "Not too worry, Stas. If the DSS agent proves herself an enemy, we will dispose of her. At the moment, we need to focus on stopping the transfer. Call me the minute the ambulance leaves."

They discussed the details of his plan, then Kozachenko pocketed his phone and rousted the brigade. The convoy consisted of ten men, two GAZ Tigr armored fighting vehicles, and a URAL-5323 with the mounted gun. While the men stowed the last of their gear, Kozachenko loaded two RPG-7s and grenades into the lead Tigr. Once that was done, he gathered them around the hood of the truck.

"Here's the situation." He filled them in on the details and then pointed to the map. "Our new mission is to take out the ambulance before it reaches the main highway. According to Stas, they will be driving this route." He traced his finger along the map. "We are going to intercept them seven kilometers short of Podil."

Barkov frowned. "Just how are we going to do this?"

"We have the same ground to cover as the ambulance. If we leave now, we'll have a head start. I'll take three men with me." Kozachenko pointed at Barkov. "You'll take one man and drive the truck. The remaining four men will bring up the rear. The truck and the tail vehicle will break off here at Shyshaky—"

"And go where?"

"Here." Kozachenko tapped a forested area on the map. "It's about thirty-nine kilometers west of here. There's a small road that crosses the Psel River. Once on the other side, I want you to pull off and disappear into the woods."

"That almost puts us in Hoholeve."

"What better place, Anatoliy?" Couldn't his second-in-command see the irony? "Once we take out the ambulance, they will be looking everywhere for us. They will throw up roadblocks, expecting us to flee. But they'll never suspect the enemy camps in their own backyard."

"It's too risky," Anatoliy said, shaking his head. Kozachenko's anger piqued. This was the second time Barkov had challenged him. Maybe it wasn't a perfect plan, but once they struck, there would be too many people looking for them to stay where they were or to push farther west, and a retreat was out of the question. Sychats'kyi Forest seemed like the safest place to be, and Kozachenko needed the entire brigade to be on board. He would not tolerate split loyalties.

"This is not a discussion, Anatoliy. The clock is ticking." Kozachenko waited to see what his second would do. Barkov hesitated momentarily and then assented with a slight dip of his head. "What will you do?"

"My men and I will intercept and neutralize the transport. Once we're clear, we'll double back and join up with the rest of you." Kozachenko looked around. "Now who wants to fight?"

All the men were eager, but in the end he selected the three who would go: Dudyk, Yolkin, and Vitaly. Dudyk was Ukrainian, and Yolkin spoke the language. If they were stopped for some reason, it would make it easier to talk their way out of trouble. He selected Vitaly because he was their best man on a rocket launcher.

No one argued with his logic. It took ten more minutes for the brigade to get on the road. Then at the intersection of H12 and Lenin Street, Kozachenko halted the convoy. From this vantage point, the two roadways stretched in four directions, shimmering like black silk ribbons in the wan moonlight. While the faint light made it easier for them to see, it also increased the chances of someone tracking their movement. But what choice did they have?

Straight ahead of them lay the small settlement of Dykanka, best known from stories of Ukrainian folklore written by the famous Russian writer Nikolai Gogol. Kozachenko had read his book about the area in secondary school. Creeping forward, he noted that there was less farmland now and more village. Thankfully, all the windows were dark, and there were no streetlamps or outside lights. The only sounds came from the occasional bark of a dog and the rumble of the convoy engines accompanied by a faint buzz from the power lines that snaked overhead.

Kozachenko kept his guard up as they rolled into the heart of Dykanka, but it appeared most of the residents were sleeping. He could only hope they'd drunk enough vodka to stay asleep while the brigade passed. They needed to get through the village without being detected.

The roads grew worse as they neared the center square. With the collapse of the Ukrainian economy had come the collapse of the infrastructure. Roadways and buildings crumbled. The GAZ's tires chattered against the cracked asphalt, and Kozachenko was forced to swerve around deep potholes pitting the road. Upon reaching the western outskirts, the sky darkened, and it started to drizzle.

Barkov grumbled over the radio. "This is all we need."

"Relax, Anatoliy. The clouds are a good thing. They block the spy satellites that the Ukrainians and Americans will eventually try to use to track us." Kozachenko reached out and flipped on the windshield wipers. "Be thankful for the small things working in our favor."

They were twelve kilometers beyond town when Stas called from Hoholeve. "The transport is leaving now."

"Good," Kozachenko said. "We'll be in position." Then he handed the phone to Yolkin. "Remove the SIM card, make sure the tracking device is disabled, and toss the phone."

He knew Stas was doing the same. Eventually someone was going to put two and two together, and there must be no way to make a connection between him and the convoy.

It took the convoy thirty minutes to reach the outskirts of Shyshaky. The town was double the size of Dykanka, and it also lay in darkness and quiet. On the far side of town, they parted company—Barkov and his men turning right onto Partyzanska Street and heading for the bridge that crossed the Psel River, Kozachenko and his men turning left and heading south. Thirty minutes later, Kozachenko reached the intersection of T1719, the road the military transport was traveling. Turning east, he drove approximately nine hundred meters before pulling off onto a small gravel road.

"Dudyk and Vitaly, get out here." Kozachenko tossed Dudyk a handheld radio while Vitaly unloaded one of the rocket launchers. "There are three vehicles coming: the ambulance, a UAZ escort, and a rental car driven by our man, Stas. He has instructions to hang back, but in case he can't, don't shoot him. Use the radio to signal when you see the ambulance, then punch out the UAZ behind it."

"And you?" Dudyk asked.

"Yolkin and I will take care of the ambulance. Once our mission is complete, either Stas will pick you up or Yolkin and I will double back."

"What if something goes wrong?"

"Nothing will."

"But if something does?" Dudyk said.

Kozachenko stared at the soldier. Was Barkov's pessimism rubbing off on him? "Then there's a wildlife refuge eight kilometers due west of here. Find the main entrance and stay out of sight. We'll come for you as soon as it's safe."

"And if we're spotted?"

"You speak the language, Dudyk. Use it."

Chapter 5

The UAZ bounced, and Jordan anchored herself with one hand on the seat and the other on the car's doorframe. Goats weren't known for their great suspension, but the ride had gotten rougher since leaving Bairak.

"Is it my imagination or is the road getting worse?" The taillights of the ambulance seemed to falter as it chattered down the stretch of highway ahead of them.

"It's worse. Between the rain and the constant abuse of heavy farming equipment, it's to be expected. Brace yourself." Melnyk swerved the UAZ to avoid another large pothole, the headlights illuminating a strip of pockmarked asphalt ahead.

Jordan tightened her seat belt. "Why doesn't the province repair it?"

"With what money?" The captain sounded bitter. "All Ukraine is crumbling. Most of the infrastructure is outdated or wearing out, while the taxes collected from the people for repairs disappear into the pockets of unscrupulous contractors or corrupt officials. Many of us had hoped to see changes after Yanukovych was ousted. Instead, we've had to deal with the invasion of Russia, increased expenses, and the loss of even more resources."

A low whistle began to overshadow his voice. Jordan recognized the sound, and the grip of fear held her paralyzed in her seat. She braced herself at the last moment.

29

A large explosion rocked the UAZ, slamming Jordan's shoulder against the window as her heart hit her throat. Instinctively she drew her shoulders around her ears and held on as the vehicle tilted onto two wheels before slamming back to the ground.

Melnyk slammed on the brakes. "What the fuck was that?"

An RPG? She shook off her daze and looked for the source of the explosion. In the passenger-side mirror, she saw a path of burning debris on the asphalt. Several hundred meters beyond that, two men dressed in camouflage stood at the edge of the road, reloading a man-based rocket launcher.

"Keep moving! We have incoming." Jordan estimated she and the captain had about thirty seconds to get out of range.

It took a beat or two for Melnyk to respond, but then he shifted gears and stomped on the accelerator. The UAZ shot forward, and he reached for the radio mic. "Hycha, come in."

Static.

He twisted the radio dial. "Hycha, command, we are under attack. I repeat, we are taking fire."

The words had barely escaped his mouth when a second explosion rocked the night. This time it was in front of them. Jordan whipped her head around in time to see the ambulance take a direct hit. Fire blazed from its undercarriage, while smoke and steam rose from the engine block. Again, Melnyk stepped on the brakes, while Jordan braced herself against the dashboard. The UAZ skidded to a stop.

She stared in disbelief as fire lapped up the sides of the transport vehicle and flirted with the windows. Then the realization that there were men inside set her in motion. Unclipping her seat belt, she reached for the door handle.

"Wait!" Melnyk's arm shot out, pinning her to the seat.

"Your men could still be alive."

"It's too late." He jerked his chin up as a large armored fighting vehicle emerged through the settling dust and pulled up near the ambulance. Two men wearing military camouflage jumped out, weapons drawn. At the front of the ambulance, they stopped, raised their rifles, and opened fire.

Jordan flinched as the first round punched through the glass, erasing any hope of the men's survival.

When the gunmen turned in their direction, Melnyk jammed the UAZ in reverse.

"Hold up!" Jordan said.

The men stood near the rear doors of the ambulance. Ignoring the growing fire, one of them yanked open the back doors and climbed inside.

Jordan scooted forward on the seat. *What the hell were they up to?*

A shot ricocheted off the UAZ's hood, forcing Jordon to duck. The soldier who had remained outside was advancing, strafing the front grill. Melnyk goosed the accelerator, and the goat bucked. Moving backward at high speed, he cranked the wheel. The goat swung around and then stalled crosswise in the road.

Jordan hit the floorboards as gunfire pounded the reinforced passenger-side door, shattering the window above her head. Sharp bits of glass rained down on her back and into her hair. More ammo rounds ripped through the thin metal of the detachable, hard-topped roof overhead and blew out the back window.

"Get us out of here!" she yelled.

"I'm trying." Hunkered behind the wheel, Melnyk tried turning the key. "Come on, come on!"

The gunfire ceased.

Jordan listened to the grinding of the starter and cautiously raised her head. The man in the ambulance exited holding something in his hand.

The envelope!

Jordan checked the location of the men with the RPG. They were eight hundred meters back, still out of range, while the two soldiers made a break for their armored fighting vehicle. No way was she going to let them get away with whatever intel was in that envelope. Not without trying to stop them.

Recognizing that her 9-mil was useless at this distance, she ripped the captain's rifle free of the dash mount and racked the gun. Bracing her arm on the window frame, she took aim and fired.

The man bringing up the rear screamed and clutched his right shoulder. His gun dropped from his hand, catching at the end of its sling and eliciting another yowl of pain. Jordan popped the latch on the passenger door. It might be too late to help the ambulance drivers, but she had a duty to try to retrieve that envelope.

"Let it go," Melnyk shouted, turning the key again. This time the UAZ growled to life. Hitting the accelerator, he swung the vehicle sharply to the left, knocking Jordan off balance and throwing her against the door.

Grabbing hold of the window frame, Jordan swung out over the road. Black asphalt moved under her feet as the UAZ jounced side to side on the pitted surface. Scrabbling for a better hold, she caught the rifle between her body and the door and wrapped her elbows over the window ledge. The toes of her shoes dragged on the road, and she pulled up her legs.

"Hey!"

Leaning sideways, Melnyk clamped a hand onto her belt and hauled her back in. "What are you doing? Are you trying to kill yourself?"

Jordan collapsed back against the seat and slapped down the door lock. She saw no benefit in pointing out that he was to blame for her near-death experience. Instead, she offered a thin smile and some bravado. "Can't a girl have any fun?"

"Just find us a way out of here."

Jordan glanced back. The soldiers had reached the AFV, and it was bearing down on them. With the UAZ quickly moving back into range of the RPG, time was of the essence.

Jordan scanned the area. Both sides of the road were lined with shallow ditches and dense forest. The headlights of the AFV flared in the rearview mirror. Ahead of them, one of the men raised the rocket launcher to his shoulder. Jordan's heart hammered against her ribs. In thirty seconds, she and the captain would be dead.

Then a slight change in the shadows on the right caught her eye. "There." She pointed. "Four meters ahead. There's an opening in the trees."

"I don't see it."

"Trust me. There's a cut in the trees." Unless it was just a trick of their headlights reflecting off the low cloud cover. But she couldn't afford to doubt herself.

Melnyk swerved left.

"Wrong way." Panic rose up, gripping her throat, until she realized he'd done it on purpose. Like a quarterback draws the opposition offside, the captain had faked. As the man with the RPG corrected slightly left, Melnyk yanked the wheel hard to the right.

The UAZ pitched up on two wheels before settling back down and rocketing toward the ditch. Time ticked by. The whistle of the incoming shell grew louder and faster. Jordan covered her ears and braced for impact.

The grenade struck, cratering the asphalt where they'd been just seconds earlier. The blast spewed forth a geyser of burning rocks and dirt. The rear end of the UAZ lifted, and the vehicle lurched forward. Visible in the soft light of the dashboard, the captain's face twisted in triumph.

Jordan watched him struggle to regain control of the UAZ. Speed carried them across a shallow ditch and sent them fishtailing along the cropped vegetation of a six-foot-wide access strip. Axle deep in the weeds, Melnyk slalomed through a row of protruding stumps. He met the challenge like a pro.

Twisting around in her seat, she could see one man trying to reload the rocket launcher while the other sprayed semiautomatic gunfire in their direction. There was no point in returning fire. No one could make a shot count from a moving vehicle at this distance—except maybe Batya Ganani. The Shin Bet agent had proven her skills during a case the women had worked together in Israel six months back. Too bad Batya wasn't here.

Light filtered through the blast haze as the AFV shot into view behind them.

"They're Russians," Jordan said.

"What?"

"You heard me. They're Russians. They're driving a new-model GAZ Tigr."

"That's impossible. Why would they be this far west?"

The inside light of the GAZ flashed on as the driver collected the two men with the RPG. In the passenger seat, Jordan spotted the wounded soldier sagging against the front passenger-side door. Now was the time to try to disable their vehicle.

"Slow down, Captain!" Snatching up the rifle, she rested her elbows on the back of the seat, braced the gun, and aimed for the GAZ's tires.

Her first shot glanced off the bulletproof glass of its right headlight. The driver backed up as Jordan fired off another round. By then the GAZ was too far back.

"Damn!"

Melnyk accelerated. "We're almost to the road."

"They've turned around." Jordan rose on her knees and watched the GAZ heading east, back toward the burning ambulance now completely engulfed in flames.

"Of course, they got what they came for," Melnyk said.

The documents.

"It doesn't make sense." Why would the Russians want those papers? If they were Chinese agents, she might understand.

"What was in the envelope?"

"How would I know? You saw it. The letter was sealed." His question made Jordan uncomfortable. It was clear Melnyk was right about what the men had been after, but *what had McClasky discovered*? Jordan turned back around. "The only way to know what was in there is to capture the bastards. Where does the road go?"

"It connects to the M03 in Podil."

"That's a major east-west highway. Can you get roadblocks set up? How many roads turn off between here and there?"

The captain snatched up the radio and tried reaching the command center.

Static.

"There are only two roads," he said. "Both go north, but they are very small."

They were nearing the edge of the farm field, and Jordan could see a narrow strip of gravel coming up fast. "Turn right."

"What if they're waiting for us?"

"They aren't." Jordan was sure of it. "They could have easily caught us back there. I'd lay odds they're looking for a doctor."

Melnyk turned right, skidding onto the gravel road and accelerating to the south. In six hundred meters, he swerved onto the Oblast road, tires squealing. At the intersection of M03 and T1720, he stopped.

"We need this road covered in both directions," he said, reaching for the radio again. "Hycha or command, come in!"

"Tak."

At last, a voice.

"Hycha? You're breaking up," Melnyk said. "We need the local police and military setting up roadblocks at all major intersections along the M03." He spoke in Ukrainian, describing the vehicle they were after and issuing orders. Jordan listened carefully, surprised by how much she understood or could extrapolate. "They have a five- to six-minute lead."

"Anything else?"

Melnyk looked over at Jordan. "Yes, one of the men is wounded. Notify the hospitals to be on guard."

"Consider it done."

Jordan could hear Hycha barking orders at someone in the background. He hadn't been behind them in the rental car as planned.

"Where are you now?" Melnyk asked. "You were supposed to be tailing us."

"I'm sorry, *Kapitan*. I stopped at IIC headquarters in Myrhorod. I'm just leaving now."

Melnyk's set jaw said what he thought of Hycha's answer. The sergeant would have some explaining to do.

"Meet us at the ambush site," Melnyk ordered. He swung the UAZ around in the road, and as he pulled forward, a speeding police car shot past with lights blazing. By the time they got back to the scene, several patrol cars were parked sideways, blocking the road. Barriers had been set up to keep back the locals and the press.

Melnyk maneuvered his way through the makeshift roadblock after an officer waved them through.

"It didn't take long for the press to get here," Jordan said, staring at the mob collected behind the barricades on the other side of the crime scene. There had to be ten or twenty reporters pressing in close and taking pictures of the charred remains of the ambulance.

"It never does with major disasters." Melnyk pulled onto the shoulder and turned off the UAZ. Jumping out, he signaled for Jordan to follow. After walking about ten feet, he stopped and pointed to marks on the road. "This is where the Russians blocked the road."

Flagging several skid marks on the asphalt, they continued looking for identifying marks. When Melnyk stopped to confer with several officers, Jordan kept on toward the burned-out hull.

The vehicle was blackened beyond recognition. The glass in the windows was gone, and the back door gaped open. Choosing her route carefully, Jordan worked her way along the side of the ambulance to the rear doors, peering inside. Charred remains were all that was left of McClasky and Zhen.

In direct conflict with the solemnity of the scene, refractions of light from the photographers' flashes pulsed through the holes in the panels, creating a strobe-light effect in the blackened interior, like a disco ball spinning in a party bus. From what she knew of McClasky, he would have enjoyed the dichotomy.

Sensing the captain approaching, she turned.

"We need something to collect the remains," she said, keeping her voice low. Even the whisper of breath might be enough to disturb the ashes. "Some way to protect them."

The captain radioed for someone to bring two bags.

Jordan looked up at the sky, fearing it might start to drizzle again. "You know that George McClasky was a hero." She glanced sideways at Melnyk. "No, you wouldn't, would you? How could you?"

McClasky had worked in the shadows during most of his service, but he was an inner-agency legend. In his forty years, he'd been credited with hunting down and bringing to justice over eighty-six fugitives or wanted terrorists and had overseen security details in some of the most dangerous places in the world. Examples of his exploits were still used for training, and stories about him were told wherever agents gathered with drinks in hand. He deserved better than to have it all end here, like this.

Another pop of light broke through her reverie, making her wince. Whoever had taken the photo was close. Shielding her eyes, she tried to pinpoint the source.

Across the road to the west, two hundred feet inside the press barrier, stood a tall man checking his camera. Was it the same man who had taken her picture in Hoholeve?

"Hey," she hollered, hoping to get him to raise his head. He responded by covering his face with his camera and snapping another picture.

Jordan considered flipping him the bird, but she didn't think the RSO, the regional security officer, would appreciate the image splashed across the newsfeeds. Instead, she held up her hand, blocking his shot of her face. He switched angles.

"Enough with the pictures," she said, moving toward him.

Lowering the camera, he nodded, dipping his head and moving away.

"Hold up. I want to talk to you."

Instead of stopping, he bolted, slipping back through the barrier and ducking into the crush of journalists. At Jordan's shout, one of the Ukrainian privates nearby made a grab for his sleeve, but the photographer dodged and disappeared into the crowd.

"*Vybachte*, ma'am." The private shrugged, and Jordan waved off his apology.

"You may find yourself on the front page tomorrow," Melnyk said after she'd made her way back. "Perhaps the picture of an American agent deep in thought will override one of the carnage."

Jordan scoffed. "You can't be serious." That was the last thing she wanted. Based on her experience with the media, the more gruesome or horrifying an image, the better. The *St. Petersburg Times* coverage of her father's murder came to mind. The picture of him facedown in a pool of blood on the front page, one of her and her mother graveside on the follow-up. Photos like that were career-makers, and today's images had the same sensational earmarks.

Another plane down and the destruction of a military ambulance transporting bodies from the scene screamed that the war in Ukraine still raged. Grisly photos were bound to find their way into the news and onto social media websites. She could only hope her face wasn't included in the barrage.

"Tell me something, Agent Jordan, and this time I'd like the truth. Why would the Russians care so much about what was in that envelope?"

It was a question she'd played over and over in her head. Zhen had known about something that happened in China, something McClasky was afraid to relay through normal channels. But she had no idea how that tied to the men who'd attacked the transport.

"The truth is I don't know."

"Would you tell me if you did?"

"No." Jordan didn't even need to think about the answer. McClasky had written "top secret" on the envelope. "Whatever was inside, McClasky had classified for a reason."

"Well, I'd like to know what was important enough for the Russians to shoot down a plane and kill two of my soldiers to suppress."

Jordan rocked back on her heels. Melnyk was suggesting the secrets McClasky knew were responsible for the downing of PR Flight 91. She tested the idea, her mind flashing on the small metal fragments she'd found embedded in the fuselage.

"What you're saying doesn't make sense."

"You suggested it yourself."

"That someone might have brought down the plane. But I never linked it to American intel."

"Do you know another reason?"

She scrambled to come up with an alternative theory—one that connected the plane and the transport vehicle. "Who else was on board the flight?"

"Mostly Poles headed home from holiday."

"We're any of them doing business in China?"

"Several, but from an early check, no one appears controversial. I imagine most were there purchasing products. Some were attending an IT conference."

"That could be the connection." Jordan knew she was grasping at straws.

Melnyk eyeballed her. "You must have some idea what your man was carrying."

Jordan met his gaze squarely. "All I know is that the letter originated in China and contained something McClasky learned in the course of picking up the prisoner."

The captain turned away, staring at the skeleton of the ambulance as if looking for answers there. "What did the fugitive do?"

"Kia Zhen? He was a computer whiz kid, a genius. For him to be charged with espionage, he must have hacked into some sensitive material, most likely by accident."

"How do you figure that?"

"He was just out of high school. He wasn't a spy."

"But if he'd come across something to trade . . ." Melnyk let the thought hang. "Why would China agree to extradite him back to the U.S.?"

Jordan had been wondering the same thing. Extradition between China and the United States was handled on a case-by-case basis. It was possible the extraction wasn't government sanctioned. "I don't really know the specifics."

"You don't seem to know much."

"I'm here on a 'need-to-know' basis." The excuse sounded lame, but she'd pried all she could out of Lory. He'd been less than forthcoming with details.

"Still, a Chinese American stealing government secrets—that's big."

Big enough for someone to justify shooting a plane out of the sky to keep him from talking? Jordan found herself feeling defensive. "The kid had ties with the Asian gangs. Do you have any of those in Ukraine?"

Melnyk shook his head. "No, but we have plenty of Russian mobsters. For the right kind of money, they would kill their own mothers."

Jordan's hands felt clammy. "Do you realize what you're suggesting?"

"That someone went to a lot of trouble to steal an envelope? Yes."

He was right, of course, but one thing bothered her. "How did they know it wasn't destroyed in the crash?"

She could almost see him churning the question in his head. When he didn't respond, she knew he'd drawn the same conclusion she had. "The timing's too perfect. Someone in Hoholeve, someone other than me, had to be looking for the envelope."

The captain's mouth twitched, but he still didn't speak.

"Who else was on scene when I discovered the bodies?" Jordan asked, filtering through her mental snapshots of the crash site. There must have been fifty people roaming around.

"A platoon of soldiers, the press, and a few local residents."

Any of whom might have supplied information to the attackers.

"We need to narrow it down," she said. "Plug the pipeline to our attackers and find them fast. If we locate the Russians and find the envelope, then maybe we'll learn the reason behind the attacks. We won't know what caused this until we have all the pieces."

"Maybe not, but we can make an educated guess."

Jordan felt a tightening in the pit of her stomach. Even the hint of a connection between the downed plane, the United States, and the destroyed ambulance would place the State Department in an untenable position. "We need to be careful what's said to the press."

Melnyk glanced over. "Are you asking me to be silent?"

"I'm asking you to be smart. There will be a lot of questions and a lot of people wanting answers. I just think it's better for both our governments if we have all the facts *before* any information is leaked. Imagine the damage it could do if the Ukrainians accused the Russians of downing the plane, and then it turns out we were wrong."

"He who licks knives will soon cut his tongue."

Was this Ukrainian adage encouraging one to hold one's tongue or to not tell a lie? Whatever it took for the captain to keep his mouth shut.

Chapter 6

Kozachenko listened as a chopper skimmed close to the tree canopy, whipping the overhead branches into a frenzy. Leaning against the hood of the GAZ Tigr, he held the phone to his chest and waited until the noise from the rustling leaves abated and then tried again. "Listen to me, Anatoliy. We've escaped detection, but we have a problem."

"Is everyone all right?"

Kozachenko stared through the windshield at the man slumped against the passenger door. "Yolkin's been shot. He was hit in the shoulder, and we can't stop the bleeding."

Dudyk and Vitaly were keeping pressure on the wound, but Yolkin was still losing blood. He also showed symptoms of shock. Kozachenko doubted he would make it. "We must find a doctor."

"You must come back here, Vasyl." The urgency in Barkov's voice puzzled Kozachenko.

"Nyet. Yolkin needs immediate medical care."

"Vasyl, you know better than anyone that one man is not worth risking the mission."

"Yolkin is crucial. We need him alive." Kozachenko felt his blood pressure spike and gripped the phone more tightly. Of all of them, Yolkin was the most knowledgeable about the workings of the gun. It's why he was chosen for this mission. Retrieving the envelope should have been easy. Having the Ukrainian and DSS agent go all

Rambo on them was the last thing Kozachenko'd suspected would happen.

"How badly is he hurt?" Barkov asked.

Yolkin's color was fading, and his breathing grew thready. "Badly," Kozachenko said. "We need to do something soon. He doesn't have much time."

"What's your location?"

Checking the GPS, Kozachenko rattled off their coordinates. They'd been forced onto the Oblast Road that ran north to Lyman Druhyi by police units heading toward them on the M03. The police response had been faster than expected. Just one more in a string of events that had gone wrong. Fortunately, the night and the cloud cover were still knocking out any hope of satellite surveillance.

Barkov snorted in disgust. "You picked a dead-end road, Vasyl."

"What?" Kozachenko reached inside the Tigr for the road map and flattened it against the hood. "What are you talking about?"

"There is no way out from where you are but to go back to the M03."

"*Derr'mo*!" Shit! Kozachenko cursed the turn of luck. "What fucking choice did we have? Just tell me where there is medical help in the area."

"There's a doctor at the end of the road, but if you go that way, you'll be trapped like a dog in a net."

Kozachenko studied Yolkin through the windshield. His skin had developed a sheen, and his lips were turning blue. "If I don't, Yolkin will be dead."

* * *

The doctor's office was located in Brateshky, a tiny village whose only reason for existence was a small train station that serviced the farmers in the area. The clinic sat directly across the street, set back from the road behind an ornate gate. Dark and empty, a sign on the door indicated the doctor lived next door.

It was one in the morning, and the town was asleep when Kozachenko pounded on the doctor's front door. A dog barked in the backyard, then a man dressed in flannel pajama bottoms and a T-shirt appeared in the hallway. He flipped on a light and pushed open the door.

"What is it?" he said, rubbing his eyes at the sight of the men. "Is something wrong?"

"Dr. Gura?"

"Yes."

Kozachenko grabbed his arm and pulled him down the front steps. "Our friend has been shot. We need you to fix him up."

The dog's barking grew more insistent, and the neighbor's dog joined in. A woman poked her head into the hall. "Gelb, is everything all right?"

"Tell your wife to shut the dog up and go back to bed," Dudyk ordered. He could feel the doctor start to shake.

"Everything's fine," the doctor called out. "There's been an accident. Nothing big, but I'm going to go to the clinic. Close the front door and tell Vadim to be quiet."

The light behind her silhouetted a shapely figure draped in a man's shirt. She reached for the door. "Do you need help?"

"No!" the husband answered. "Go back to sleep, *kohannja*."

She hesitated, spinning and revealing a pair of long, slender legs. One of the men blew out a sharp breath.

"Don't!" the doctor said. "Leave my wife alone and I will help you."

Kozachenko ordered Vitaly and Dudyk to guard positions near the front gate, then spurred the doctor toward the passenger side of the GAZ. Once the doctor had taken a look at Yolkin, Kozachenko leaned in. "Well?"

"This man needs to be in a hospital."

"We are here. What can you do?"

"The bullet has gone through, but it appears to have nicked the axillary artery. This man needs surgery."

"Then get started." Kozachenko signaled to his men. "We need to move Yolkin into the clinic."

Gura protested. "I cannot perform that type of surgical procedure. I don't have an operating room or the experience."

"I'm sure you'll do fine, Dr. Gura." Through his tone, Kozachenko conveyed that the doctor didn't have a choice.

Gura glanced between the men. "I'm guessing this wasn't a training accident."

Kozachenko offered a cold smile. "You're very astute."

Five minutes later, they had Yolkin laid out on a table in the clinic. Kozachenko posted Dudyk to watch the front door and ordered Vitaly to help with the procedure. The doctor gathered supplies. He was shaking his head, and sweat beaded on his forehead.

"We need to put him to sleep," Gura said. "But in his condition, too much anesthetic could kill him."

"He must not die," Kozachenko said. The consequences were implied.

Gura mopped his brow with his sleeve and signaled to Vitaly. "I'll need you to stand by his head. Make sure he keeps breathing. You." He pointed to Kozachenko. "While your man monitors the patient, I'll need you to assist me with the surgery. Once I cut open his arm, we won't have much time."

Yolkin moaned as Gura inserted an IV and thrashed about as the doctor cleaned the area where he planned to make the incision.

"You need to keep him still," Gura ordered, draping the shoulder with a sterile cloth. He picked up a syringe, drew some medicine, and reached for the buffalo cap on the IV line. "Are you ready?"

"Whenever you are," Kozachenko said.

Gura administered a small dose of medicine, waited for a short count, and then picked up a scalpel. Yolkin bucked as the knife sliced into his shoulder. Kozachenko felt his stomach flip as blood saturated the blue drape, and Yolkin let out a yowl.

"Keep him still."

Jumping partway onto the table, Kozachenko pinned Yolkin down. "Give him more anesthetic."

Gura tapped the IV line, and within seconds, Yolkin went limp.

Kozachenko slid off the table. Yolkin's face had gone slack, and his eyelids were half open. "Is he breathing?"

Vitaly put a finger under his nose. "Barely."

Gura signaled Kozachenko over. "We need to work quickly. I have no way of knowing how long he'll be out."

It didn't take long for the doctor to slice the shoulder and find the bleeder. Kozachenko assisted, while Dudyk and Vitaly did their best to avoid watching.

"Hand me that clamp."

Kozachenko passed over the instrument. The artery spurted blood like a whale's spout. Gura clamped it off below the bleed.

"Now hand me the needle and thread." He seemed to take pleasure in the men's discomfort. "For being such tough guys, you're all a bit squeamish."

Kozachenko's smile only went as far as his lips. "Shut up and sew."

Chapter 7

They placed McClasky's and Zhen's charred remains into new bags, which were tagged and transported to the police morgue in Reshetylivka along with the burned bodies of the ambulance driver and his fellow soldier. Jordan and Captain Melnyk accompanied the remains.

The police station was new, with shiny tile floors, rows of metal chairs, and an information desk restricting access to the elevators. Except for the investigators assigned to take their statements about the ambush, it was virtually deserted.

Having given their stories about what happened, they'd both been released. Now standing in the empty lobby, the captain handed Jordan her car keys.

"Hycha finally made it. Your car's outside in the car park."

"Thanks." Jordan could see the rental, parked in plain view under a streetlamp in the virtually empty parking lot. "Any news about the attackers?"

"Do you mean, have we found them?" Melnyk shook his head. "No. There's no trace."

"In other words, they've escaped, and we have no idea where they've gone or what they plan to do next."

"The theory is they headed east, back toward the Russian encampments. Once they travel outside of the Poltava Oblast, we have less coverage on the roads. The farther east they go, the more protection they have from Russian insurgents. Our chances of catching them now are slim."

"What about hospitals and medical centers?"

Melnyk bobbed his head. "We've checked with all of them. There have been no gunshot wounds." He grinned. "Perhaps your shot was superficial."

"Or maybe he died." Jordan was confident in her marksmanship abilities, proud to shoot like a girl. "They could have found help somewhere else. We know there's an insider feeding them information. What about a smaller clinic or a local doctor, even a veterinarian?"

The captain looked skeptical. "Rural doctors in Ukraine treat multiple villages. None of them is equipped to deal with a gunshot wound."

"That doesn't mean our guys wouldn't pay them a visit." Heading for the unmanned information desk, she came up with a phone book and thumbed through the pages. "Limiting our search to the Poltava Oblast should narrow it down some."

Melnyk reached over and took the book out of her hands. "The Poltava has a population of just over 1.5 million," he said, flipping quickly to the listing of physicians. "There are at least one hundred health care providers listed." His finger skimmed down one side of the book, then the other.

"Take out the dentists, the hospitals, and the big clinics."

"That leaves approximately twenty-five names."

Jordan handed him a pen. "Which ones are outside of the bigger cities?"

Melnyk ticked down the list, circling a name here and there. "These are worth trying, but not the others. Some are in areas too far north, or the cities are too large."

"That's good," Jordan said, trying to sound encouraging. "Go through the others."

Eventually he whittled the list down to five, and Jordan picked up the desk phone. "I'll dial, you talk."

The first three calls turned up nothing. One phone rolled over to an answering machine. They didn't leave a message. The other two woke up the doctors. Neither had been disturbed until the phone rang.

Melnyk banged down the handset. "This is a waste of time."

Jordan picked it up and dialed the next number. "Humor me. There are only two more names on the list."

This time a woman answered with the name of the clinic. Jordan held out the phone.

"*Vitayu? Chy mozhu ya dopomohty?*" the woman said when no one spoke. Jordan guessed she wanted to know who was there.

"Please?" Jordan said.

"*Vitayu?*" Hello. The woman sounded nervous.

Melnyk grabbed the phone out of Jordan's hand and launched into his script. Halfway through his spiel, his expression changed. Holding his hand over the mouthpiece, he said, "This is the wife of the doctor at the Brateshky Clinic, about twenty-three minutes from here. She says her husband was called out for an accident about an hour ago. She has offered to get dressed and walk over to the clinic."

"No!" Jordan violently shook her head. "That would be dangerous, for both her and her husband. Tell her to stay where she is until we get there. Give her my cell number." Jordan jotted it down in the margin of the yellow pages and shoved the book toward him. "Tell her to call back if the doctor returns, but by no means should she try to contact him." Jordan heard the faint bark of a dog in the background. It sent a shiver of fear along her spine. "Tell her to lock the doors."

It had taken Jordan and Melnyk thirty minutes to get to Brateshky. They'd arrived before the police. Stopping near the clinic gate, Jordan noticed there weren't any vehicles parked out front, but the lights were on, and the front door stood slightly ajar. Next door, a dog in the backyard had taken up the steady, rhythmic barking of an animal in distress.

"This doesn't look good," Jordan said, drawing her weapon as she climbed out of the UAZ. The captain, she noticed, also had a gun in his hand. The gate squeaked as she pushed it open.

Crossing the front yard together, protecting each other's backs, Jordan paid special attention to the shadows around the buildings. At the front door, she waited for Melnyk to position himself before going in. They cleared the reception and two exam rooms before they found them. The doctor and his wife seated on the floor of the back room near a metal procedural table littered with bloody surgical sponges. Both had been shot in the head, execution style.

"Clear," she said.

Melnyk squatted down and checked both victims for a pulse. "Both are dead. It's hard to tell how long."

"Long enough that we missed their killers." Jordan's gaze took in the scene, the bloodstained drapes with the blood still drying, the bloody surgical instruments in the sink. The door of the medicine cabinet on the far wall had been jimmied open. There was no way to know what shape the man she had shot was in. However, one thing was clear. The Russians were in the wind.

Chapter 8

The U.S. embassy was situated in the Podilskyi District of Kyiv, housed in a sprawling complex anchored by two modern four-story buildings. Lory's office was at the back of the property on the second floor with a view through the fence of Nyvky Park. Per orders, Jordan had come directly from Reshetylivka that morning without stopping at the Intercontinental Hotel. She was hot, filthy, and thirsty—not to mention tired. She'd stopped in the ladies' room only long enough to use the facilities and pull her hair back into a ponytail.

"Glad you're back." David Lory gestured for her to drop her go-bag near the door and waved her to a chair across the desk from him. He stood about her height—above average for a woman, short for a man. Small-boned and wiry, he wore a dark-blue suit and tie that made him look more like a diplomat than an agent. He also looked like he'd gotten a good night's sleep.

"Do you want something?" he asked. "Coffee? A Coke?"

Jordan perked up. "Diet?"

He hit the intercom button. "Mary, do you mind getting us a couple of Diet Cokes with ice?"

"Right away."

By the tone of her voice, Jordan imagined Mary minded, but would bring them anyway.

"So what happened out there?" Lory asked. "It's not even ten thirty AM and the media's having a shit storm. Mary's been fielding

51

calls all morning from reporters. They all want to know whether we had someone on board that flight carrying top secret information worth killing for. I'd like to get my hands on the person who started that rumor. Thank God no one can prove it."

Jordan wasn't sure who'd leaked the information. Melnyk? Hycha? Frankly, any number of people could have seen her with the envelope.

Shrugging out of her jacket, she leaned back in her chair. "I'm sorry to say, but *where there's smoke, there's fire.*"

"You think there may be some truth to it?"

"I do." She spent the next few minutes filling him in on the last twenty-four hours. As she was wrapping up, Mary arrived with the two glasses full of ice and two sodas. Lory barely acknowledged the woman, while Jordan thanked her profusely.

"Not a problem. It was my pleasure."

Jordan doubted it was.

"Thanks, Mary," Lory said, indicating she should shut the door. "Now where were we?"

"There isn't much more I can add," Jordan said. "Any chance you know what was in the envelope?"

Lory broke off eye contact. Not a good sign.

"The State Department is not aware that McClasky was in possession of any classified documents."

That was a different story than the one he'd given her yesterday morning.

"I saw the envelope, sir. And I distinctly remember you telling me McClasky had stumbled upon some intel he wouldn't share while still in country."

Lory looked back. "Whatever he had on him didn't go through official channels, so officially he was not carrying any top secret information for the U.S. The buzz is that he knew something he refused to talk about until he was out of China."

"Who's the source?"

"The political officer at the U.S. consulate in Guangzhou. He claims McClasky called and requested assistance in getting Zhen from the Ynagjiang Bureau of Public Security office to Guangzhou Baiyun International Airport. The PO complied, but McClasky wouldn't tell him anything." Lory tented and flexed his fingers. "Look, Jordan, for all I know, McClasky was carrying around his letter of resignation. The PO claimed something had spooked him. Maybe he just wanted out."

It surprised and ticked Jordan off that a man who had served the State Department well for forty years could be painted as some sort of loose cannon. "He wouldn't mark his resignation letter as top secret. If McClasky broke service protocol, he must have had good reason."

"I'm not so sure about that. From all reports, his handling of Zhen's extraction was a tad unorthodox."

"How so?"

Lory seemed to turn inward, and Jordan wondered if she'd pushed him too far. She took a sip of her Diet Coke and waited while he wrestled with how much to tell her. With luck, patience would tip the scale in her favor.

"Have you ever been to China, Agent Jordan?"

"No, sir."

"Well I have. It's crowded, smoggy, and difficult to know who you can trust." His eyes locked on hers. "When the DSS received information that Zhen had been located, McClasky went to pick him up. The local police liaison, a detective named Yang, tracked Zhen to an apartment in a suburb of Guangzhou. Unfortunately, before Detective Yang and McClasky could move in, Zhen was swept up in a drug crackdown."

"Wouldn't Yang have known about a sting operation?"

"You'd think. Unfortunately, it's not that easy. The Chinese don't always like to share." Lory started tapping his fingers on the desk. "In an effort to get a handle on their growing drug problem, they've instituted some of the harshest drug laws in the world. But since users and dealers exist in all levels of government, crackdowns are initiated with no warnings or interagency cooperation. Anyone caught trafficking in large quantities faces execution, while the local police have the authority to bypass the court system and send any casual users to compulsory drug rehabilitation centers. We're basically talking labor camps."

"Zhen was facing possible execution for the drug charges then?"

Lory nodded. "He must've figured he'd do better facing charges in the U.S. While McClasky worked with the police to get him released, Zhen was busy talking to the embassy. That's how the political officer at the consulate got involved. He was able to arrange for Zhen's release into U.S. custody, but by then the Triad had put a price on his head. McClasky had no choice but to load him onto the next plane out—Flight 91 to Krakow."

"So no one but McClasky knew what Zhen had to offer?"

"According to the political officer. But if you ask me, the PO is our resident spook, the CIA chief of station in Guangzhou. He made some quick arrangements. The powers that be were ready to grant Zhen immunity from prosecution and protect his family in exchange for what he knew. Unfortunately, no one ever had a chance to cash in."

Jordan ran the scenario. If the PO was CIA, his cover was working as a Foreign Service officer for the Department of State, and he would be trained in negotiating with foreign government agencies. In order to maintain his cover, he would have had to let DSS transport Zhen back to the States.

"Whatever Zhen knew, it must have been good for the CIA to be willing to barter for his freedom, in light of the fact he would be in the custody of Homeland Security."

"Tom Daugherty told me you were sharp."

It surprised Jordan to hear him say her boss had complimented her. It was no secret that she and Tel Aviv's RSO didn't always see eye to eye. She didn't know how to respond.

Lory reached for his drink. "Though, personally, I think Zhen would have disappeared once he was stateside."

"So what's our next step?"

"To call the director and write up the report." Lory glanced at his watch. "It's five thirty PM in Washington. Let's see if he's still in his office."

She sipped her Diet Coke while the call connected. Lory exchanged a few pleasantries and then brought his boss up to speed.

"About the envelope Agent Jordan claims to have seen . . ." Lory broke off, nodding his head to whatever the director was saying. "We're in total agreement." More head bobbing. "I'll have to get back to you on that."

Lory cast Jordan a pointed look, and she felt her bullshit meter go off. Why did she have the distinct impression he was about to ask her to lie? The last person who'd made that request was Dan Posner, her first RSO, and look at how that had turned out.

She thought back on that fated night. She and Dan staked out in the alley behind the Lebanese consulate waiting for a suspected terrorist to exit the garage. Posner'd reacted too quickly, gunning down the terrorist and killing the Lebanese consul's daughter while they were still on consulate grounds. She could still hear Posner asking her to back up his story and tell the FBI that the terrorist had shot first. She'd opted for the truth, and they'd both been reassigned—she to the embassy in Tel Aviv, while he'd been placed on the Secretary of State's protection detail.

"Yes, sir, we've expedited the process," Lory said. "Repatriation of the remains should happen in the next day or two." More head bobbing. "I'll do that, and I'll let you know when we're sending them home."

Jordan's apprehension grew when Lory cradled the receiver and said, "He's not happy."

She shrugged. From her perspective, there were no positives in this scenario. "Did you expect him to be?"

Lory smiled grimly. "He would like you to write out a full statement of what happened in the Poltava Oblast, from your arrival in

Hoholeve to the ambush to Brateshky." The RSO pulled a form out of his drawer and pushed it toward her. "He also asked me to remind you of the State Department's official position."

"Which is?" She figured she would sweat him a little.

"That George McClasky was *not* in possession of anything other than travel documents."

"Is he asking me to falsify my report?"

"Absolutely not. He just wants you to be sure of what you saw before you put it into record. Regardless, I intend to continue looking into the matter."

The last time she'd spoken up and told the truth, the director's nod had gone in her favor. That wouldn't be the case now. Lory had put her in a tough position. If she made reference to the envelope in her report, it couldn't be substantiated. Sure, Captain Melnyk, Sergeant Hycha, and a handful of soldiers could corroborate its existence, but not one of them could read English. She would be the lone dissenter on the official position, which would do nothing to further her career. On the flip side, if she omitted the envelope in her report and then it later turned up, she made the perfect scapegoat. It was a no-win situation.

The safe bet was to forsake her ethics and go with the crowd, but when had she ever played it safe?

"Do you have any questions for me?"

"No, sir, I understand the department's position."

"Good." He picked up his glass of soda. "The last thing the ambassador or the Ukrainian government needs right now is another diplomatic headache."

Based on the current state of affairs, she found it hard to disagree. Still, if the contents of that envelope had been worth downing a commercial passenger jet and ambushing a military transport, Jordan figured it merited a mention.

"Agent Lory, aren't you at all curious about the contents of that letter?" she asked.

"What letter?" Lory laughed at his joke. "Truthfully? Right now, I'm more interested in resolving this situation without ushering in another diplomatic ice age between the U.S. and the Russians. If we fan the rumors, governments will get testy, and threat levels will rise. Before you know it, everyone will have an interest. I'm telling you, we make one wrong move here, and the DSS comes out smelling like shit."

"Unless the rumors are right, in which case there's more to worry about."

"Especially if they're right." Lory set his glass down hard. "Then everyone will want to know how we let a lowlife like Zhen board a plane for home without first divesting him of his secrets. The truth is what would a scumbag like Zhen know anyway?" His temper seemed to cool slightly before he spoke again. "Don't misunderstand me, Jordan. I think it's great we captured the hacker. But I also believe it's coincidence, misfortune really, that caused this plane crash. And I think it's misinformation fed by the press that prompted the attack on the transport."

Jordan swirled the Diet Coke and ice chips left in her glass. "Except that I'm not misinformed, Agent Lory. I know what happened out there, and trust me, those men came for the envelope."

"I wish I had your idealism and lack of cynicism." He gazed off as though remembering a different time and then looked her square in the eye. "I only wish your appreciation for the delicacy of the situation was as strong as your sense of righteousness. Right now my bosses, both the director and the ambassador, feel it makes sense to wait until the IIC investigation is complete before we go substantiating any claims or releasing any information. Everything we've talked about stays in this room. We can't afford to have anyone going off half-cocked."

The exchange left a bitter taste in her mouth that had nothing to do with her flat soda. "I understand."

"Good. I'm glad you're on board." Lory leaned back in his chair. "You know, what you accomplished in Israel was remarkable, especially for a rookie. The brass has its eye on you." He jerked his head at the paper on the desk. "Now what's your gut telling you?"

She stared at him for a moment, trying to put her thoughts into words. Finally she picked up the incident report form. "To quote the late, great Flannery O'Conner, *The truth does not change according to our ability to stomach it.*"

Lory's smile froze in place. "You're going to document the envelope, aren't you?"

"You can always classify the information," she said, knowing it was not the outcome he'd expected. It put the ball back in his court. If he censored her report and the rumors proved true, his name would be the one people dragged through the mud.

"Think it through, Jordan. Do you like your job?"

"Is that a threat?"

"That's not my call."

She sat there awkwardly staring him down. Finally he stood up and showed her to the door. "You can finish writing your report in the waiting area, Jordan. Just leave it with Mary."

"I'd be happy to track down the envelope, sir."

"I think you've done enough." He paused, and then as an afterthought added, "I'll be sure and let your RSO know how much we appreciated your help."

She nodded at the closing door, knowing it was more likely he'd give Daugherty an earful, which he would pass along.

Sitting down on a cushioned chair in the waiting area, Jordan finished her report, fleshing out as many details as she could remember in addition to the main event. She stopped at the point where she found the bodies.

Lory's question ping-ponged around in her head. Yes, she liked her job. What wasn't to like about it? As an ARSO in Tel Aviv, her job was backing up the regional security officer in conducting criminal investigations of passport and visa fraud and keeping an eye out for travelers with criminal histories or terrorist connections; in protecting U.S. diplomatic facilities, personnel, and information; and by serving as a law enforcement liaison to Israel. Then in the last six months, she'd taken some additional training and earned a new job classification: assistant regional security officer-I.

Officially the *I* stood for investigations. Mostly she worked the same details, only now she was trained to assist in tracking down and apprehending U.S. citizens wanted for serious crimes back home or help in the apprehension of U.S. citizens committing crimes on foreign soil. On rarer occasions, she pulled a protective detail, like traveling to Kyiv with the ambassador's wife.

Jordan had requested this assignment. Had she known it would turn out like this, she might not have come.

Refusing to be intimidated by the director and Lory, she wrote down her observations, including her concerns about the hole in the fuselage, the envelope, and the ambush. Something bad had happened out there. She wished she could shake the feeling that things were just heating up.

Jordan signed the report. Then she remembered the fragment. Retrieving it from the toiletry case in her go-bag, she held the evidence bag up to the light. She still wanted the piece tested. She had no idea what she expected to find, but she had a gut feeling that an analysis of the metal might offer a clue to its origin and from there the cause of the crash.

"RSO Lory asked me to leave this with you." She handed the woman the report and one of her business cards. "Thanks for taking care of the filing."

"Not a problem."

Jordan guessed that wasn't true and that she'd probably just added to Mary's workload.

"Just one more thing."

Mary looked up, and Jordan realized for the first time that the woman was not much older than herself. Her roots showed she'd dyed her hair an ash blonde, which added age, but her skin was smooth and wrinkle-free. "Shoot."

"I need to have this analyzed." Jordan held up the fragment. "Can you point me toward the lab?"

Mary opened up one of her desk's side drawers, pulled out a form, and scribbled her name on the signature line. "Take the elevator to the basement and follow the signs. Give this to the tech," she said, handing Jordan the form. "He'll send me the results, and I'll let you know when they come in."

* * *

The forensic lab occupied a corner of the basement. If staff needed crime scene materials analyzed, such as fingerprints or photo identifications, this was the place. Pushing through a set of double doors, Jordan found herself standing in front of a long Formica-topped counter. A tech in a white lab coat with horned-rimmed glasses and spiky hair was the only one present. Tall and thin, he sauntered over and leaned against the counter in a manner he must have intended to be attractive.

"What can I do for you?" he asked, eyeballing her from head to toe.

Jordan held out the fragment. "I need this analyzed yesterday."

"That's my specialty. Do you have a form?"

She handed him the paper Mary had given her. He took a quick look and handed it back. "You need to finish filling it out. Don't forget to leave your contact numbers, both your office and personal cell."

"The results should be sent to Mary in RSO Lory's office."

The tech looked disappointed. "Too bad. I wouldn't mind delivering them personally."

Jordan pursed her lips and focused on filling out the request. She'd gotten used to the come-ons, always being the new girl in town. The last thing she wanted to do was encourage him. Still, having an ally at the embassy couldn't hurt. She smiled and handed back the form. "You know, I didn't catch your name."

"Henry."

"I'm Rae. I did put my cell number down. I'd like to know what you discover. Maybe when you're done with your preliminary analysis you could give me a call?"

Henry perked up. "Really? I mean, you got it!"

Chapter 9

The Intercontinental Hotel occupied a small triangle of land on the corner of Rylskyi Lane and Volodymyrska Street. The lavish eleven-story guesthouse occupied a spot across the square from St. Michael's Golden-Domed Monastery. It boasted a five-star classification and luxury accommodations that—according to its literature—were "designed to satisfy the most pretentious guest." Upon seeing her room, Jordan bought into the propaganda.

Mrs. Linwood had booked herself into the Royal Suite with a connecting executive room for Jordan. Hers was a third of the size with no free minibar, but the room came with a large king-sized bed, a soaker tub, full use of the Club Intercontinental, and floor-to-ceiling windows that offered stunning views of the city. The weather had cleared, and the sun reflected brightly off the golden domes of the cathedrals.

The first thing Jordan wanted was a shower. After doing her best to scrub the stink of the crash site off her skin, she drew a fresh tub of water and tried soaking away the memories. Images of the burning wreckage, the shattered bodies, and the car explosion had become rooted in her mind. She couldn't shake the thought that in spite of all the devastation that had occurred, there was ultimately a bigger price to be exacted.

If only she could figure out the end game.

A half hour later, she toweled off and reverified the duty schedule. She had four hours before she needed to report. That gave her plenty of time to pay a visit to the Kyiv Medical University of UAFM. It was the school where Jordan's father had allegedly studied and taught prior to playing goalie for the Russian National Hockey Team. It was also where he'd allegedly met Ilya Brodsky and been recruited as a KGB spy. *Allegedly.*

Just the thought of Brodsky caused her stomach to tighten and her insides to crawl. She had blocked all memories of the man until their paths had crossed in Israel. A former Russian soldier, he'd emigrated to Tel Aviv after her father's death, where he'd reinvented himself as a Shin Bet colonel. Their meeting hadn't been friendly.

Since then, she couldn't shake the childhood memories where he played a role. The times at her home, out for dinners, at the hockey rink. She remembered her father encouraging her to call him *dyadya*, uncle, as one sometimes did with close family friends. She remembered Brodsky drank too much, his icy-blue eyes, and how her mother always seemed fearful when he was around. And then there was the endless loop of him threatening her father just two nights before he'd died.

Jordan exited the Intercontinental and headed south. UAFM was located twenty-five minutes away and a straight shot down Volodymyrska Street. As she walked along, she tried imagining what life had been like when her father had lived in this city. She imagined a more stark and monochromatic world. Long before his birth, the Soviets had banned all manifestations of Ukrainian patriotism, while today the colors of Ukraine festooned the buildings. Yellow-and-blue flags draped the balcony railings, colored the alcoves, and served as neckerchiefs on the statuary in defiance of the politics that divided them. The pro-Russians on one side and those who believed Ukraine's future lay with the west on the other. One constant thread bound them together—nationalism.

Her father's legacy had helped forge a different kind of unity among the Soviet people. Born in Ukraine, he had risen to fame as the star goalie of the Russian National Ice Hockey Team. His countrymen had loved him, and Jordan had never tired of hearing the stories of his glory days or of how he had captured the heart of the beautiful Frances Jordan. Theirs had been a fairytale romance, the Russian and the American. Defying all odds, they'd married, had two children, and then, when Rae was six, her father was murdered.

She recalled the sound of her mother keening at the news; the images of her father resting in his casket at center ice. The sadness and confusion that surrounded that day had never completely dissipated. It steered her life, driving her into her present job.

Looking back, she could see the clues suggesting her father was more than he seemed. There was the large number of soldiers in attendance at his funeral. There were the dour men in suits who came to offer their condolences, men like Ilya Brodsky. And then there was the speed with which her mother had whisked them back to the States. Within months, Frances had changed their last name and begun the slow process of excising their father from their lives. Until six months ago, when she'd met Alena Petrenko, and he'd once more become the specter in the room.

That meeting with Alena had turned her world upside down. Jordan would never forget escorting the Americans under her protection to that appointment and meeting the tall, ethereal person who called herself a doctor. A Russian Jew, she claimed she knew Rae's father and insisted he was more than just a talented hockey player. According to Alena, he was a gifted teacher of alternative medicine and worse—a spy.

When Jordan's mother refused to discuss it, Jordan was left with no option but to launch her own covert investigation. So far, she didn't like what she'd turned up.

A honk pulled her out of her reverie. Jumping back to the curb, she raised a hand in apology to the driver and chastised herself for her lapse of attentiveness. She'd reached an intersection where the street narrowed, with Shevchenko Park closing in on one side and the bright red buildings of Taras Shevchenko National University pressing close on the other. Not only were there more cars and bicycles, but the pedestrian traffic had also changed from business types to hordes of hurrying students.

Waiting at the corner for the light to change, she caught sight of a tall man with unruly dark hair who looked vaguely familiar. When she turned, he ducked into a doorway.

A student, or was he following her?

Paying closer attention to the people around her, Jordan crossed with the light. Within a few moments, the same man exited the doorway and started traveling a route behind her. He looked to be about her age, wearing a dark T-shirt and blue jeans. Then catching a glimpse of his face in a window reflection, she realized where she'd seen him before. He was the journalist who'd taken her picture at the site of the ambush.

But why was he following her now? There was nothing newsworthy in what she was doing.

Maybe someone had put him up to it.

Her heart raced. There was only one person she could think of who might care where she went and who she talked to in Ukraine—Ilya Brodsky. She might not be able to expose him as a former KGB agent without exposing her father and thus jeopardizing her job, but she might find proof he'd had something to do with her father's murder. Other than herself and her immediate family members, he was the only one who might be harmed by the information she uncovered about her father. Did Brodsky intend to stop her from digging? Or maybe he just wanted to know what she discovered.

Jordan forced herself to think rationally. There were any number of other reasons the journalist might be following her. He might be connected to the Russians, acting as their eyes and ears here and in Hoholeve. Or he might have seen her lifting the fragment or concealing the envelope. Hell, maybe he just fancied himself the next Anderson Cooper.

So what's the play, Rae? she asked herself. At this point, she needed either to shake this man, confront him, or abort her mission.

She'd been trained to know that if you spot someone once, it's likely an accident. If you spot someone twice, it's apt to be a coincidence. If you spot someone three times, it's an enemy action. At this point, she had to consider her tracker an adversary. The next step was to figure out if he was operating on his own or as part of a team.

A quick scan of the area pulled up some potential accomplices—the young mother with a stroller sitting on a bench near the park entrance or the man standing idle near the open gate. If he had a team, and they were any good, she would likely never pick out any others.

Keeping the reporter in her peripheral vision, Jordan moved toward the park entrance. While she was well-trained to ID people following her, shaking them was a different matter. At the Federal Law Enforcement Training Center, FLECT, they'd been taught a variety of surveillance techniques. The preferred method for dealing with someone following you was to bore him to death. The basic concept was to let the person, or persons, follow you around while you lead them nowhere in hopes they'll eventually move on. Other tactics included the "pause and turn," where you let your tracker know you've spotted him, and "the acknowledgment," where you actually confront your tail.

Right now, the latter seemed the most plausible option, provided she could lure him into a trap of her own.

Cutting toward the park, Jordan kept tabs on her tail out of the corner of her eye. Stopping at the park entrance, she made a show of photographing the ornate gate before flipping the camera to selfie mode. After snapping a few photographs of her tail as he crossed the street, she uploaded it through a secure link into the DSS facial recognition software. With luck, she would get back a name.

Putting away her phone, she cut into the park, quickening her pace to put a little distance between herself and the journalist. The young mother rose as she passed, only to be greeted by another woman with two small children in tow. They headed off toward the playground. The man standing near the gate ground his cigarette out and turned away from the park. Her man appeared to be working alone.

According to the map she'd consulted before striking out for UAFM, a shortcut through the park was the quickest route to her destination. Now with all the path choices and outlets, the park seemed tailor-made for a game of cat and mouse.

Jordan slowed her pace and assessed her surroundings. Like everything else in the Ukraine, what once showed signs of grandeur had crumbled under the strain of the economy. Grass grew deep on either side of the cracked asphalt pathways and encroached on the small garden areas already choked with weeds. Paint peeled off brightly colored benches, streetlamps were devoid of bulbs, and yet people were everywhere.

Men and women walked with purpose, dressed for business, but with no jobs to go to. Screaming children ran circles around their mothers. Couples strolled hand in hand. Students lay in the weedy grass in the shade of the trees, more interested in their study partners than in the books cracked open beside them.

After a few minutes of walking, Jordan pivoted and doubled back. The plan was to confront the man following her, but he was nowhere in sight. Had she lost him, or had he realized what she was up to and hidden himself? Maybe spotting him on the road *had* just been a coincidence, or maybe she'd been wrong. *Maybe.*

Chapter 10

She spent the next few minutes zigzagging through the park until she was sure she had lost him, then headed for the Lva Tolstoho Street exit, the one nearest the Kyiv Medical Institute-UAFM. Housed in a single-story building kitty-cornered from the main university, UAFM was painted baby blue instead of red like the primary institution. It occupied the entire block but had only one entrance, an oversized double oak door.

Jordan scanned the crowds one more time, then jaywalked the street. Entering the foyer of UAFM, she was struck by a blast of cool air that stunned her into thinking maybe she'd been wrong to come here. The last words Alena Petrenko had said to her whispered through her mind: *Sometimes it is better to let the dead sleep.*

"May I help you?" a receptionist called out in English from behind a circular desk opposite the entrance.

It didn't surprise Jordan to be identified as a Westerner. To blend in here, she would need to have worn stockings and high heels and be dressed to the *n*th degree. Instead, she'd opted for her casual uniform—comfortable leather shoes, cotton socks, khakis, and a short-sleeved, dark-blue knit shirt. Her 9-mil was locked up tight in the Intercontinental's hotel room safe.

"Come, come." The receptionist impatiently waved her closer. A stout woman in her fifties, her hair was dyed a uniform shade of brown, her makeup artfully applied. A worn black jacket strained to button over a white polka-dot shirt. Her name badge read, "Zlatta."

"Are you interested in the school?" she asked.

Jordan made sure the door was closed and then crossed the white-tiled entryway. "Actually, I'm looking for some information."

"That's why I'm here."

"I'm looking for some information on my father. I was told he taught classes here back in the late '70s or early '80s."

Zlatta knit her eyebrows. "I'm afraid that's impossible. That was before this school even existed."

Jordan mirrored Zlatta's frown. "Are you saying the Ukrainian Association of Folk Medicine didn't exist?"

"Not as a university. We now offer fully accredited doctor of medicine degrees in a number of alternative specialties." She reached for a brochure.

"Then this *is* a recognized school?" Jordan immediately wanted to snatch back the words or at the least strain the incredulity out of her voice.

Zlatta straightened her carriage. "Of course! UAFM holds level one through level four accreditation."

After witnessing Alena's alternative healing methods, Jordan found it hard to believe. "Does that equate to a Western PhD?"

"Better! Our graduates are all certified MDs. They take a mixture of traditional and alternative medicine classes for over six years."

"When did the first class graduate?" Jordan hoped her rapid-fire questions didn't stop Zlatta's rapid-fire answers.

"1998."

Jordan ran the math in her head. *Seventeen years.* "Have you ever heard of a Dr. Alena Petrenko?"

Zlatta's face looked blank. "That name is not familiar."

"She practices medicine in Tel Aviv, has for over thirty years. She claims to be a graduate of this university." It was those claims that had led Jordan here. When Zlatta shook her head, Jordan added, "What about a man named Ilya Brodsky?"

Even saying his name was distasteful to Jordan. But if Alena was telling the truth, he'd been the one who'd brokered her father's connection to the Russian program designed to study the use of psychic discovery in warfare and spying known as PSI.

Zlatta nodded her head. "The name seems familiar. I can't place where I've heard it."

Jordan was treading on thin ice. Any connection between her father and the KGB put her job in jeopardy. The DSS wasn't likely to allow her to work for them if it turned out she was the daughter of a KGB spy. At the very least, she'd be considered a security risk. So she decided to switch tacks.

"Do you know if there was instruction offered here before this became an actual school?" she asked.

"Not that I'm aware. The only person who might have known that was our founder and former CEO, Pokenevich Valeriy. Unfortunately, he's dead."

"What about his colleagues? There must be someone here who goes back before this school was accredited." Jordan didn't want to sound desperate, but this was her only real lead for information on her father's past. She needed to know the truth.

The woman scrunched her eyes in thought, pressing her fingertips against her lips. Then as if consulting her conscience and receiving an answer, she reached for a business card.

"Dr. Pokenevich did have one associate who might know something. They were close friends from childhood." Zlatta wrote down a name and number, then handed the card to Jordan. "The man's name is Professor Fedorov."

Jordan thanked the woman and tucked the card into her jacket pocket.

Realizing she wouldn't get more, Jordan said her good-byes and made her exit. This time, instead of cutting across traffic, she headed to the crosswalk. Pushed along by an eddy of pedestrians and swirling emotions, her mind flitted back through all the things she'd learned about her dad over the years. Each revelation had left an impact.

His death—caught in the crossfire between an assassin and a guard detail—had led Jordan to her current job, which had led her to Alena. But not only had the doctor insisted her father's death was intentional; she'd alluded to his nefarious past. If what she had told her was true, chasing ghosts might very well cost Jordan the job she loved.

A sense of being watched, the hairs rising on the back of her neck, made Jordan look up. She caught sight of a tall thin man with dark ruffled hair and tensed. The man ducked into the corner coffee shop, but she knew it was him.

Damn. It wasn't a coincidence that he'd found her. Which meant he must have watched her enter the school and been waiting for her to exit.

Jordan weighed her options. She could confront him inside the café or choose a quieter, more secluded spot for a conversation. She went with the latter.

Crossing the street, she turned toward the park. From the corner of her eye, she watched him exit the café and thread his way toward the light. At the entrance to the park, she stopped to give him a chance to catch up and pulled out her phone. Maybe there'd been a hit on the facial recognition software. It would be nice to know who she was dealing with.

Sure enough! The system had come back with five possibilities. Scrolling through the photos, she stopped when she landed on a picture of Nye Davis. The database information was sparse: 6'2″, brown eyes and hair, age thirty-four. He traveled on a United States passport, had served four years in the Army, and was purported to be a stringer for Reuters, an international news agency headquartered in London. She waited for the light to change and for Davis to step off the curb. Once he reached her side of the street, she moved quickly into the park. If it was a cat-and-mouse game he wanted, she'd play.

Jordan picked up her pace, forcing him to give chase. The quicker he had to move, the more he'd have to think on his feet and the more mistakes he was apt to make.

Rounding a corner near the playground, she moved out of his line of sight. Here, the path split in three directions, but she ducked behind a food wagon and kept watch for her quarry in the mirrored facade of the light post. Within several seconds, he appeared and faced the separate paths with a look of frustration that caused Jordan to smile. Then after what seemed like a short game of "eeny meeny miny moe," he selected the most direct route toward Volodymyrska Street.

Jordan fell in behind him. He had to be headed back to the Intercontinental. But the questions remained: Who did he work for, and why had he been following her?

Jordan glanced at her watch. The clock was ticking. She had little over one hour before she had to report for duty. Ahead of her, Nye Davis moved slowly along the wide bricked sidewalk that abutted an even older bricked street. He'd soon reach the opera house, where the sidewalk melded with a wider stepped terrace. Cover would be hard to maintain. She weighed her options. Her best hope of surprising him was to take a parallel route and intercept him near the Golden Gate. He was texting as he walked, so it shouldn't be hard to beat him into position.

Turning left, she jogged down the cross street and then turned right at the next intersection. The street cut through an upscale neighborhood of trendy apartments fronted by flower planters painted in the national colors. In this area, the buildings were devoid of the usual graffiti. Uniformed guards stood at the doorways, and a few storefronts were marked with subtle and tasteful signs.

At the end of the block, Patrons crowded the outside tables of a stylish café across from the Golden Gate's monument park. Often called "the sky gate" because of the way the sun passed through it every morning, the Golden Gate, Kyivans believed, saved the city from darkness and death. Jordan found it ironic that in 1648, Russian ambassadors solemnly passed through announcing the reunion of Russia and Ukraine. It stood like so many of Kyiv and Ukraine's famous monuments as a symbol of Russia's power. No wonder the citizens were so conflicted.

Jordan cut through the park and stopped at the top of a small set of stairs that led down to the sidewalk on Volodymyrska Street. The park grounds were elevated, ringed by a low stone wall.

Spotting Davis in the distance, his head still buried in his texts, she crossed the sidewalk to stand behind a soda machine next to a small street kiosk and waited. When Davis pulled even, she stepped in front of him. "Nye Davis?"

The man looked up from his phone. Surprise then resignation marked his features. *Busted.*

"That's me."

"Why are you following me?"

"You have the wrong guy." He tried to walk around her, but she blocked his path.

"I don't have time for games. I want to know why you've been tailing me."

He smiled and gestured to a corner of the wall. "Want to sit down?"

He was taller and better looking than she'd realized, and his smile was disarming. Jordan reminded herself he was a journalist. "No, I want you to answer my question."

He shrugged and boosted himself up on the wall. "I find you interesting."

It wasn't what she expected.

"Why?"

Again the smile. He took a beat too long looking at her, and she felt her face heat.

"I saw you at the crash site," he said. "You seemed to have a different agenda than everyone else. It makes me curious."

He set his phone down beside him.

"Are you recording our conversation?" she asked. "Turn it off."

Davis thumbed open the phone and clicked off the recording device. "You can't blame me for trying."

"What is it you want?" She felt off-kilter, hating the fact she was standing while he perched comfortably on the wall looking down at her.

"I'd like to know why a U.S. Diplomatic Security Service agent was out at the crash site in Hoholeve, and why the ambulance she was escorting to the morgue was ambushed en route."

"That's classified information."

"But you admit you work for DSS?"

Jordan drew a deep breath, then dragged her fingers through her hair and twisted it into a knot at the nape of her neck. She was good at interrogation. He might be better. "That isn't a secret. I see you've done your homework."

"The rumor going around is there was a courier on board that flight carrying classified information and that somebody downed the plane in order to keep that information out of the hands of the U.S. government. Can you confirm that?"

This was where the party line came in handy. "Yes, there was a DSS agent on board, but he wasn't carrying any official documents."

"What about the second body?"

"Excuse me?" *How did he know about Zhen?*

"There were two bodies transported."

An observation any of the press could've made. The information was bound to come out. "The agent was escorting a fugitive back to the States to stand trial."

"Name?"

"We're not releasing it at this time. We haven't notified the family yet."

"Did this fugitive know something worth crashing a plane over?"

Jordan tensed. It was time to nip this line of questioning in the bud. "From what I've heard, the IIC believes the crash was an accident, mechanical failure."

He seemed to weigh the answer. "Then why the escort?"

"For your edification, escorting the body of a U.S. DSS agent killed in the line of duty from site of his death to a secure location is procedure. I wouldn't read too much into it if I were you."

"Thanks for clearing that up." He bounced his heels against the wall. "That leaves just one more question. Why the interest in UAFM?"

Jordan felt her breath stop halfway to her lungs. Aware that he was watching her, she forced a smile. "That's personal. It has nothing to do with my job."

"Then if I go back there and ask the person at the desk what the pretty redhead came in asking about, I'm only going to learn more about you?"

"Leave it alone. I've answered your questions."

"Really?" He jumped down off the wall. "Because I think you've only told me what you and the government want me to know."

Chapter 11

Jordan took over the protection detail at 6:00 PM. Keeping a low profile, she waited as Tracy Linwood used the facilities, then trailed her back to the dining room, where she joined a table of five women, a few of which Jordan had to work to ID. She recognized the woman to Linwood's left. She was Willa Hamish, a British Labor politician. Next to her was Ellis Quinn, CEO of Quinn Industries, a defense contractor. The others presented a challenge.

This was the eighth year of the Women's Leadership Alliance, a group of high-powered women from all walks of life, who served as examples for young girls around the world. Their goal—to set an agenda for progress and change in the coming year—seemed a bit lofty.

After a keynote speech, delivered by a European actress Jordan thought looked vaguely familiar, the dinner party dissolved, and Linwood headed for her suite. There was the normal chitchat and then she asked Jordan about the plane crash. Jordan gave her the condensed version. Back in the room, she did a quick sweep and secured the main door.

"Do you need anything else, Mrs. Linwood?"

"A glass of wine. Care to join me?"

"I'd love to, but duty calls."

* * *

Jordan escorted Linwood to breakfast the next morning, then went back upstairs and slept. The sound of her phone ringing at 1:00 PM woke her with a start.

The number belonged to the U.S. embassy in Ukraine.

Linwood? Not likely. If something had happened downstairs, she would have known.

Henry? It couldn't be. It hadn't been twenty-four hours since she'd dropped off the fragments.

It turned out to be Mary with an order for Jordan to report to Lory's office immediately. Since she didn't work for him, Jordan hung up and phoned her boss.

"You're being temporarily reassigned," Daugherty told her. "Something about the situation there on the ground. They have a problem. You know the backstory. The director issued the orders."

"Is this about the plane crash?"

"Lory'll have to fill you in. Just be sure you pack up your gear. Someone else has been assigned to Linwood. They'll need the room."

"That's it? No sage advice?"

"You want some advice? Here it is. Good luck, Jordan. Watch your back."

* * *

It took her forty-five minutes to reach the embassy, and Lory was pacing. As soon as she entered his office, he gestured for Mary to close the door behind her then got right to the point. "We have a problem."

Jordan didn't like the way he said "we." Had something else happened? Her mind immediately flew to her conversation with Nye Davis.

"What's wrong?"

"This." He threw a piece of paper across the desk. It was a lab report.

"I can explain."

"You can? Then I'm all ears because I'd sure like to know how in the hell we ended up with the wrong guy."

Jordan frowned and picked up the report. She'd assumed it was the report on the fragment she'd taken down to the lab. Instead, it was a copy of the repatriation documentation required by IIC.

She skimmed the results. "Sir, this has to be wrong."

"They ran the DNA comparison twice."

"Are you saying McClasky was escorting someone other than Zhen?"

"Either that or our guy got mixed up with another body at the morgue."

"That's not possible. I secured the remains myself and verified the bag reached the morgue. My initials were even on the seal. The tech would have had to break it when he pulled the first sample." She shook the paper. "This test was run on the man I found handcuffed to McClasky."

"Which is why you're headed to China, Agent Jordan."

"Excuse me?" It seemed impossible that she'd heard him correctly.

"How's your Cantonese?"

"Rusty." In truth, she spoke only a little. Enough to say hello, good-bye, and ask where the nearest bathroom was.

"Then I suggest you brush up because I need you to locate Zhen. Or find out what happened to him and who took his place on that airplane. I don't think I need to explain what a diplomatic nightmare this is turning into, for both the U.S. and Ukraine." He reached down, picked up another piece of paper, and handed her a printout of a boarding pass. "You're booked on the next flight for Guangzhou. It leaves in two hours."

That didn't give her much time.

"Mary has the contact information you'll need. I've spoken with our FBI legal attaché in China. He's stationed in Beijing. He put McClasky in touch with Yang, but otherwise the legat has taken a hands-free approach. However, he expects to be kept in the loop. So do I." He drilled her with his stare. "I'm reporting straight to the director on this one, Jordan. Good luck. Watch your back."

Jordan nodded.

On the way out, Mary handed her a packet. "I e-mailed you all the intel, but I thought these might help. There's a guide book of Guangdong Province and a language dictionary."

"Thank you, Mary."

"No problem. Good luck."

"What, no watch your back?"

Mary tossed her a wave, and Jordan headed for the exit. It was the third time in the last three hours that someone had wished her luck. She wondered what they knew that she didn't.

Chapter 12

Jordan made one stop on her way out of the building—the lab. Rather than wait for an elevator, she took the stairs.

"I was just about to call you," Henry said when she came through the door. For some reason his hair looked a little spikier today, like a rooster in full display. "I put a rush on your request. I just got it back."

"What does the report say?"

The fact that she was only interested in the paperwork didn't go unnoticed. Henry stopped preening and started moping. He grabbed a single sheet of paper off his desk and handed it over. It was a list of components found in each fragment, categorized by element. She skimmed to the bottom but found no written analysis of the findings.

"There's nothing that explains what this means."

"That's because I haven't gotten to the writing-it-down part yet. I can get it for you by tomorrow."

"It can't wait. I need the information now." She watched him waffle. "Seriously, Henry. I'm booked on a two o'clock flight."

"Fine, come on back, and I'll walk you through it." He opened the gate in the counter and gestured to an island with a large monitor. "Want to tell me what you were hoping to find?"

"How about you tell me what was found first," she said, not wanting to lead him toward any conclusions. Better he draw his own.

"Not even a hint?" He grinned, his cheeks pushing up his glasses. "God I love a challenge." Directing a mouse on the laptop, he put a

PDF of the breakdown onto the screen. "The very first thing that jumped out was the lack of explosive material or any type of propellant on the fragment. You said it came from the crash site, so one would expect to find some residue. *Nada*."

"So that rules out a missile?"

"From any traditional weapon."

There was only one weapon she knew of that didn't use explosive materials and could shoot a projectile that high in the air with enough punch to bring down a plane—the railgun. But it was still in the testing phase, not land-based, and presently designed only for ocean-going vessels.

"Any possibility the piece came from the engine?"

Henry bumped his glasses up the bridge of his nose and looked over at her. "It can't be entirely ruled out until we know more about the aircraft, but from what I discovered, People's Republic Airline flies primarily Boeing jets. The odds of one of their engines being made out of metal containing the elements found in the fragment are slim."

"That means we've hit a dead end."

Henry grinned. "Not entirely. It took me awhile, but I finally located a manufacturer that's producing steel with the same basic amalgams in nearly identical ratios."

Jordan perked up. "Which one?"

"I can't definitively prove the fragment came from their stock, but . . ." Henry paused, pulling up the PDF of a company report and positioning it next to the lab report on the screen. "This company, REE Manufacturing, exports steel that's nearly a perfect match to the fragment."

"Henry, you're amazing!"

His face grew pink. "If we had some samples of REE materials to compare with the fragment, we might be able to prove it's the source. The content of your piece indicates the presence of ion-absorbed ore with significantly higher than normal traces of dysprosium and terbium. It's the exact same content ratio of the ore listed in the metal exported by REE. Do you know the odds of that?"

"No. Explain it to me, in layman's terms, the encapsulated version, please."

"Basically ion-absorbed ore is multicolored loose sand clay that's rich in soil, granite, volcanic mineral weathering, and rare-earth elements." He pointed to the screen. "Dysprosium and terbium, the two listed here, are what we call heavy rare-earth elements, mostly used in manufacturing *green* items. For example, small amounts of dysprosium can make magnets in electric motors lighter. Terbium helps cut the electricity usage of lights. Light rare-earth elements like cerium and neodymium are more abundant, but—"

"Henry!" Jordan circled her index finger in the universal sign for "hurry up." She'd already spent fifteen minutes down here, and it was a forty-minute cab ride to the airport in good traffic.

"Gotcha. Anyway, once I knew we were dealing with rare-earth metals, I started looking at the other minerals present. In this case, iron and granite." He started talking faster. "I can absolutely say that there is only one place on earth where you would expect to find the components listed here all together."

"You can give me an exact location?"

"More like a vicinity. The ore comes from a remote mountainous region of the northern Guangdong province."

"In China?" She'd been expecting him to say he'd found evidence pointing to the Russians. This supported the theory that the downing of the plane had something to do with Zhen.

Henry nodded. "Science doesn't lie, and REE has a mill there. I'll send the report to your phone."

* * *

It wasn't the in-flight time of long-distance overseas travel that drove Jordan crazy, it was the layovers—this one for three hours in Bangkok. When she tried napping, images of the crash site and the flaming ambulance haunted her. But what really kept her from sleep was the idea of a state-of-the-art weapon making its way into the heart of Ukraine.

Finally giving up on rest, she settled into a seat near an outlet with her back to the wall, pulled out her tablet, and started searching the Internet.

The U.S. Navy had recently publicized upcoming trials on their railgun system. She started there. Logging in through a secure server, she searched the federal database for everything on the U.S. development of the railgun.

The Navy contracts belonged to Quinn Industries, the same Quinn as the woman who'd been seated next to Tracy Linwood at the Women's Leadership Alliance. Her company was based out of San Diego. The latest reports showed field testing on the railgun currently under way. There was a land-based version mentioned that was in the early stages of development, but up until now, the size of the power source required to fire the gun prohibited making it portable.

Jordan wiggled up straighter in her seat. Zhen could have hacked the Quinn Industries computers. It would explain the charges. But if he'd traded or sold secrets to the Chinese, they wouldn't want that to get out. There was no way they would've allowed his extradition from China.

Frustrated with hitting dead ends, she opened the Quinn Industries website and read its overview. The company specialized in drone, railgun, laser, and advanced guidance and defense system development. Privately owned, analysts estimated the company value at $2.5 billon. Ellis Quinn, age forty-five, was listed as the CEO. No wonder she was being feted by the International Women's Leadership Alliance.

Pulling up the dossier on Quinn, Jordan was surprised to find she was actually one of three women heading up major U.S. defense companies. Born and raised in Seattle, she professed a lifelong dedication to aviation and earned a PhD in astronautical engineering from MIT. Some D.C. analyst had attached a five-year-old photo from when she was voted *People* magazine's hottest bachelorette over forty.

Jordan studied the photo. Dark-haired and strong-boned, Quinn had a hawkish air about her. Jordan couldn't see her risking a billion-dollar company selling weapons technology to the Chinese.

Next Jordan searched the report database for anything suggesting Quinn Industries had ever been hacked. She came up empty. By all reports, there had never been an external or internal cyber threat. She found it hard to believe.

According to Henry, the fragment had originated in China, so she went there next, searching everything she could find on China's "new concept weapons" program—*xin gainian wuqi*. The program included lasers, high-powered microwaves, particle beam weapons, coil guns, and railguns. It was clear from the intel that when it came to hypersonic and laser weaponry, China was winning the arms race.

The railgun was the only weapon listed in the Chinese program that used a projectile but no propellants or jet fuel, so Jordan searched for intel suggesting they might be close to producing a transportable electromagnetic weapon. Nothing popped up. Either there wasn't one currently in development or China excelled at keeping secrets. Jordan was betting on the latter.

Flipping through the documents, a definite pattern jumped out. With every advance in Chinese weaponry, somewhere in the world there existed a corresponding technology heist.

Chapter 13

Kozachenko moved away from the camp and placed the call he'd been avoiding since rendezvousing with Barkov and the other men.

"Pakhan," he said in a show of respect. In truth, he didn't care much for the man. However, he was the leader of the *bratva* and currently the only one who could help them out of this jam. "We need to talk."

"What happened?"

Kozachenko filled him in on the events since leaving Dykanka. "We're safe here, and Yolkin is improving. But with the helicopters flying overhead and the increased patrols on the highways, we have no way to move. The window is closing on our opportunity."

"This mission cannot fail." His tone carried a rebuke.

Kozachenko's face burned, but he kept his voice level. "It was a combination of decisions that brought us to this point, Pakhan."

His words were measured, but he hoped his message was clear. Kozachenko and his men had fired on the plane on the pakhan's orders. He was not willing to shoulder the blame.

The pakhan remained silent.

Finally, Kozachenko asked, "What do you want us to do now?"

"Stas is working on a plan."

"Do you think it wise to keep him involved? Aren't you afraid they might figure out he's our man on the ground?"

"Nyet. He's been very careful. Besides, he is who we have."

"Forgive me if I lack confidence." After all, they were talking about a man who'd shown a certain impotency when confronted with a simple task.

"Vasyl, you may not trust him, but I believe you trust me." The pakhan's voice held the timber of a threat. The head of the Russian bratva was not someone used to being challenged, and it was clear to Kozachenko that he had crossed a line.

"Of course, Pakhan."

"Once Stas works out the details, he'll be in contact. Now tell me, what was in the envelope?"

Kozachenko had been dreading this moment. He hesitated to tell him the truth for fear the pakhan would think he was lying.

"There was only one thing written on the page. It must be a password of some kind." Kozachenko read it out loud. The pakhan repeated it back. "That's right. It seems odd, but we must look on the bright side. It means Zhen gave him nothing."

"Or everything." There was a pause on the pakhan's end of the line that made Kozachenko's skin itch. "Now tell me why Agent Jordan's being sent to Guangzhou."

Kozachenko was caught off guard. "The DSS agent is going to China?"

"You didn't know? You sound worried, Vasyl."

Kozachenko couldn't deny it. It made him angry he wasn't informed and uneasy to think of Agent Jordan in Guangzhou digging for information. "That one is trouble, Pakhan. Don't underestimate her."

"You worry too much, Vasyl. She won't be a problem. I have already arranged a special welcoming committee."

Chapter 14

The Guangzhou airport teemed with people. Not unexpected at the start of business on a weekday in a city of forty-four million, but Jordan wasn't a big fan of crowds. Stepping into the sea of people, she allowed herself to be swept along toward baggage claim and worked to ignore the overt stares of the other travelers. She couldn't decide if it was her red hair, the way she dressed, or the fact she stood half a foot taller than most of the women that garnered all the attention. Near the immigration counter, the humidity from outside overwhelmed the air conditioning. Sweat dampened her collar. She could see the exit and handed the customs official her passport, waiting impatiently while he scanned it through the system. Under normal circumstances, the diplomatic passport worked in her favor. This time, the customs agent questioned her.

"Do you have a weapon in your bag?" he asked.

"No."

Knowing she wouldn't be allowed to carry her weapon off mission grounds, Jordan had left her 9 mil in a gun locker at the embassy in Kyiv. She figured that if she really needed a weapon, the RSO at the consulate in Guangzhou could provide her with one.

The customs agent didn't believe her. He insisted on searching her bag, and by the time he let her pass, she was hot, testy, and running late for her meeting with the local RSO.

As she exited the customs area, the chatter of Cantonese, Mandarin, and Hakka in the main terminal mixed with the techno-style music pulsing through the terminal speakers plucked at her fraying nerves. People pushed and shoved as they hurried for the doors, and Jordan felt her patience slipping. After sixteen-plus hours of travel from Kyiv, all she really wanted was a decent cup of coffee.

She waited in line for a Starbucks, then headed outside to find the driver Lory had said would be there to meet her. He stood in a queue of other drivers holding a sign with her name on it.

"*Néih hóu*," she said. Hello.

"Welcome to Guangzhou."

That ended the small talk, and the driver turned his attention to maneuvering traffic. The rule of thumb seemed to be whoever nosed in first had the right of way. After a few minutes acclimating to the braking, accelerating, and weaving, Jordan turned her attention to the information that Mary had sent, skimming the pages for a second time.

Once DSS verified the victim with McClasky wasn't Zhen, Lory had ordered a full-scale investigation into what'd happened. The primary goal was to find Zhen, ID his doppelgänger, then determine who had ordered the switch and why.

Most of the intel related to Kia Zhen showed a few petty juvenile offenses and some affiliation with the Triad, but it was hard to be a Chinese American living in *Dai Foa*, or Big City, as the Chinese called San Francesco, who didn't have some contact with the gangs. After graduating from high school with honors, he'd taken a gap year. He clearly hadn't used it productively.

Leaning her head back, Jordan closed her eyes. Lory expected answers. Finding them might not prove to be easy.

Thirty minutes later, she was jarred awake. Blinking her eyes, it took her a moment to get her bearings. The driver was parked against the curb in front of the U.S. consulate. A long line of Chinese citizens were queued in front of the door.

"What do I owe you?" she asked the driver.

"Nothing. I work for the consulate."

She collected her bag, handed him twenty-five yuan as a tip, and headed for the main building. Four stories of stone and teak wood, it anchored the 7.4-acre consulate complex and was intended to welcome visitors. Jordan thought it looked like a giant loaf of bread.

Skirting the line, she walked up to the desk and flashed her badge. After signing in, she passed through a metal detector and was directed to the third floor. RSO Jennifer Todd was waiting when she stepped off the elevator.

"I'm glad you made it, Agent Jordan," Todd said, extending her hand. "The traffic can be brutal this time of day."

Jordan returned the woman's handshake. "It was customs that gave me the most trouble."

"That, too." Todd's blue eyes twinkled. "I mean, what about *immunity* don't they understand?" Fit and fifty, the RSO could have passed for twenty-five. Small and compact with blonde hair that hung straight to her shoulders, her sleeveless dress showed off a set of guns that would make most men jealous.

"Did Agent Lory fill you in?" Jordan asked, following Todd down the hall to an office that faced the river.

"As a matter of fact, he did. This plane crash is a horrible thing. I'm not sure how much help I can be, but I'll try to answer your questions."

"I can only imagine the phone calls you've been fielding."

"Between the press and the family members, we've been under siege." Todd crossed to her desk. "Of course, it's the families that my staff and I care most about."

"How's the government reacting?"

"They seem more concerned with keeping the families in line. Yesterday we saw protests. Always unnerving, considering how unusual that is here and how the Chinese government tends to react."

Jordan thought of the iconic images of Tiananmen Square. She'd only been a small child, but between the recorded violence and the disparate numbers reported of the dead and injured, the tongues of the free world had wagged. It hadn't helped China's image.

Rather than offer Jordan a seat, Todd knelt down beside her desk. "Lory tells me you want to know how we tracked down Zhen."

From her use of past tense, Jordan wondered if she'd heard the news of the switch. "Didn't Lory brief you?"

"About the plane crash?"

"About Zhen."

Todd stood up, clutching a small purse. "He told me we got the wrong man."

Jordan nodded. "We need to find the real Zhen and ID the man sent home in his place."

"Then the best bet is talking to Detective Yang Li." Todd toed the bottom desk drawer shut with her foot. "He's our Foreign Service officer. He and McClasky were the ones who located your fugitive, and they were present when the other officers moved in. If anyone can shed some light on all this, I'm betting Yang can."

Chapter 15

The Sing Kee restaurant was located on Di Shi Fu Road near a busy shopping district. Tall buildings lined the street, the upper stories protruding over the sidewalks, creating arches protecting pedestrians from the rain and sun. Colorful signs with cascading Chinese characters bedecked the structures and delighted the eye, but an acrid odor caused Jordan to wrinkle her nose in disgust.

"What *is* that smell?"

Todd grinned. "There's nothing quite like the odor of fermented bean curd. It's a delicacy called 'stinky tofu.' You get used to the smell."

Jordan wasn't convinced, but her own stomach growled as she followed Todd into the restaurant. The eatery was busy and crowded, and it took a moment to adjust to the chatter of voices floating on the techno beat. The chartreuse and white tiles covering the walls and floor offered little in the way of acoustics. Glass chandeliers hung from high ceilings, lighting up round banquet tables. Green metal chairs cushioned in brown vinyl provided the seating. One small countertop station to the left was used to pass food from the kitchen to the wait staff.

A young Chinese man with a neatly trimmed beard and square black glasses sat in the far corner, his back to the wall. Detective Yang, Jordan guessed.

He stood as they entered, and Todd made a beeline toward him. "Li, I'm so sorry we're late."

"Not a problem. I am enjoying my tea."

"May I introduce Agent Raisa Jordan."

Introductions made, Yang gestured to the chairs around the table. "Please, sit."

A true cop, he'd already secured the best seat at the table for himself—the one with a full view of the room. Jordan chose the second best. The one to his left. From there she still had close to a full restaurant sweep. They ordered more tea, then a variety of steamed and fried dim sum: prawn and pork dumplings, chiu chow dumplings with peanuts, chicken claws in bean sauce, duck rolls, and crispy calamari. Once the waiter walked away, Detective Yang got right to business.

"Agent Todd says you want to know about the apprehension of Kia—"

Todd cut him off. "I haven't told you yet, but you didn't get him, Li." She filled him in on the details. The detective looked dumb struck.

"That isn't possible."

"Except it is," Todd said. "Somehow his picture was switched in the system. The photos and IDs we used to get him out of the country are an exact match to the man pretending to be Zhen. It suggests an inside job."

"And I'm telling you, it's not possible," Yang said. "Agent McClasky showed me a picture of Zhen taken in San Francesco."

That surprised Jordan. Pulling her phone out of her pocket, she scrolled to the picture of Zhen. "Was it this picture?"

Yang squinted at the screen, moving it closer to study the picture. "It's the same photograph, different man."

"This is the *real* Kia Zhen," Jordan said. "We believe McClasky received doctored photos and or falsified documents allowing someone else to be transferred."

"On whose orders? Someone at the consulate?" Yang looked genuinely surprised.

The U.S. consulate employed more than four hundred people in various capacities and processed over one million visa applications a year. Someone could easily have been paid to alter or delete Zhen's photos. And considering what little she knew about Chinese cyber-crime and their rampant government corruption, it didn't seem too much of a stretch to believe the People's Republic had at least one hacker capable of doing the same.

"Or someone at the police district," Jordan said, not willing to let all the blame fall on the Americans.

Todd bobbed her head in agreement. "We've got our experts looking into it, but I'm afraid it's possible we'll never know who per-petrated the act."

"To be honest, I'm not that interested in *how* it happened," Jordan said. "I'm more interested in finding Zhen. Detective Yang, can you walk me through what went down that day?" She dredged a dumpling through the *char siu* sauce and popped it into her mouth, savoring the tender pork while concentrating on Yang's recounting.

"Agent McClasky came to my office with that picture and a sus-pected location. We headed straight there and spotted Zhen. Then before we could move in, the Guangdong police department initiated a drug raid on the apartment complex. They brought a full contin-gent of men and moved door to door, arresting everyone. The chief inspector was even on scene. The police took thirty-seven people to jail that day, including Kia Zhen."

"Did you or McClasky tell anyone on scene why you were there?"

"We tried, but no one listened. We ended up going back to police headquarters. Your legal attaché is stationed in Beijing, so Agent McClasky contacted the consulate's political officer while I spoke with the chief. Together your PO and my chief arranged for Zhen to be released into U.S. custody."

From where Jordan was sitting, it appeared that one of two things had happened. Either the Chinese had substituted someone for Zhen in order to keep him in China or the PO had used Zhen's capture as a means to smuggle someone out of the country. The question was, which scenario fit best? And what made silencing the man on board

PR Flight 91 worth the lives of over three hundred men, women, and children? More and more, it seemed that Zhen was the key.

"What can you tell me about the Guangdong Triad?" she asked, reaching for another dumpling. "According to our sources, they'd put a hit out on Zhen."

Yang heaved a sigh. "The gangs are the biggest disgrace in our country. The Guangdong Triad is one of the largest, with a membership of approximately forty thousand worldwide. They and their numerous subgroups control the drug and weapons smuggling throughout the region and have their fingers in all the illegal gambling and extortion rackets in the Guangdong Province. They're also heavily involved in the illegal mining of rare-earth metals."

Jordan blew out a soft whistle. They had enough members to fill two towns the size of the one she'd grown up in. "It's rumored the Triad has strong ties with the police and a significant number of the communist elite. Could they have had a hand in this?"

"Unfortunately, yes. The Guangdong Triad is unstoppable," Yang said. "*Chinaweek* even lists its *dragon head* as one of the fifty most powerful people in Asia."

Todd, who'd been picking at the rice on her plate with her chopsticks, looked up. "It's hard to combat them. Many of the communist leaders consider the gangs *patriotic*. Leaders have even called on them to disrupt protests in times of civil unrest."

Yang nodded, swirling the tea in his cup. "The worst part is that the Guangdong Triad is only one of our gangs. We have documented as many as twelve hundred others. It is the scourge of my country."

Jordan glanced up as the waiter approached carrying a fresh teapot in his left hand.

Odd. She remembered him being right-handed.

A knife flashed in his hand. Instinctively Jordan threw up her arm, deflecting the blow. The teapot fell to the floor and shattered.

Yang jumped to his feet and reached for his gun. "Stop! Police!"

The dining room erupted. Patrons jumped up and fled, knocking over tables, streaming toward the exits. Jordan spotted eight young men in various sizes and shapes, dressed in black and wearing bandanas across their faces, coming through the front door and pushing toward them through the crowd.

The waiter jumped up before Yang could clear his gun from his holster.

Jordan lunged. Grabbing the waiter's wrist, she twisted the man's arm. He spun, his sleeve riding up to reveal the bottom half of a dragon's tail tattoo. Jordan forced him to face her, then jabbed him hard in the throat, and he fell to the ground.

Yang wrestled his pistol free and fired it once in the air. "Police."

Again the waiter staggered to his feet, hitting Yang hard on the back of the neck. The detective grunted and went down, falling on top of his weapon. Just as quickly, Jordan slammed the waiter back to the floor. Behind her, she could see Todd grappling with an assailant.

"Run," Todd yelled.

The attacker lunged, then stepped back holding a bloody knife. Todd screamed and gripped her side, blood streaming through her fingers.

"Go!" she yelled.

Jordan sized up the advancing team. They carried knives, no guns, and they were focused on her. If she ran, they would follow, hopefully leaving Todd and Yang alone. Still, she found it hard to abandon them.

"Go!" Todd yelled again.

Jordan bolted. Taking the emergency exit, she found herself on the busy street. "*Gau mehng ā*!" Help!

People all around ducked into doorways. Only two men remained in the open. They approached and didn't look friendly.

"Stop her," yelled a man running into the street behind her. He grabbed hold of her hair, and Jordan instinctively stepped back, releasing the tension that threatened to pull the strands from her scalp. Grabbing his hand with both of hers, she rotated until his arm bent backward and then pulled back his pinky finger until she heard the bone snap. He quickly released his grip, and she kicked him hard in the groin.

Seeking an avenue of escape, she found herself face-to-face with one of the men in the street. He was big. A dragon tattoo wrapped his arm. He looked like he thought this was fun.

"You want to fight?" he said, grinning.

Jordan feinted to the right. He dodged in front of her. She moved left, and he dodged left.

"You want the police?" He threw back his head. "*Gingchaat!*" he shouted, then looked around, spreading his hands wide. "What, no officers coming to help you?"

The group of assailants had formed a semicircle at her back. Through the restaurant window, she could see people bending over Todd and Yang. Help may have been summoned, but she would likely be captured or killed before they arrived.

The first rule of defense was "when placed in a dangerous situation, find an escape route." Her best option was through the man blocking her path. With luck, he would trip up his friends.

Reaching into her pocket, she pulled out her "tactical pen." She'd carried one since academy training. It looked like an ordinary writing instrument, but it was made out of aircraft-grade aluminum and had a strong pointed end that could be used as an ice pick. It was the next best thing to a gun.

Palming the pen in her right hand, she raised her hands as if ready to fight.

"Ooohh, the lady wants to box," the man said. Pulling back his right arm, he took a swing.

Jordan raised her left arm, and his fist connected with her elbow. She braced for the jolt. At the same time, she swung her right hand and drove the point of the tactical pen hard into his pectoral muscles. When the man dropped to his knees, Jordan jumped over his body and ran.

"Catch the bitch!" the man yelled, one arm clutched tight to his side, his right hand cradled in his lap. Two blocks down, Jordan could see the entrance to the Di Shi Fu Shopping Mall.

She pushed herself faster, putting the results of her daily physical training to the test. She held a thirty-second lead when she hit the front door.

With no time to assess her best move, she pushed through the crowd and jumped on the escalator to the second floor, taking the steps two at a time, pushing past angry customers while ignoring their angry protests.

"There she is!"

Jordan looked down from the top of the escalator. A gangster pointed up at her. Three others were already on the moving stairs.

She bolted to the right. None of the storefronts she passed appeared to have exits. At the end of the corridor, wide doors opened into a department store. Racing inside, she spotted another escalator. Running through the accessory department, she snatched up a pink silk scarf, then rode up a floor, again threading her way through the people above her. She kept her eye on the store entrance.

One of the men entered and pointed straight at her. "There."

Damn! Reaching the top of the escalator, she turned to the sales women manning the floor and begged for help. *"Mh'gōi bōng ngóh."*

Several turned away, but one woman stepped forward. "Come with me."

She moved swiftly, and Jordan stayed tight on her heels. Her only hope was for the woman to show her an alternate way out of the store.

"In here." The saleswoman ushered her into a stock room full of racks of women's clothing and pointed to an emergency exit. "This leads into the warehouse. You can get back to the ground from there."

"Mh'gōi."

"You don't have much time. Cover your hair."

A commotion outside indicated her time was up.

"Hide!" the saleswoman ordered.

Jordan slithered behind several racks of dresses and ducked down. Through gaps in the fabric, she watched as four men pushed into the room.

"Where did she go?" one demanded.

The saleswoman pointed to the door.

Three of the men took the ruse. Shoving the woman aside, they ran for the warehouse exit. The fourth man paused, casting his gaze over the racks of clothing. He tossed one rack to the side, pawing his way toward the back of the stacks.

The saleswoman fled the stock room. Jordan was on her own.

"Come out, come out," the man said. "I know you're here. I can smell you."

Jordan held her breath and remained still.

"Don't be foolish, girl. This will be much easier if you just surrender. We don't want to hurt you. We just want to talk."

Which is why the waiter came at me with a knife?

"You should have let sleeping dogs lie," the man said, flinging another rack to the side. He was within spitting distance now. Jordan gripped her pen tighter.

The man's hands grabbed the edge of the rack Jordan was hidden behind. She glanced up. Their eyes locked.

He flung the rack sideways, and Jordan sprang to her feet. She lunged, driving the tactical pen deep into his sternal notch.

The man grabbed his throat. Blood gurgled out between his fingers.

Jordan sprinted for the exit. Drawing a deep breath, she pushed through the door, hoping no one waited behind it.

Inside, the warehouse appeared to be empty. Pallets of boxes formed long rows, bisected by wider aisles on either end and down the middle. Jordan chose the center aisle and headed for the back of the building. Finding a set of stairs, she descended to the ground floor that ended at an exit presumably to the street. Above, footsteps pounded on the floor.

The gang members must have circled around. Shouts indicated they'd found their friend. Jordan had no choice but to push open the door.

She found herself in a narrow alleyway with only foot and bicycle traffic. No one waited for her. People moved in both directions past multiple vendors hawking their wares. Quickly, Jordan wrapped the scarf around her head hijab-style, stooped her shoulders to appear shorter, and fell in step with the other pedestrians. To hurry would draw attention. Right now, her best chance of escape was trying to blend in.

A few moments passed before she heard the shouts of the men reaching the alley. By then she was at the intersection with Di Shi Fu Road. She could see the gang members in the glass reflection of the storefront on the corner. The men were searching the crowds in both directions, while one man studied his phone.

Was he tracking her?

Pulling out her cell phone, Jordan removed the SIM card and dropped the casing into the birdcage of a vendor walking past in the opposite direction. With luck, they would follow the signal, and it would buy her some time.

At the corner, she merged with the crush of pedestrians moving away from Di Shi Fu Street, aware the gang members were searching for her and unsure where to go next. She had to assume the Triad didn't want her to find Kia Zhen. But why? And how had they known she was there? How had they known she was even in China?

First things first, Jordan told herself. Right now she needed to put some distance between herself and the gangsters. Once she was safe, there would be time to figure things out.

Chapter 16

Stopping next to a bronze statue of a man pouring tea out of an oversized pot, Jordan took stock of her surroundings. The gang wouldn't be far behind her. She needed a change of clothes.

Shangxiajiu Commercial Pedestrian Street teemed with people—tourists and locals alike—looking for cheap fashions. The wide granite-tiled street stretched into the distance flanked by a mixture of Qi Lou, veranda-style architecture, and more European buildings. Adding to the business, horizontal signs of every color advertised a variety of stores. The area pulsed with energy.

Across the street was a four-story building bearing an H&M sign. Ducking inside, she bought herself a pair of skinny black pants, a white T-shirt, and a black purse. After changing in the dressing room and transferring the money and rest of the items from her jacket pockets into the purse, she plaited her hair, winding the scarf in to disguise the color, then discarded her clothes in a trash receptacle on the street. Moving onto the next store, she bought a pair of black flats. Two stores down from there, she purchased a pair of sunglasses, a parasol, and three cell phones, topped up with minutes, from a vendor who didn't ask to see her ID.

Back on the street, Jordan found an open bench and opened the parasol. Many of the women walking the street were using them for shade. Hers was for cover. Then pulling one of the new phones out of the bag, she dialed RSO David Lory's direct line.

When he answered, she got right to the point. "I don't know if you've heard, but things have gone south."

"What the hell happened?"

The details poured out. "I have no idea how the others are. Detective Yang's likely to have a headache. Todd was stabbed in the stomach. She lost a lot of blood."

She heard Lory dialing on the main office phone. "Mary, put a call through to Todd's office. Get me an update, now!" Then he was back talking to Jordan. "You need to get back to the consulate."

"The Triad knew I was here," Jordan said. "How did they get that information? Who can we trust?" She couldn't help but remember that McClasky hadn't trusted anyone in his time here. He'd jumped the first flight out of the country and look where that had gotten him.

What she wanted to know was who knew she was coming who also knew about McClasky's having been here? Five people jumped to mind: the legal attaché, RSO Todd, the consulate's political officer, Detective Yang, and his bureau chief. Giving Yang and Todd the benefit of the doubt narrowed her choices to three: the legat, who worked out of Beijing and had minimal contacts in the Guangdong province; Yang's chief, a potentially corrupt Chinese police official; and the PO, who—if Lory was correct—was Guangzhou's CIA chief of station.

"Don't trust anybody," Lory said, confirming what Jordan already suspected. "Sit tight. I'll call you right back."

Minutes after the phone went dead, Jordan spotted the first gang member weaving his way through the crowd. He was easy to pick out. If the dragon tattoo spiraling his forearm and the bandana looping his neck weren't enough, the parting of the crowd leaving him wide berth was a dead giveaway.

Jordan lifted her phone and snapped a picture. He turned and looked in her direction.

Hunkering down under the parasol, she kept track of him in her peripheral vision and texted the photo to the forensic lab in Kyiv. She considered processing it through the lab in Israel, but it was Lory's case. Besides, no sense in depleting her own office budget when she knew she could trust Henry. With luck, he could help her ID the gangster, or at least tell her something about the tattoo. Until then, her best hope was anonymity.

Several more gang members entered the street, moving through the crowd and scattering people before them like schools of fish. Jordan stayed seated, feigning interest in her phone.

Finally, Lory called her back. "Todd is in the ICU. It doesn't look good. Yang was checked out at the hospital for a possible head injury and then released. Can you find your way back to the consulate?"

"Yes."

"Good. We've just received an official request from the director-general of the Public Security Department of Guangdong Province to stop our investigation into Kia Zhen's activities in China. From here on out, the local police will handle the case. They will inform us when they learn something. Pack it up, Jordan. We've been benched. Your job is done."

"But sir—"

He cut her off. "It's not open for discussion. They view our investigation as a means for the U.S. to gather intel on China."

"They think I'm spying?" Jordan wished she had some water. The Chinese had been known to execute spies.

"They haven't gone that far, but we can't afford to antagonize them. Not with what's happening in the South China Sea. As far as the Chinese are concerned, they gave us our guy and got rid of a drug dealer. End of story." An ice cube clinked into a glass, and it sounded like he was pouring a drink. "Just get back to the consulate, Jordan. We're bringing you home on the first flight out."

"I don't think that's smart."

"It isn't a choice." Frustration infused his voice. She wasn't sure if it was directed at her or the situation.

Jordan's wet her lips. She needed to come clean about the fragment she'd taken from the PR Flight 91 crash site. She hadn't intended to withhold information, but there had never been an opportunity to bring it up—until now.

"Agent Lory, there's something I should have told you." She described her find and told him what Henry had figured out.

"Go back to the beginning. Did I hear you right? Are you suggesting it was a Chinese weapon that brought down that plane?"

She understood his incredulity, but things were starting to take shape in her head. "Think about it, sir. The person McClasky brought out of the People's Republic, the man claiming to be Kia Zhen, swore he had information of vital importance to our national security. It would make sense that the same information could be harmful to China."

"Keep talking."

"So who orchestrated the prisoner swap? Our government, the Chinese government, or the Triad? Probably not China, they would want to keep whatever Zhen or his replacement knew from reaching the U.S."

"Motive to shoot down a plane."

"Maybe the crash victim was a valuable asset the CIA needed to get home. What better way to smuggle someone out of China?"

"Another motive for China to shoot down the plane."

"And what if you're Zhen? Can you think of a better way to get the U.S. off your back than to fake your own death?"

"Are you suggesting the Triad had something to do with this?"

"They knew I was coming."

"What are you proposing we do, Jordan?"

"First we have to find Zhen. Then we need to figure out who the actual victim was and why he was on the plane. And let's not forget the men who ambushed the transport. They were Russian."

"I don't get where you are going with this."

Jordan puffed out a breath. He still hadn't connected the dots. "The Russians. The Chinese. It takes a pretty big gun to shoot down a plane."

She heard him set his glass the down hard as the ramifications sank in.

"*Shit*. You're thinking this has something to do with a weapons deal."

"Bingo." From the noise, Jordan figured he'd spilled his drink. "What is Zhen accused of stealing?"

"Sit tight, Jordan. I'll call you right back."

Famous last words, she thought when the line went dead. Slipping the cell phone into her purse, she folded up the parasol, stood, and stretched. He'd deflected her question, and she'd been sitting so long, her muscles were stiffening up from the fight in front of the restaurant. Plus she was beginning to draw curious stares. As the sun moved low in the sky, neon lights had flared on, creating the illusion of a Chinese Times Square where tourists and locals congregated once the night descended.

Jordan knew one thing for sure. She needed to get off this street.

Pulling up a map on her phone, she headed down a narrow side street toward the nearest place she might find a taxi. Hemmed in on both sides by tall buildings and vendors manning pushcart stands, she felt slightly claustrophobic, amplified by the feeling of being watched. She glanced back over her shoulder and felt her heart skip a beat. She wasn't being paranoid. Nye Davis stood talking to a vendor two kiosks back.

Quickly she reversed directions, moving with the crowd until she was up in his face. "What the hell are you doing here?"

A woman behind her pushed her hard, and she found herself slamming against his chest. He steadied her and pulled her out of the pedestrian traffic.

"Nice running into you, too."

She took a step back. "Cut the crap, Davis. Why are you following me?"

He held his hands wide. "Let's just say I'm intrigued."

"How did you even know where I was?"

"I have contacts."

They had to be good. Only a handful of people knew she had left Ukraine. "You need to back off. This situation is dangerous."

"I get that." He jerked his head in the direction of Shangxiajiu Street. "I considered jumping into the fray back there, but you handled yourself like a pro."

"It's my job." Though, clearly she'd lapsed in employing her observational skills. How had she not noticed him sooner? "Where were you when that went down?"

"The café across the street from the restaurant. I was trying to find out who you were meeting with. I recognized Todd from my research, but who was the guy she introduced you to?"

Worried someone might overhear their conversation, Jordan looped her arm through his and leaned in close. "Let's walk."

He duplicated her visual sweep, then pulled his arm free and draped it across her shoulders like they were a couple. "Why not?"

Turning around, they headed back along the street. She had to admit it was the perfect cover. Anyone searching for her would be looking for a lone American woman, not one half of a duo out for a stroll. Yet it bothered her how safe she felt in the circle of his arm. "Why so much interest in what I do?"

"Like I told you back in Kyiv, you look like a girl with a story." When she tensed, he hugged her closer. "It's true, Agent Jordan. Every other journalist I know is camped outside IIC headquarters. They're all being fed the same cock-and-bull story. I chose to follow a hunch. I think you know something we're not being told. And from what happened at lunch, it's clear I'm not the only one who thinks so."

As much as she wished for a confidant, a Reuters reporter didn't fit the bill. Anything she said would be fodder for his reports. So for the second time, she fed him the party line. "I'm only here tying up loose ends."

"Like finding out what your dead agent or Kia Zhen knew that got PR Flight 91 blown out of the sky?"

How did he know about Zhen? His name hadn't been officially released. "I told you before, the crash is being ruled an accident. McClasky didn't know any—"

Davis spun her toward him, gripping both of her shoulders tightly. "Don't play me for a fool, Agent."

"Lower your voice and let go of me, now," Jordan said.

Davis dropped his hands. "Sorry, Agent Jordan, I—"

"Shhhhh." She glanced around to see if anyone was watching them. "Drop the job title. Call me Jordan or Rae."

"Okay, *Rae*. Why not play straight with me? We both know there's a story in here. Maybe we can help each other, maybe we can—"

Her phone rang. It was Lory.

"Hold that thought," she said.

Raising a finger, she stepped away and answered the call.

"I've taken this up line, Jordan. The consul general was unavailable, so I spoke with the ambassador in Beijing. He says you need to come in. The director agrees. With the tension in the South China Sea, the trade alliances, and China's dumping of steel, the diplomatic situation is touchy at best. No one feels we can afford to ruffle feathers right now, not based solely on conjecture. I've had Mary book you on a flight for Ukraine leaving tomorrow afternoon."

"Any concern someone might try to shoot down my plane?" She hadn't meant it to be funny, and he didn't take it that way.

"Do you have a problem with that, Jordan?"

"As a matter of fact, yes." She knew she'd pissed him off. *Too bad*! Still, she chose her next words carefully. "My packing up and leaving without Zhen plays directly into somebody's hands. Whoever that someone is, he doesn't want us to find the kid. You've got to ask yourself why."

"Why?"

"Because they don't want us to recover whatever it is Zhen stole, or maybe they still need him? The fact that the NSA is guarding the information on the espionage charges just backs up my theory."

Lory fell silent. Maybe she was getting through.

"The police are looking for you, Jordan. They want to question you regarding what happened at lunch. If they get to you before you can get to the consulate, you will be detained. The ARSO is a little overwhelmed by what's happened, so let me give you the PO's cell number in case of emergency."

She committed the number to memory. "What about Zhen?"

"We've been over this, Jordan. Let's work on an extraction plan for you."

"I understand your concern, Agent Lory. I'm just not sure we can afford to walk away. If Zhen sold the weapons plans, it may still be possible to retrieve them. If they've built prototypes, we need to destroy them."

"You're not a spy."

"I know that, sir."

"At best you've got some rudimentary training in covert operations. Hell, without the police liaison, you have no authority to operate on foreign soil."

"I also swore an oath to protect my country and its national security."

"What are you asking for, Jordan?"

"Just a couple more days. I've got a feeling Zhen is alive. Let me keep looking for him. Give me forty-eight hours. If I don't have something tangible by then, I'll get on the plane." She could hear Lory's fingers drumming the desk. Maybe he'd listen if she sweetened the pot. "Look, if I come away empty-handed, tell them I disobeyed your orders. If I find what I think I'll find, you take the bows."

"Daugherty warned me about you."

"Did he now?" Jordan wasn't surprised.

Chapter 17

She had barely put away her phone when Davis slipped his arm around her shoulders and started guiding her back toward Shangxiajiu Pedestrian Street.

"We can't stay here," Davis said.

Instinctively Jordan pulled away.

"Listen," he said, tightening his grip and bending his mouth so close to her ear she could feel his warm breath. "There are two Triad members coming up the street. We need to backtrack, now!"

She peeked over his shoulder. Two gang members moved swiftly in their direction. She wasn't sure if the two men were dialed in on them yet, but it wouldn't be long before she and Davis hit their radar. Then all hell would break loose.

Tucking her head against Davis's shoulder to hide her red hair, she matched his stride toward Shangxiajiu Commercial Pedestrian Street.

Davis leaned in. "When we get there, you need to be quick. Turn right and try to blend in with the crowd, then when you get to Upper Ninth Road, hail a cab."

Since when did he give the orders?

"What are you planning to do?" she asked.

"Run a diversion."

His words caused her to slow her pace. "I can't let you put yourself in danger."

"Keep moving, Rae," he said, guiding her forward. "I can handle myself."

"Right, because all international correspondents receive specialized training." Or because of the mentioned military background? When she had a chance, she would ask him about that.

"In my case, yes."

They locked eyes, and she saw a sharpness there that made her believe it was more than a little. He had a look she'd seen in the eyes of agents and Marines prepared to put their lives on the line to protect those entrusted into their care. She'd seen the same look in Batya Ganani's eyes when they were running for their lives in Israel, the same look in the captain's eyes when they had come under attack outside Hoholeve. It was a look that belonged to someone with combat experience, someone on a mission, someone with training who had a plan.

She had a better view of the men now. Both were small and slight, the dragon tattoo curling around their biceps. "Maybe they can tell us what happened with Zhen?"

"Don't even think it." It almost sounded like an order.

Jordan peered up at him, but he never looked down, his gaze sweeping the crowd like a built-in sonar device. "If we work together, I think we could take them."

"Please, can we just go with my way? Where there are two of these guys, there are more, and at the moment they're not interested in me. It's you they want to kill, and I'm not about to let that happen." His tone had softened, but his voice still held an impervious quality that made her want to rebel and acquiesce at the same time.

"Since when did you become my guardian angel?"

He didn't respond, but she felt his arm muscles bunch like a cat getting ready to spring. "We're almost there. When I tell you, veer right and get to the end of the street. Catch a cab and go straight to your hotel, not the consulate."

For a split second, she wondered if this might be a trap. Why was he waving her off the consulate, when Lory told her to go straight there?

Not that it mattered. There was no way Jordan was going to serve him up as a decoy.

Before she could come up with an alternate plan, they reached the intersection at Shangxiajiu Pedestrian Street. "Listen to me, Davis."

He ignored her, forcing his way into the passing throngs of people while keeping his arm firmly around her shoulders. Then as the crowd closed ranks behind them, he spun her away to the right and disappeared. Jordan found herself caught in the current of people, swooped away like a fish in a fast-running river. Managing to twist herself around, she stumbled along backward while moving sideways against the tide.

Focused on keeping her feet, it took her a moment to spot Davis. He stood a head above the crowd moving swiftly in the opposite direction. Then two gang members breached the crowd and loomed before her. They looked both ways before spotting Davis, then taking the bait, moved off in his direction. His gambit had worked.

Afraid of what might happen if the gangsters caught up to him, Jordan started following. Then suddenly, as if fulfilling a prophecy, four more gang members materialized. When two of them headed her way, there was nothing she could do except turn around and head for Upper Ninth Street.

She had almost made the taxis when someone grabbed her arm.

"Where you going, lady?" asked a recognizable voice. The man wrenched her arm, spinning her around. The gangster from Di Shi Fu Road, the one she'd stabbed with her tactical pen, grinned.

"Let me go." She tried pulling her arm away, but he held tight. When she tried twisting out of his grasp, he laughed and clamped down harder.

"You're not getting away this time, bitch."

She saw light flash off a knife blade and noted the swoop of his arm as it skimmed toward her. She arched away, but there was nowhere to go.

Jordan braced for the strike. When it came, the blow knocked her down, but the only pain came from her elbow slamming against the ground. She moved her hand to her side. No blood.

It took her another beat to realize the gangster was laid out cold on the tiles beside her. The other gang members had scattered, and suddenly Davis loomed above her.

"Where did you come from?" Jordan sat up. Pain shot along her arm as she tried to plant her hand and help herself to her feet.

"I'll explain later. Right now, we need to go!"

A crowd was gathering, forming a blockade around them, growing and tightening as people pressed close to see what all the commotion was about. From somewhere down the street, she heard a police whistle.

Realizing that getting caught like this, with a Triad member down, would do nothing to help her present situation, she reached for Davis's hand. He pulled her to her feet.

"*Mhgòi*, excuse me," he said, plowing a path to the street.

There was no shortage of taxis at the corner and no hesitation on the part of the driver to spirit them away in the face of the descending police once Davis flashed a hundred dollar bill. Jordan gave the driver the address. Once clear of the area, she drew a deep breath, exhaled slowly, and settled back in the seat.

"Thank you for back there."

Davis waved off her gratitude. "You would have done the same."

"I would have thought about it."

He grinned. "You know how you can pay me back."

Jordan stole a look at him from the corner of her eye. From the way he'd disarmed the gangster and laid him out cold on the ground, it was clear he was more than just a news correspondent. Just like her father had been more than a hockey player. This man had skills. The question was how current they were and where they'd been acquired.

"How?"

"With a story."

"If that's what you're really after," she said.

"What's that supposed to mean?"

"Nothing." Jordan shrugged. "Except that once we're free of this cab, I've got a couple questions for you."

Chapter 18

The taxi driver made two passes around the consulate. The first one established that the Chinese military had set up camp. The second showed military placed strategically at every entry point.

"I told you it wasn't a good idea to come here. Any other thoughts?" Davis asked.

"One." Mary had booked Jordan at the Guangzhou Mei Ling Hotel several blocks from the U.S. consulate. The small building was wedged in between the Zhujiang New Town subway station and the Union store, a seller of basic Western and imported foods. Large red lettering in both Chinese and English festooned the hotel's portico, while inside the front desk glistened in gaudy tiles of shiny gold. "May I help you?" asked a woman behind the desk. She saved her brightest smile for Davis, who stood behind Jordan in line.

"I have a reservation," Jordan said.

"Passport?" After verifying Jordan's documents and swiping a credit card, the woman handed everything back. "Would you like two keys?"

Jordan looked over at Davis. "Oh, we're not together. He needs his own room."

"Do you have a reservation?"

Davis shook his head and flashed a smile. "It was an unexpected trip."

"I'm sorry, but the hotel is full. There is much going on in Guang-zhou this week. I'm afraid you'll have trouble finding a room in the city." The woman glanced between them again. "Perhaps your friend would reconsider?"

"Does it have two beds?" Davis asked.

Jordan looked at the woman and shook her head.

"Let me make a few calls and see what I can find." After phoning five of their backup hotels, the hotel clerk cradled the receiver. "Sorry, no luck. Everywhere full."

"How about a rollaway?" This time he looked beseechingly at Jordan. "You wouldn't really put me out on the street, would you?"

The woman tapped on her keyboard. "I can have the houseman bring up a cot, but there will be an extra charge."

"I'll pay for it," Davis said. "In fact, I'll pay for the whole room."

"Nice expense account," Jordan said, feeling her resolve crack despite her better judgment. It didn't help that he was so damned good-looking or that he'd just saved her ass. She waited a moment longer before giving in. "You're buying dinner, too."

Their room was on the third floor, and she almost retracted her goodwill offer upon seeing the layout. Only slightly more muted in tone than the common areas, the bedroom walls were covered in gold-and-white wallpaper descending to planked hardwood floors. The cot had already been delivered and was crammed into the tiny space along with a double bed, a flat-screen TV, a small desk with an electric kettle and ergonomic chair, a clothes rack, and a sitting area consisting of a small table and two chairs looking out at a small French balcony.

"Look at it this way, it's bigger than most New York City hotel rooms," Davis said, dropping his backpack in the middle of the cot. "Where's your luggage?"

"I'm guessing at the consulate."

"I take it you had your go-bag with you?"

"In Agent Todd's car."

Davis stepped to the window and looked out. "Does anyone know you're staying here?"

"Not unless someone hacked my e-mail, which is always a possibility. But seeing as we weren't ambushed upon our arrival, I'm fairly certain we're okay for the night."

He seemed content to take her word for it. "Hungry?"

"Starved." She'd hardly eaten anything since yesterday morning. Just a bite or two before lunch had been interrupted.

While Davis ordered take out from the in-house restaurant, Jordan checked out the bathroom. Separated from the main room by an etched glass wall, it was designed more for aesthetics than providing privacy. After washing her face, she conducted a quick survey of her newly acquired cuts and bruises. Her elbow was red and slightly swollen, leaving her forearm and hand slightly numb. She needed to put ice on it. There were dark fingerprint marks on her arm. Bruises deep enough that if Henry were there, he might have been able to pull fingerprints and ID her assailant. Last, there was a welt where the tip of the gangster's knife had grazed her stomach. She'd been lucky not to have suffered Todd's fate. She owed that to Davis.

Which was a big part of why he was in the next room. That and the fact he was incredibly handsome. She couldn't deny her attraction. Still, it didn't earn him a pass on explaining where he'd learned to disarm an armed assailant and knock him out cold.

Davis was sitting at the desk typing something on his computer when she reentered the room, so she brewed some tea and then settled into one of the chairs beneath the window. The view was of another wing of the hotel and a small courtyard.

While Davis worked, Jordan pulled out her phone and called Henry. She'd sent him the photo only a few hours ago, so there was a good chance he hadn't even looked at it yet. Still, identifying the men who tried killing her—twice—was high on her list, and it was worth a try.

Henry sounded pleased that she'd called. After a few seconds of chitchat, she got down to business. "Did you get the photo I sent?"

"Yep."

"Any luck identifying the gang member?"

"I'm one of the best forensic specialists you'll find, Rae, but even I'm not that good. The facial recognition software is running, but do you have any idea how many Triad members or suspected Triad members there are?"

"Over forty thousand." High enough numbers that the odds of the database coughing up a match to one of the men was slim. "What about the tattoo? Did you find anything on it?"

If he was surprised she knew, he gave no indication.

"We had better luck there. The Triad is actually composed of a lot of little Triads, and that particular tattoo is associated with one called the Danxia Triad. It's a subgroup of the Guangdong Triad, based out of Shaoguan."

Jordan set down her tea and reached for the small pad of paper and the pen on the table. "Can you spell that?" She scribbled as he parsed out the letters. "Isn't that close to the area where the fragment originated?"

"Spot on."

There was the connection she'd been looking for. "I owe you, Henry."

"Bring me a souvenir."

Davis glanced up as she set down the phone. "Good news?"

Jordan picked her tea back up and considered how much she should tell him. She needed to be cautious. "Henry ID'd the tattoo."

"What's the connection with Shaoguan?"

He had been paying attention. She would have to be more careful. A rap at the door saved her from answering. "I'll bet it's the food."

"Don't think we're done here," Davis said, pushing back the desk chair and crossing to the door. His hand caught the handle, and then at the last minute, he looked through the peephole.

Davis yanked back his hand, and sharp pinpricks of fear propelled Jordan out of her chair. "What is—"

Davis cut her off with a hand signal, but it was his hard expression that made her swallow her words.

"Who is it?" she mouthed, starting forward to see.

Davis blocked her path. "It's the police. How the hell did they find us?"

The girl at the desk! They'd shown her their passports, and she must have entered them into the system. It was a rookie mistake. Jordan should have realized that the Chinese would be monitoring the hotels and watching for credit card usage. The Communist Party was notorious for tracking foreigners' movements—especially foreigners they wanted to question.

The Chinese detention centers carried their own reputation—thirty people jammed into a ten-by-ten cell with no blankets, chairs, beds, or pillows. Whether or not a prisoner was brought up on charges, all detainees were made to work for food, and corporal punishment was common. Once in custody, the police could detain them for as long as they wanted—forever unless someone at the consulate found out. Maybe even if they did.

They needed a way out.

Jordan flung open the windows to the French balcony and looked with dismay at the ornamental railing bolted to the outside of the building. Sticking her head out, she could see all the windows were decorated the same and there was not a fire escape in sight. She and Davis were four floors up with no way down.

Leaning out to look at the ground below, she was discouraged to find the night blanketing the small common area that stretched between the two buildings. The dark made it nearly impossible to gauge the distance to the ground or to see what lay directly beneath them. She would guess it was thirty feet to the ground from the bottom of the railing. Farther out, some of the passage had been converted to parking spots, and the lights and action of the city lit up the streets at either end.

The police tried again, this time pounding on the door. Jordan could hear them talking to each other.

"We need to get out of here," she whispered. "It sounds like one of them is heading back to the front desk for a key. That will only buy us a few minutes. Any ideas?"

"Only one." Davis picked up one of the chairs near the window and jammed its back under the doorknob.

Jordan smiled. That might buy them an extra fifteen seconds, if they were lucky.

Yanking back the covers on the bed, she stripped the sheets and knotted one to the other. Based on the average length of a queen-sized bed, and subtracting the inches tied up in the knots, one bed provided close to ten feet of makeshift rope. Quick on the uptake, Davis grabbed his camera off the bed, looping it around his neck; stripped the cot; and added his sheets to one end of the chain while Jordan tied the other end to the bottom of the balcony railing. Hung for decoration, she could only hope it would bear their weight.

Davis held up his end of the makeshift rope. "It won't make it to the ground."

Jordan reached for the sheet and tossed it over the edge. "It doesn't have to. If I've done the math right, we'll run out of sheet with just over ten feet to go. That's a single-story jump. It's doable. When you get to the end of the sheet, just hang and drop. Let your knees and body absorb the shock." She could see he wanted to discuss it, but there wasn't time.

"Go!" she ordered.

"Why me?" Davis moved toward the window. "Oh, I know. It's because you want to see if this thing will hold?"

Jordan grinned. "That, and I'm trained to go last."

He hesitated a moment, then swinging his camera around to his back, he clutched the window casings and lowered his weight onto the wrought-iron fencing. Jordan felt a tsunami of relief when it didn't strip away from the building. Swinging his legs over the top rail, Davis lowered himself down and grabbed onto the sheet.

The policeman outside the door shouted to someone. Jordan tried to listen. "I think they're back with the key, Nye."

She watched him rappel down the side of the building, like a climber slipping along the line, holding the sheet above and below his body and using his feet to push off the side of the building. It looked like he'd done something like this before.

As he reached the end of the line, she heard the click of the door.

Behind her, the chair Davis had jammed under the doorknob scraped along the floor. Then its back legs bit and held, giving her a few more seconds of time. Looking down, she spotted Davis waving from the small patch of grass.

Her turn.

The chair splintered as she jumped the railing. Clinging to the backside, she watched the door swing inward and catch on the security chain. *Another few seconds.*

Ignoring the pain in her arm and elbow, Jordan shimmied down the bed sheets hand over hand. Nearing the end of the makeshift rope, she felt a jerk on the fabric and looked up. A head poked through the window, while someone else's hands reached through the iron and grabbed hold of the sheets.

"Stop, police," yelled the man peering down on her. Then came another tug, and the hands started pulling her up.

"Drop," Davis yelled.

The policeman barked an order. "He's sending someone to cover the back," she yelled to Davis. Another pull hoisted her another foot.

With a quick *Oh Lord*, Jordan let go.

The air swirled upwards all around her. She registered the startled look on the policeman's face above her and then braced for the landing.

She slammed into Davis's arms, which was better than hitting the ground. "Where to?" Davis asked, setting her onto her feet. "The consulate?"

She shook her head. It was a six-minute walk or a three-minute run, but that's where the police would expect them to go. Not to mention the Chinese military had locked down the perimeter. "Head for the subway."

The Zhujiang subway station sat on the corner, with trains departing in four directions every couple of minutes. Entering through the glass doors, they raced down the escalator while pushing past people on the steps. A cavernous room opened to a series of shops and was divided up by a row of royal-blue columns marching across the white-tiled floor. Signs over the portals to the tracks signaled the arrival of trains and listed their next destinations.

On the far wall, a bank of six or seven self-service ticket machines spit out travel cards for cash or credit. People queued three or four deep. Jordan chose one line, Davis another. Impatiently she tapped her foot, watching the escalator for any sign of the police. Based on the snippets of conversations around her, this was a shorter than usual wait.

Thank God for small favors.

Upon reaching the ticket kiosk first, she signaled to Davis and, pooling their money, came up with the right cash to buy two one-day passes. It gave them on-and-off privileges for the next twenty-four hours. If they could get in and out of a station quickly enough, they'd have time to change trains and disappear before the police figured out in what direction they'd gone.

The next scheduled train departed on Line 3 to the north. Standing on the platform, Jordan had a clear shot of the escalator. Simultaneous with the train pulling into the station, two policemen rode into view. Grabbing Davis's sleeve, she pulled him along the platform, keeping her face averted. A rush of commuters poured off the train when it stopped, and Jordan took advantage of the crowd. Pushing against the flow, she urged Davis to keep up and boarded the last car. Grabbing two seats in the back, she bent forward and pretended to tie her shoes until the train cleared the station, leaving the two cops behind.

Chapter 19

Jordan sat up and studied the subway map that spanned the windows. Davis slumped against the seat and stared at her. "What's really going on here, Rae?"

She pointed to the sign. "We're on the Northeast Branch. We need to get off at the next station."

"You know what I meant."

She looked him straight in the eyes. "Let's get out of this first, and then we can talk."

"And you'll tell me the truth?"

A voice announced the next stop, and Jordan jumped to her feet. "We need to catch Line 1 to the west."

"Answer the question."

Jordan shifted her weight, maintaining her balance as the subway train slowed. He'd put his life on the line for her twice, and now he was a fugitive. If anyone had a right to know, he did. "I will."

After switching trains twice, Jordan and Davis got off at Quzhaung station on Haunshi East Road, an area known for its restaurants and clubs. Spotting a pay phone near a cybercafé, Jordan pulled Davis aside.

"Do you have any money?" She had a few coins in her pocket, but most of her money was in her purse back at the hotel.

"We can't go in here," he said. "The *wǎng kā* require you place an ID on file."

Of course, he was right. China regulated the use of the Internet and most electronic communication devices. Any person connecting you to a server was required by law to enter your name, birthdate, and ID number into the system. The same was true with any electronic purchase, such as a new SIM card for your phone. It meant the Chinese government knew—among other things—where everyone was, who they were talking to, and what type of social media they preferred.

"I just want to use the payphone."

In addition to his camera, Davis still had his passport, credit cards, and a wad of cash.

"How about coins? Do you have any coins?" She dug deeper in her pockets and produced a few jiao, China's equivalent of a dime. Davis produced his own handful. Between them it was enough.

The first person Jordan tried reaching was Lory. When his answering machine picked up, she was asked to deposit two yuan for three minutes, the equivalent of a dollar. She left a detailed message, explained she no longer had a phone, and ended up telling him she would try again later.

"What now?" Davis asked.

It was after midnight, and she had one local cell number, the one for the PO that Lory had given her earlier. She punched in the digits. If this didn't constitute an emergency, she didn't know what did. The PO was expecting her call. "What the hell have you gotten yourself into, Agent Jordan? The Chinese have posted military details outside the consulate gates, and I've been fielding calls from my local police contacts for the past hour."

"Is your phone secure?"

"As secure as you can get in China. Start talking."

Jordan told him about the attempts on her life, starting with the attack at the restaurant and ending with what had happened at the hotel.

"Any idea why they're so hot to find you?"

"I asked questions about Zhen." Jordan didn't feel comfortable giving him details over the phone. "Apparently I touched a nerve."

"That may be an understatement." He hemmed and hawed for a second, then said, "The quicker we get you off the streets the better. Where are you?"

"Are you sure the phone is safe?"

"I need to know where to send the driver."

Not really an answer, but she'd accept it. "We're near the Quzhaung subway station."

"We?"

She told him about Davis.

"Are you sure he can be trusted?"

"He had my back today." She could hear the PO breathing softly and wondered what he was thinking. Finally he spoke. "Okay, there's a twenty-four hour noodle and congee shop on Ziniu Road. Travel west on Huanshi East one block and turn left. The shop will be on your right. I'll send Charlie to pick you up. It will be at least an hour. He'll get you somewhere safe until we can sort this mess out. He's a good guy. You can trust him."

"And if things get dangerous?"

"Don't worry about Charlie," the PO said. "It wouldn't be his first rodeo."

* * *

Twenty minutes later, they were sitting at a table inside a small diner, bowls filled with food, looking out at the street. At this time of night, it was mostly young people their age who were out—men in white button-down shirts and black pants; women in various shades of silk teetering along on their three-inch stilettos. Between them they had a full view of the block.

Davis poured two glasses from a bottle of *Baijiu* and handed her one.

Jordan held up her hand and refused to take it. "I'm not sure this is a good idea."

"Come on, you haven't experienced China until you've tasted the sorghum wine." He set the glass on the table in front of her and raised the other in a toast. "*Ganbei*. It means 'dry the glass.' The locals drink it straight down."

Jordan studied him for a moment, then reached for the small cup on the table. *What the hell*, she thought. She was stiff and sore, and a drink would help take the edge off the pain. Clinking glasses, she wrinkled her nose at the strong aroma and braced herself for the shot. The amber liquid surprised her. It went down easy. Showing Davis her empty glass, she set it down.

"So are you going to tell me what's going on?" he said.

Jordan picked up her chopsticks and twisted them into her noodles. She knew she owed him some answers. He'd saved her life and now, because of her, he also was wanted by the Chinese police. But where did she start, and how much should she tell him?

"Come on, Rae. I think I've earned your trust enough to be read in. Consider me an asset."

"In the first place, DSS agents don't have assets. In the second, you do realize that assets can sometimes become collateral damage, right?"

"And sometimes they're disposable. I'm willing to take the risk."

He'd proven that. The question was, how much risk was she willing to take? After all, he worked for Reuters.

"Will you answer a few questions?" she asked.

"If it will get me some answers." Davis poured them another round of Baijiu. The second shot warmed her insides, and she felt herself thawing toward him. It was hard not to warm to the smile lighting up his handsome features.

"Where did you acquire your skills?"

"You mean my writing talent?"

"No. I mean your street fighting abilities, rappelling off a building. Those aren't typical everyday talents."

"Would you believe me if I told you I was raised in a tough neighborhood and used to frequent the climbing wall at the local gym?"

"No." Maybe in another place or time, but something in his eyes and the way he'd reacted to both situations convinced her there was more to it.

"When I joined the Army, I had some Special Forces training. I've kept active. It helps when you're a reporter asking to be embedded into war zones."

"Why become a reporter?"

"Do you have a thing against all journalists, or just against me?"

The gruffness in his voice surprised her. "I don't know what you mean."

"Sure you do. You struggled to even say the word."

She looked down at her glass, the drops of liquor like garnets on crystal, then she lifted her gaze. "I just don't understand how you can justify making a living capitalizing on other people's pain and misery."

"Is that how you see my job?" His dark eyes locked on hers. "Let's get something straight, I do what I do because someone needs to tell the stories. A lot of people died in that plane crash, a lot of people were left without mothers, fathers, sisters, and brothers. But what you see as capitalizing on the survivors' misery, others view as a ferreting out of the truth in order to find justice for the victims."

Jordan sat in stunned silence. He sounded impassioned enough to be believable. "If that's true, I owe you an apology."

"But you don't really buy it, do you? What happened to make you so cynical? Is it so hard to believe that some of us wear white hats?"

She had to admit, he had a good shtick. She'd painted him with the same brush as she did all reporters. Maybe she was wrong about him. "Let's just say, it hasn't been my experience."

"That's what happens when you bring your own baggage to the party."

"Sometimes I need a bellman."

"Don't we all?" He poured the last of the Baijiu into their glasses, then lifted his in a toast. "To second chances."

She raised her glass. "Second chances."

Chapter 20

Kozachenko eased his finger off the trigger of his Tokarev TT-33 and lowered his weapon. "We weren't expecting you."

Stas lowered his hands, wiping the sweat off his palms. "I can see that. You nearly blew my *fucking* head off."

"Next time instead of walking in unannounced, you really should call ahead."

"I thought the pakhan had done that."

Kozachenko grunted. "He told me you would contact us. He didn't say you'd be foolish enough to come here. How do you know you weren't followed?" Kozachenko stepped to the side and looked past the soldier, peering into the dark. The risk of a face-to-face seemed unwarranted.

"No one is there," Stas said, pushing past Kozachenko. "I came because we must move the gun tonight."

"To where? Why haven't I been told of the plan?"

"It has only just been arranged. We're taking it to Nyzhni Yares'ky." Pulling a map from his pocket, Stas walked over, spread it open on the hood of the GAZ, and pointed to a small town south of their location. He detailed the plan, then refolded the map. "We need to get this right, Vasyl. Timing will be everything, and there won't be a second opportunity."

* * *

Several hours later, with Yolkin riding shotgun where he could keep an eye on him, Kozachenko pulled the truck from the cover of the trees onto the unnamed road. It was 1:50 AM, three minutes after the moon-set, and dark clouds muddled the sky. Stas had gone ahead to make sure the road was clear to the turnoff. Barkov and three men had gone ahead to ready the gate. Dudyk was behind with the others.

Once he'd turned the truck onto Partyzanska Street, they were committed. The only thing Kozachenko could do now was to keep the engine noise steady as he lumbered the truck through the sleeping town.

Turning onto Lenin Street, a lone car approached from the south, and Kozachenko's heart accelerated. He watched as the car passed and disappeared from the sideview mirror. The driver never even tapped his brakes. Still, with all the televised accounts of the ambush, he radioed Dudyk to keep an eye out for the vehicle.

"I see it. Do you want me to follow?"

"He's still moving?" Kozachenko asked.

"Yes."

"Does he seem curious?"

"Nyet. If you ask me, by the way he's driving, I'd say he's drunk."

"Then keep moving. The sooner we get off the road the better."

To Kozachenko's relief, at the outskirts of town, the landscape opened up, alleviating the claustrophobia created by the towering trees on either side of the road. Here there was farmland to the east and forest and river to the west, and the few houses lay dark and far back from the road. They were only nine minutes out from their destination. What could possibly go wrong?

At Yares'ky they faced one last section of road bordered by houses. Kozachenko downshifted and was halfway through a turn when Stas broke radio silence.

"We have a problem. There are cop cars coming up the road from the highway."

Then Dudyk jumped in. "That's not all. There are cops on the Shy-shaky bypass road. I can see their lights in my rearview mirror."

They were close enough to their endpoint that Kozachenko could smell the winter wheat. Two more kilometers and they would be at the turnoff. He hit the accelerator. "The driver of the car we passed must have called it in. Dudyk, go straight. Draw them away, and then lose them."

He downshifted when he saw the road and cranked the wheel hard to the right. The truck was moving fast and tipped up on two wheels. Kozachenko held the turn until the truck righted. Tires slamming back to the ground, he braked.

"I can see you, Vasyl," Barkov said. "Turn right in two hundred meters. If you pass the road, you'll be trapped with no way to turn around before being seen."

Kozachenko braked harder but still was forced to reverse.

"Good," said Barkov once the truck was off the road. "In another hundred meters, turn left. You should be able to see us."

Kozachenko followed the directions and spotted the GAZ parked near the back entrance gate to the Yares'ky silo and processing plant. It was here that the farmers of the Poltava region brought their harvest and where they processed the grain and packed it into railroad cars for transport.

Barkov doused his lights. Kozachenko followed suit.

"Stas said to drive past the silo to the end of the track," Barkov said. "There should be seven railroad cars. The middle one will have a ramp for loading the truck."

Kozachenko could hear the sirens drawing closer. "We aren't going to make it."

In the distance, he could see the turnoff from the main road. He watched Dudyk go straight, two police cars in hot pursuit. A third police car turned left.

"They've separated. One came this way."

"And two just passed me headed north," Stas said through the radio. "You have maybe three minutes to get out of sight."

"Quickly, follow me." Barkov gunned the motor and sped down the dirt road. Kozachenko followed him through the gate, careening along in the dark, pitching back and forth on the rutted gravel. On the right, he could see the large warehouse and on the left, a small mechanic's shed.

Barkov pulled up short, and Kozachenko nearly ran into him. "What the fuck?"

"We're out of time," Barkov said. "We need to put the truck in here." The doors of the shed were padlocked shut, and one of the men pulled out his gun.

"Are you crazy?" Kozachenko said, knocking the barrel toward the ground. "Someone will hear the shot."

The police car had reached the first turn off the road.

"You want to just wait for them to catch up to us?" Barkov asked. "We'll be forced to kill them all, and then what? We'd have the entire force upon us."

"First, we need to be smart." Kozachenko pointed to the mechanic's shed. "We'll park the vehicles next to the building where it's blocked by the trees. Everyone, get out and help. Quickly," he ordered. "Barkov, run back on foot, lock the gate, and then get out of sight."

Without turning on the lights, they maneuvered the trucks into position with only seconds to spare. From the shelter of the trees, Kozachenko heard the shouts of the policemen as the cars pulled up near the gate. Suddenly a bright spotlight flared, sweeping the side of the silo.

"They didn't come past us," one officer said, climbing out of his cruiser and walking over to rattle the gate. Another officer joined him. Together they circled their flashlights along the trees, the side of the large warehouse, down toward the train cars. The beams crisscrossed as they neared the small mechanic's shed, and Kozachenko sucked in a breath, fearful even a whisper of sound might give them away.

"I say we check the warehouse," said one of the officers.

"There wasn't enough time for them to hide in there. I say we check the forests along the river."

"We can do both. We'll check the forests and rivers first and come back once someone comes out and opens these gates."

Making a final sweep with their spotlights, the officers got back in their cars, turned around, and drove away. Once they were out of range, Kozachenko keyed his radio. "Barkov, get back here now. Dudyk, come in?"

No response.

"Dudyk?"

This time there was a crackle on the radio, but his words were garbled. Either he was out of range or there was a problem. Regardless, they needed to load the vehicles here onto the train and out of sight.

A few minutes later, Stas showed up along with two other men.

"This is how things will go from here, Vasyl." Stas spelled it out for Kozachenko, who decided the plan was simple, if crazy. Tomorrow morning, a train would pass through and pick up the seven cars on the track before proceeding on to Hoholeve. There the task of loading the crash debris into the cars would commence. Once the train cars were loaded, the rubble would be freighted to Krakow.

"And we're supposed to just get on the train?" asked Kozachenko.

"Nyet, the trucks will be hidden in here." He pointed to a car that looked longer than the others. "This one is designed for the vehicles to be parked snug to the walls on either end. Once they're correctly positioned, my men and I will fit false walls into place, sealing you in. To anyone loading the cars, it will appear to be the same amount of space."

"Someone is bound to notice the difference in length and question why the car holds less than it should."

"Yes, but I'm the one in charge of loading them. I'll make sure no questions are asked."

Watching the men as they maneuvered the truck and SUV into position, Kozachenko felt a wave of fear. He hated tight spaces. Even as a child, he'd hated playing hide-and-seek and tucking himself away in dark, cramped places. "How long will we be inside?"

"Three days, provided the train runs on schedule."

"That doesn't leave us much time at the other end. You're sure this is the fastest route?"

"It's the best that could be arranged on short notice."

Kozachenko had the feeling Stas enjoyed being in charge, but his plan was far from foolproof. If they managed to avoid detection in Hoholeve, there was still the Polish border crossing and the need to keep the bodies fresh.

"How cold will these cars get?"

"They will be set between two and four degrees, just cold enough to keep the bodies from decomposing anymore, not cold enough to cause them to freeze."

That meant, even bundled up inside their sleep sacks, it would barely be tolerable. Kozachenko also hated the cold. If ever there was a time to become a believer in God, it would be now.

"You're sure there is no other way."

"Don't worry, Vasyl. Take heart. I've made arrangements for extra blankets and vodka. Lots of vodka."

Chapter 21

A blue VW pulled up in front of the noodle and congee shop, and Jordan recognized the driver. It was the same man who had picked her up from the airport.

"Let's go, Davis. Our ride is here."

While he paid the check, Jordan stepped outside under the awning. The rain had backed off to a light drizzle, but the heat and humidity were relentless. After making a quick survey of the street, she hurried toward the car.

"Néih hóu," she said.

"Long time no see, Special Agent Jordan," he replied, holding open the door to the backseat. He jerked his head toward Davis, who was exiting the restaurant. "Who's this guy? He wasn't with you yesterday."

"He's a friend."

Davis held out his hand. "Nye Davis."

"Charlie, everybody calls me Charlie." He shook Davis's hand, waited until they were both inside, then climbed in behind the wheel, rain spatter glistening on his dark hair. "I don't know what you did, Agent, but you did it good."

"That seems to be my forte," she said. "Is there a plan?"

"No good plan. We can't go back to the consulate now, too many Chinese police outside. The PO says to lay low, and he'll be in touch once he figures something out. We have a safe house north of town." Charlie dropped the car into gear. "For now, I'll take you there."

A safe house. Another indication that the PO was CIA. A secure, secret residence wasn't something the consulate would keep. And since Charlie knew about it, that made him either CIA or an asset.

"How did you make everyone so mad?"

The PO had told her to trust Charlie, but what if the PO couldn't be trusted? There was still the question of who engineered the prisoner swap.

Not willing to tip her hand, she offered up only a piece of the puzzle. She told him she'd been on a quest to figure out what Zhen knew that had spooked McClasky, not that Zhen might still be alive.

"Plus, I found something at the crash site." Jordan had said it casually, but it dropped like a bomb. Davis twisted in the seat beside her. Charlie stared back at her from his rearview mirror. Then she told them about the fragment.

"I knew it! I knew that plane was intentionally brought down," Davis said.

"Except there's no real proof. The crash is still under investigation, and the IIC is leaning toward ruling it an accident."

"Is that what you think?" Charlie asked.

"No." She thought the plane had been shot down.

"How much have you learned about the fragment?" Davis asked.

"Our forensic guy sent it out for testing."

"Henry?"

Jordan eyed him suspiciously. "You know him?"

Davis raised his hands in the universal sign for surrender. "I talked to him. For the record, he refused to tell me anything."

"Good man." It made sense to Jordan that Davis would try, but she was glad to know Henry had shown discretion.

"So what did he find?" Charlie asked.

"It came back high for rare-earth metals."

"Chinese metal," Charlie said.

"You came to that conclusion fast," Davis said.

"China manufactures ninety percent of the rare-earth metals. They use them in making all kinds of specialty items, cell phones, wind turbines. China is also one of the world's leading steel exporters."

"Could the plane have been made with Chinese steel?" Davis asked.

"Not according to Henry. He claims the plane manufacturer doesn't use Chinese steel."

"Then it came from whatever brought down the plane," Davis said.

"That's the theory. Henry was able to pinpoint the composite of the metal to a specific area north of here." She explained to them about the content analysis and its connection to REE Manufacturing. "If they produced the steel, they should have records of where it was sold. If we can track the shipments, maybe we can figure out who used it to build a weapon."

Both men remained quiet, and she waited for one of them to speak.

Charlie looked up at the mirror. "Did you ever think maybe they built it?"

"It makes sense," Davis said. "The charge against Zhen is espionage, right? Maybe he hacked some weapons plan."

"Great minds think alike," she said. The right weapon schematics could be worth millions, but any buyer would want a prototype to ensure the plans worked. "The only caveat is it appears to be Russians who shot down the plane."

Charlie whistled softly. "You're talking about a weapons sale."

Davis was nodding. "Zhen steals the plans, REE builds the weapon and then sells it to the Russians."

"Are you thinking the sale was government sanctioned?" Charlie asked.

Jordan shook her head. According to her research, the rare-earth metals mining industry had started out state-owned. Then, with the onset of the market economy, some private entities had moved in. Then China tried driving up prices by limiting trade, and the Triad had waded in through the sludge of illegal mining operations. "More likely it was the Triad. Why else would they come after me?"

"In China, sometimes the two are intertwined," Charlie said. As he gave them a crash course in the Chinese mining industry, an idea began forming in Jordan's head.

"Hey, guys," she broke in. "We have some time, don't we?" Lory had given her forty-eight hours, though now with the change in current affairs, time had become a non sequitur.

Charlie narrowed his eyes in the mirror. "Why?"

"How about we make a trip to Shaoguan?"

"Why would we want to go there?"

"According to Henry, that's where the metal in the fragment was mined, and there's an REE Manufacturing plant located just south of the city. Either we use our time waiting around for the PO to call, or we use it figuring out what Zhen knew that got his plane blown out of the sky."

"I vote we go to the Great Wall," Charlie said. "It's much better for tourists."

"Are you saying we won't blend in in Shaoguan?"

"You'll stick out like a sore thumb."

Jordan looked at Davis. "What do you say?"

"I'm in."

Charlie looked between them in the mirror. "I say you're crazy. But if you want to go to Shaoguan," he shifted the car into overdrive, "fasten your seat belts. I'm taking you on the scenic route."

While Davis snapped pictures out the windows, Jordan soaked in the landscape. At first there were skyscrapers shrouded in the polluted air of the city that soon gave way to suburbs. For a stretch, neat rows of blue and pink patio homes marched in lines up the rolling green hillsides, colliding with areas of incomplete construction until they eventually climbed into the mountains, leaving behind all traces of town.

Lulled by the slap of the tires on concrete, Jordan dozed in and out until she felt the car slow. Scooting up on the seat, she checked the clock on the dashboard. They'd been driving north for nearly two hours. Out the windows, small farms began dotting the landscape.

"Are we getting close?" she asked.

"To the mines." Charlie slowed even more and pointed off to the right. "They come in these mountains before we get to the city. Maybe it's time you make a plan. You can't just walk in and ask to see their sales records."

"He's right," Davis said, "but this is where what I do comes in handy."

The three of them outlined a plan. Davis and Jordan would go in together while Charlie stayed with the car. Davis would introduce himself as a journalist doing a story on illegal mining in the area. How in addition to destroying the rivers and poisoning farmland, the illegal mines were cutting into the profits of legitimate companies like REE. Then he'd ask to speak to the man in charge.

"It would help if we knew something about him," Jordan said.

"You want to use my laptop?" Charlie passed a laptop over the seatback. Davis snatched it out of his hands.

"Okay, I've got something," Davis said after tapping a few keys. "His name is Ping Mu. In 1995, he graduated with a master's degree in engineering, joined the Communist Party of China, and started working as an engineer at REE's steel factory in Hainan. After eighteen years with the company, he was promoted to head of manufacturing at the Shaoguan plant. Five years later, he's on the fast track to being one of REE's next deputy general managers. Here's a photo of the plant."

Jordan moved close to see the screen. If you discounted the number of tattooed persons showing up in the aerial, Ping sounded like a standup guy. Suddenly aware she was leaning against his shoulder, Jordan pulled away. "So you're playing you. Who am I supposed to be?"

"My assistant, of course."

As the person who should be in charge, Jordan wasn't keen on being relegated to minion status. "Let's not forget who's running this operation."

"It gets us in the door," Davis said.

"We're here," Charlie announced, pointing off to the right.

The mine at Fanshuikeng loomed before them, a blight on an otherwise tranquil landscape. Mine tailings scarred the top half of the mountain, while the REE Manufacturing plant squatted at its base, dwarfed by the scope of its digging operations.

"Good, just park in front," she said. Charlie pulled through the gate, turned the car around, and backed into a parking space across from the main entrance.

"REE Manufacturing." Charlie gestured to the sign in front. He waved a hand up and down, then across the letters. "Top-to-bottom, right-to-left reading. Do you want me to come in and translate for you?"

As an asset, it was probably better for him not to be seen with them.

"Thanks, but just stay with the car."

"You're the boss. But you should take these." Charlie handed them each a phone. "For now they're safe to use. I preprogrammed them with my number and the number of the other phone."

Spotting a face in an upstairs window, Jordan tapped Davis on the shoulder. "That's our cue. We don't want to give them too much time to get suspicious." Climbing out of the car, she patted the window frame. "Thanks, Charlie. Keep the engine running. We won't be long."

Davis joined her outside the car, and together they crossed the parking lot. With each step, Jordan took measure of the complex. The main building was a large, two-story warehouse that appeared to house the offices and serve as storage for finished product. In the near distance was a cluster of other buildings where she figured the actual production took place. Behind the heavy metal entry door, a staircase ended on a landing.

"Ladies first," Davis said.

"You go," she replied, making it clear who was in charge.

Climbing the staircase, she spotted a motion detector high on the wall and another security camera.

The heat and humidity seemed to weigh them both down. At the top of the stairs, Davis paused. "Here you should go first."

"Fine." Jordan opened the door marked "Office" and reveled in the blast of cold air that raised goose bumps on her arms. Standing in the doorway, she blinked and let her eyes adjust to the lighting. In front of her was a long, high counter separating the entry from the receptionist's area. To her left, a bank of windows covered in blinds looked out toward the parking lot. To the right, another, taller bank of windows revealed a cavernous warehouse filled with pallets of steel product, the view reaching across the plant floor to what appeared to be a mirror-image office on the opposite side.

Jordan noted the two cameras mounted in the corners of the room and then stepped forward to the counter. A woman about her own age stood behind it watching a row of flat-screen monitors, each showing a different view of the property: the warehouse floor, the offices, the back door, and the parking lot.

"Néih hóu. *Nĭ douh yáuh móuh yàhn sīk góng Yīngmán a*?" Does someone here speak English? Jordan said, butchering the Cantonese.

"I can help you."

Jordan smiled. "We'd like to speak to your employer. My boss is a journalist doing a story—"

"I'm sorry, Mr. Ping is out."

Across the warehouse, a man stood at the window. Jordan figured the girl was lying. "Do you have any idea when he'll be back?"

"No."

She was either efficient or stonewalling.

So much for Davis's plan.

"A man named Kia Zhen recommended we talk to him," Jordan said. "Is he in by any chance?"

At Zhen's name, the woman recoiled slightly. Jordan was sure she recognized it.

"We have no Zhen working here." The woman shook her head, straight black bangs swishing across her brow. "I'm afraid I can be of no help."

Davis looked unhappy, and Jordan considered her options. There was nothing to gain by being pushy and everything to gain by waiting to see what happened after they left.

"I guess we'll have to come back, then."

Davis pulled out a business card and handed it to the woman. "Please tell your boss I was here."

The woman barely dipped her head.

Jordan made another visual sweep of the room, this time noting the location of the filing cabinets and additional exits.

Walking back to the car, Davis gripped her elbow and caught one of the bruises. Jordan winced.

"What the hell was that back there?" Davis asked. "That wasn't part of the plan. The plan was to find a way in to talk to Ping, not make us both personae non gratae by bringing up Zhen."

Jordan glanced back. The woman was back at the window pacing like a shark gliding back and forth watching the swimmers wading into the water.

"Your plan wasn't working," she said.

"You didn't give it a chance."

Charlie waited until they were back in the car and then asked, "Did you get what you wanted?"

"Not even close," Davis said.

"That's not true. The receptionist claimed the owner wasn't in, but someone was watching from the office window across the way. And I'm sure she recognized Zhen's name, though of course she denied it."

"Where to now?" Charlie asked.

Jordan was curious to see if anything came out of stirring the pot. "Head toward Shaoguan but pull over at the first place you can park and not be seen."

"A stakeout!" Charlie seemed almost exuberant. "Maybe now we'll get a look at the bad guys."

They didn't have to wait long. The car engine was barely cool when two blue pickups full of men peeled out of the REE parking lot and headed north. Davis instantly identified the man sandwiched into the back of one of the trucks.

"Wait a minute. That's Kia Zhen." He looked accusingly at Jordan. "All this time you knew he was alive?"

"I can explain, but right now we need to follow those men." She reached forward and grabbed Charlie's shoulder. "Can you tail them and keep from being spotted?"

Charlie's face hardened in the rearview mirror. "You understand these men are Triad. A dozen of them to three of us."

"The PO told me you were the man for the job."

"There's a difference between driving dangerous and being dead," Charlie said, starting the engine. "This is a very bad idea. The Triad will kill you if you mess with them."

"It won't be the first time they've tried," Davis said.

Jordan shot him a glare. "You're not helping." She looked back at Charlie. "Just don't get too close."

Charlie switched his gaze from Jordan to Davis in the rearview mirror. "This is either one brave or one crazy girl you have."

"Possibly both."

"Just drive!"

The road wound up the mountain and joined with another one at the top of the hill. To the left was concrete, to the right dirt. Fresh tracks in the red clay soil combined with the rev of the pickups signaled which direction they'd gone.

Instead of peppering her with questions about Zhen, Davis slid forward to the edge of the seat and craned for a better look. Jordan was glad for the reprieve. She knew at some point she would be made to explain.

Charlie glanced up at the mirror. "This could be a trap."

"It could." Jordan rolled down her window and listened. "But I don't think so. Both trucks are still moving. Turn right up here."

Following the sound of the vehicles, they wound back along the damp clay road, becoming more and more isolated. Jordan began to question her logic in following when she heard one of the truck motors cut out.

"Pull over," she said, gesturing to a small side road that angled off through the trees. "Cut the engine!"

Jordan jumped out before the car bucked to a stop and listened for the men's voices. She could hear them talking, but it was impossible to tell how close they were. Shutting the car door with barely a click, she leaned in the window.

"You guys, stay here," she whispered.

"And miss getting the action shots? No frickin' way." Davis picked up his camera and slid out of the car on the driver's side.

"I'm going to climb the hill and find out what I can see from above," she whispered. "I need you here, ready in case we need to make a run for it."

"You're not going up there alone."

"Believe it or not, Davis, I can take care of myself."

"It's not up for debate."

By his expression, she knew he would never be dissuaded. At least not in the amount of time they had. "Then stay close, keep low, and be quiet! Got it? And if we get jammed up, you do what I tell you."

"Got it."

Jordan turned to Charlie.

"I'll wait with the car," he said.

"We may need to make a quick getaway."

"No sweat." He must have seen concern on her face. "Don't worry, Agent Jordan. I'll be fine. I know kung fu."

Jordan pulled out her phone and checked for his number. "Make sure your phone is on vibrate only. If we're not back in fifteen minutes, get the hell out of here and call the PO."

Charlie leaned across the front seat as they started away. "Break a leg."

Chapter 22

Jordan slowed her climb as she neared the crest of the hill, carefully watching where she placed her feet. The red clay was slick underfoot, the soil saturated by monsoons. Sensing Davis close on her heels, she signaled him to stop. The men's voices were louder, and she could make out some of their words.

"How did the American agent know where to look for you, *zuk-sing*?"

If she had her Cantonese right, the man had to be talking to Zhen, zuk-sing being a derogatory term used for a Chinese person born away or who identifies too closely with Western culture.

"Are you eager to go back to the U.S., Zhen? You no longer want to be in China?" The voice sounded like it belonged to her favorite aggressor, the man Davis had laid out in the street.

"Why would I want to leave?" That had to be Zhen, and he sounded scared. "The Americans want to try me for espionage. I'm as good as dead if I go back."

"You're as good as dead here."

"Please, dude, I'm telling the truth. I don't know why the bitch was here."

"Mr. Ping wants to know what happened at the police station."

"Nothing happened. It was total chaos. The police held me for a while, asked me some questions, then they just cut me loose."

"Why would they do that?"

"How should I know? I was just glad to be free."

Inching forward, Jordan could see Zhen now. He looked younger than eighteen, the age listed on his dossier. Fear had drained the color from his face, and he was trembling. From the look of things, it wouldn't be long before he was begging for his life.

Unless she did something before things escalated. She considered leaving him to the Triad and saving the U.S. taxpayers the expense of a trial. After all, he was a traitor. An *alleged* traitor, she reminded herself, which meant turning her back on him wasn't an option. He was an American and as such deserved a fair trial by a jury of his peers, a group that would no doubt remand him to prison. How long he stayed there would depend on what kind of deal he cut for himself, how forthright he was about what he knew, and what he'd done. None of which concerned her in the least. Her only job was getting him home.

Davis's camera clicked, and Jordan turned, making a chopping motion across her neck. He snapped her picture and then twisted his camera around to rest on his back. Jordan pointed to a spot on the path with a little more height.

From either vantage point, she couldn't see much—Zhen and the feet of the man he was facing. Otherwise, she only had a view of the backs of the trucks. There was no way of telling how many Triad members were below them or how well they were armed. From what she'd seen when the trucks left REE, there were at least eight gang members, and they'd been armed to the teeth.

Signaling Davis, she backed off the ridge, and he followed. They needed a diversion, some way to draw off the guards.

Charlie!

Once back in the safety zone, she filled Davis in on her plan. "He just needs to drive the car farther up the road toward the mines. If we can lure some of the Triad members away, it would leave Zhen with minimal supervision, at which point we could attempt a rescue."

"Are you nuts?" Davis said.

"I know it's a risky plan, but I know you can fight, and there's no reason for the gangsters to hurt Charlie. By most accounts, they simply run locals off."

"Except these guys are on edge. What if this is the time they decide to send a message?"

She'd texted Charlie while they talked, and now her phone emitted a tiny beep. She held up Charlie's reply for Davis to read. "He's good with the plan."

"Only because he knows kung fu."

"This'll work." It had to. It was their only window of opportunity. "Are you in or out?"

"In."

"Great. Let's hope we at least cut the number of guards by half. I'll go for Zhen. You disable any vehicle left behind." It went without saying they'd have to take out the guards. "Any chance you carry a knife?"

Davis shook his head. "I'm a weapon-free zone."

"Not anymore." She handed him her tactical pen. "The end is razor sharp. Stab the tire sidewalls and tear sideways."

"Perfect. And if we're caught, I can use it to commit harakiri."

"Not in China. That's a Japanese custom." She started up the hill, then turned back around. "Just remember, you're the one who wanted to come."

The two of them returned to their perch on the ridge and watched as Charlie snaked the car up the red dirt road. Her instructions had been for him to get as close to the mining operation as possible in order to lure as many gang members away from Zhen as he could. It worked, with one exception. The gangsters piled into both pickups, which meant the Triad still had both sets of wheels.

"Let's go." Jordan slid down the side of the hill with Davis behind her. Wrapping her arms around small tree trunks, she worked to stay on her feet before pushing through the undergrowth. At the sound of breaking branches, the two remaining gang members turned.

She moved in one direction. Davis moved in the other. One gang member charged into the brush after Davis, while the other kept a tight grip on Zhen.

Circling around behind Davis's attacker, Jordan scooped up a rock and struck him in the back of the head. He dropped like a stone. Then a sharp blow from the side drove Jordan to her knees. The other gangster had left Zhen and was about to come at her again. He grabbed her from behind, pinning her arms to her sides and lifting her off her feet.

"Get Zhen," she yelled at Davis.

"If it isn't the bitch from Guangzhou." The gangster's breath, warm on her neck, reeked of garlic.

It was the man from Shangxiajiu.

He tried lifting her off her feet again, but Jordan hooked her legs behind his. As he struggled to get a good grip, she grabbed one of his fingers and snapped it back. He loosened his hold and she twisted, jabbing her thumb into his eye socket.

The gangster screamed and backed away, and then his hand came up with a knife. Flight was no longer an option.

Ignoring the pain in her ribs from his earlier blow, Jordan sucked in a breath and assumed a fighting stance. When he thrust the knife at her, she sidestepped and circled out of range.

"You think you're tough?"

Jordan didn't react to the taunt. She kept her eyes on him and the weapon. She didn't know where Davis was, but she hoped he had collared Zhen and headed back to the rendezvous point.

The gangster lunged again.

Jordan deflected the blow. Then using a move she'd only trained for, she slid her hand down his forearm, grabbed his wrist and bent it inward. To her surprise, it worked. Next thing she knew, she was standing behind him, hyperflexing his wrist. Applying pressure, she stepped forward, tripping him and sending him to the ground. He let go of the knife as he fell, and per training she followed him to the ground. In the final move, she locked her feet around his torso and brought his right arm down on her leg, twisting until she felt his elbow give.

His scream shattered the quiet of the pullout. It was time to go. "Davis!"

"Here." He had Zhen by the collar, his hands bound by the laces from Davis's shoes. Between them they dragged their prisoner back up the hill.

"Any sign of Charlie?" she asked.

"He passed by a few seconds ago. If we can outrun the gang, he should be in place." Davis gestured behind them toward the oncoming trucks. "We've got to move."

It took the gangsters a few moments to realize what had happened. By then Jordan and Davis were dragging Zhen down the hill toward the car.

"Get in," Jordan yelled, taking shotgun.

Davis pushed Zhen into the backseat and climbed in beside him. Jordan slapped her hand on the dashboard. "Let's go!"

"I also took race car driving lessons," Charlie said, lurching onto the road. Jordan spotted a blue pickup in the rearview mirror. Davis looked over his shoulder.

"Then why are they gaining on us?" he asked.

A gunshot shattered the back window of the car, and Davis pushed Zhen onto the floor.

"You going to have to pay for that," Charlie said, looking at Jordan.

"Just go!"

Hunching over the wheel, he pressed down hard on the accelerator, and the car leapt forward. The lead truck closed the gap, pulled up tight, and rammed the back bumper of the sedan.

"You're going to pay for that, too."

"Move it!" Jordan yelled.

The pickup veered toward them, and Charlie slammed on the brakes. Jordan braced herself against the dashboard as the truck careened across the road in front of them. Then punching the accelerator, Charlie clipped the truck's back fender, sending it into a spin on the mud. Jordan caught a glimpse of the terror and anger on the gangsters' faces as the pickup climbed the embankment and the sedan shot past. The truck flipped, coming to rest in the middle of the road like a turtle on its back. The second truck slid to a stop.

"Didn't I tell you I know how to drive?"

Chapter 23

After crossing the bridge into downtown Shaoguan, Jordan used the GPS on the phone, directing Charlie into the parking garage of a three-star hotel near the main intersection of Fengdu Street and Heping Road. As soon as he'd put it in park, Davis asked to talk to her privately, outside of the car.

Leaving Zhen with Charlie, the two of them walked a few feet away.

"Why didn't you tell me Zhen was alive?" Davis asked.

Jordan went with honesty. "I didn't know for sure, and I didn't know how far I could trust you."

"Care to fill me in now?"

His dark eyes drilled her, and she self-consciously looked away. "There's not much to tell. According to the DNA test we ran in order for the U.S. to repatriate the body, the dead prisoner with McClasky wasn't Zhen. Someone else came out of China that day."

"Who?"

"We don't know. He hasn't been ID'd yet, but someone went to a lot of trouble to make the switch."

"Who?"

Jordan looked at Davis. "You tell me."

"Who benefited most by getting him out?"

"My guess? The Triad."

"There are no other possibilities?"

148

"Well, sure," she said. "It's possible the imposter wanted out of China and arranged for someone to help him switch places with Zhen."

"I can buy that."

"There's the Chinese. Maybe they needed someone from their camp back in the states. There's the CIA." Jordan's frustration mounted as they ran through the possibilities. Every scenario pointed to someone having access to classified U.S. intel. "The only thing we know for sure is that whoever arranged for the switch knew McClasky was coming."

"How many people knew?"

Davis's question brought her up short. Up until now they'd been talking in broad hypotheticals, but now he was asking her to boil it down to specific individuals. He'd helped her out of a couple of tight situations, but that didn't mean she would throw her colleagues under the bus or that she could trust him with secret information.

"I've already said too much," she said, turning back toward the car.

Davis reached out and grabbed her arm. "Don't cut me out now, Jordan."

"Take your hands off me."

He let her go, and she took two steps back.

"Sorry." Davis held his palms up. "Look, this isn't about my being a reporter. I'm smart enough to know that there's more at stake here than a story. This is about you deciding whether you can trust me. Let me help you figure it out."

Jordan trusted very few people. Not as a child, not as a woman. It made her tough, focused, and hard to manipulate—one of the reasons she was so good at her job.

"Would it help you to know I'm still an active Special Forces Reserve officer?"

It caught her attention. "That wasn't in your file."

"Only because it would make me a target in some of the places I go. I'll make it easy for you, Agent. Either I'm all in or I'm all out."

The switch in tone and manner made his position clear. He was done screwing around.

Slowly she turned to face him. He waited calmly while Jordan wrestled with her demons. On one hand, her instincts urged her to put her faith in him. On the other, she feared his betrayal. She wanted nothing more than to have someone to collaborate with, someone she could count on to have her back. If he was still active reserve, he had the best interest of his country at heart. But it also meant involving another command structure. Plus there was his affiliation with Reuters, which wasn't going to make Lory happy. Unless, of course, it turned out to be some sort of cover.

"What's it going to be?"

"You better not be playing me."

"I'm not."

Said the wolf to the lamb. "RSO Lory knew about McClasky. He was the one who sent me to Hoholeve to retrieve the bodies. But he definitely didn't know anything about the exchange."

"Then we rule him out. Who else?"

"The DSS director knew."

"Apprehending Zhen was their mission. Why would he sabotage his own operation? What about the CIA?"

"I thought that, too. The political officer at the consulate knew. He's possible CIA." She jerked her head toward the VW. "Charlie's likely an asset."

"Do you think the PO's chief of station?"

"It's what I was told."

Jordan ran the toe of her shoe along a crack in the cement. It was like the dividing line in a group of variables. "The PO helped negotiate Zhen's release from jail. RSO Todd and Detective Yang knew McClasky was coming, but I'm confident we can rule them out. Then there's whoever handled the prisoner swap inside the jail, whoever McClasky might have told, and the Triad's involvement. We have too many unknowns."

"There has to be a way to narrow it down. How do you think the prisoner swap happened?"

Jordan told him about the sting operation.

"*Damn*. That cracks the suspect pool wide open."

"Of course, you don't know any of this," she reminded him. "Any splashy headlines would end my career. Besides, I think the longer we keep all this under wraps, the better."

"Based on your reception in Guangzhou, it seems somebody has gotten the word."

"Either that or someone doesn't want me uncovering Zhen's secrets. For all we know, he could have staged his own death to avoid an indictment for espionage."

She heard tires squealing on pavement as a car turned into the garage. She whipped her head around as a car full of teenagers drove past, openly curious about the two tall Americans standing in the middle of the parking lot. A car door opened, and then Charlie called out over the top of the car. "Hey, you about done? We need to get out of sight. You two don't blend in so well."

Jordan glanced around the cavernous parking garage. Until the teenagers, she hadn't seen anyone else coming in or out. She also hadn't been paying attention.

"I'm on it," Davis said. "Stay here, and I'll go get us a room."

"What about your passport?"

In the end, Charlie had gone inside while Jordan and Davis waited in the car with Zhen. Ten minutes later, he came back holding the keys to a suite in the Shaoguan Hotel.

"We're all set," he said, handing both Jordan and Davis a key card.

"Do we need to worry about hauling Zhen through the lobby?" she asked, conscious of how disheveled they must look. She still wore the clothes she'd purchased in Guangzhou, and they'd taken their share of abuse. Her white shirt was streaked with red clay, and there was a tear in one of her pant legs. Davis hadn't fared much better, and Zhen's hands were tied behind his back. "Any chance we'll set off some hotel employee's alarm bells?"

Charlie gave them the once-over. "It could be a problem."

"What's the layout of the lobby?" Davis asked.

"The elevators are to the left through the door. The desk is across the lobby. To the right is a seating area."

"I've got this," Davis said. "Give me a thirty-second head start."

Unsure of the plan, Jordan counted off the seconds, feeling apprehensive as she pushed through the hotel doors. She quickly realized she'd worried for nothing. Good to his word, Davis strode in through the street access, requesting assistance in finding an address and commanding the attention of everyone in proximity. His lanky carriage and easy smile offset the ugly American routine and captured the full attention of every woman in the lobby while eliciting glares from the men. No one even looked at the three of them.

Nudging Zhen toward the bank of elevators, Jordan felt him balk and exerted pressure on his bound wrists. "Don't even consider it."

Once they were headed up, she released her grip on his ties.

"This sucks," he said. "Why is this necessary? No way I'm going to run. I'm better off with you. The Triad will kill me if I go back there."

He'd said something similar to the gangsters about returning to the United States. She figured both statements were true.

Charlie began to respond, but Jordan headed him off.

"No more talking until we're safe in the room." Call her paranoid, but she didn't want to risk someone overhearing anything they talked about. It could spell disaster if the wrong people put together what they were doing in Shaoguan.

* * *

The living room of the deluxe suite looked like a miniature version of the lobby. Its overstuffed furnishings included a red couch and two red chairs across from a buffet holding a flat-screen TV. Near the floor-to-ceiling windows were a desk and chair.

Charlie swiveled the screen toward him, picked up the TV remote, and sat down at the desk. "You mind?"

Jordan shook her head and deposited Zhen on the couch. After making a quick sweep of the rooms for cameras and listening devices, she stepped to the windows. The suite was on the seventh floor, with no balcony. In the distance, purple mountains backed a city landscape gleaming in various shades of sunset yellow. Once satisfied the room was secure, she untied Zhen's hands.

Rubbing his wrists, he stretched and propped his feet on the coffee table. "Any chance of getting something to eat or drink?"

Before Jordan could answer, Davis let himself into the room. "What'd I miss?"

"Nothing," she said. "We were just about to order room service." She also needed to check in with Lory. By now the PO would be aware they hadn't gone straight to the safe house, but the more information she could give her boss when she called, the better.

"Sounds great," Davis said. "I'm famished."

They settled on a variety of dim sum, tea, and two Diet Cokes—one for Jordan and one for their prisoner. While Charlie called in the order, Jordan turned back to Zhen. She wanted some answers. Talking in front of Charlie was chancy; likely anything said would find its way back to the PO. But her need for answers outweighed the risks, and she'd already granted Davis a pass.

"Tell us what you're doing in China, Kia." She went with his first name, hoping to develop rapport. "Maybe you could start by telling us how you ended up in the hands of the Triad."

"I'm not sure how much I'm allowed to tell you."

Jordan wondered what was that supposed to mean. "You're wanted on charges of espionage. Now isn't the time to be cagey."

Zhen flipped back his mop of hair. "It's not what you think. My cousin Eddie works for the government, undercover. He asked for my help hacking into this company's servers. It was all on the up and up. He said he'd pay me one hundred thousand dollars."

"Are you saying the hack was sanctioned by a government agency?" Davis asked.

"Exactly. It was all for show. Eddie just needed the files as bait. He never intended to sell them."

"Did he tell you what branch of the government he worked for?" Jordan already had a good guess what his answer would be.

"The CIA. His contact was someone at the consulate in Guangzhou."

The fact Eddie'd divulged his affiliation with the CIA to Zhen made Jordan suspicious. No one working for the agency was that forthright, not while they were still employed. Though, if Eddie was telling his cousin the truth, it supported the theory that the PO helped orchestrate the prisoner swap—the kid for his CIA asset. Even if Eddie was Triad, it made sense to export him in place of Zhen. Eddie likely knew more, which also made him a target.

"Does Eddie have a last name?" Davis asked.

"Zhen, same as me." The kid leaned forward, elbows to knees. "Where the hell is he anyway? I haven't seen him since we got busted."

Jordan skipped past his question. "Tell me what you took."

The kid's eyes narrowed. Did he suspect she was holding back? Finally, he shrugged and told her what she wanted to hear.

"They were plans for a new military weapon under development for the U.S. Navy."

"What was the name of the company?"

"Quinn Industries."

If Zhen was telling the truth, her hunch that Quinn Industries had been cyberattacked was correct.

"And you bought into your cousin's bullshit?" Davis was mimicking Zhen's posture. It was an interrogator's technique designed to put the subject at ease, given you asked the right question.

"Eddie's my cousin." Zhen sounded defensive. "I didn't think he was doing anything illegal, if that's what you mean. I still don't."

Jordan leaned forward, too. "Eddie lied, Kia. The CIA would never sanction this type of bluff."

At least that's what she wanted to believe. She looked at Charlie to gauge his reaction. He appeared to be watching TV.

Zhen's face contorted in anger. "You're wrong. Eddie's mission was to infiltrate the Triad and ID the buyer. The Chinese respect a good hacker. He was forced to produce the goods. The plans were never supposed to leave his hands."

"So what happened?" Davis asked.

"Once I delivered the plans to Eddie, he told me I was done. He said he was going to take things from there, and I could expect payment in a couple of weeks. The next thing I know, my name is on the top of the Feds' Most Wanted List. Eddie said it was all a mistake. He told me to lay low, that he'd straighten things out. Then he showed up, saying we need to get out of the country. It was supposed to be temporary. He said someone was onto him, and the only way to salvage the op was to pretend to go through with the sale."

"And that didn't seem sketchy to you?"

"I trusted my cousin," he reiterated. "I still do. Eddie's a brave dude. I'll admit I had reservations about messing with the Triad, but not Eddie."

"Did you ever meet his CIA handler?" Davis asked.

"Hell, no! That was top secret shit. The only person I ever met was Ping Mu. He was the buyer. To be honest, I was starting to think Eddie was still working his way up the Triad food chain."

Jordan hated to break it to Zhen, but it sounded to her like Eddie was just out for a big score.

Davis scooted closer to the edge of his seat. "He had the plans, so why bring you to China?"

If looks could label you "idiot," Davis would be a drooling mass of Jell-O.

"It was just as dangerous at home. What do you think would have happened if I'd been picked up in the States? I would've been screwed, and it would've blown Eddie's whole op. Besides, he needed me to tweak the plans."

That caught Jordan's attention. "What do you mean?"

"The guidance system specs totally sucked. The U.S. government has been telling everyone they were ready to roll out the gun this year, but that's a load of crap. Eddie asked me if I could come up with a fix." Zhen spoke as if he'd been asked to tweak his cousin's high school science project.

"Were you able to fix it?" she asked.

"Frickin' A I did. It's not perfect. The portable power system still has flaws. It works great for one firing. After that it has to be recharged or needs to be hooked up to some type of continuous power source."

Davis suddenly straightened. "Hold on a minute. What kind of weapon are we talking about?"

She and Zhen looked at each other, then answered in unison. "A land-based railgun."

Chapter 24

At the word *railgun*, Charlie's head came around. "What did you say?"

Davis rolled his eyes and laughed. "Let's get real."

"It's no joke," Zhen said.

"It's bullshit!" Davis said. "You're talking about a fantasy weapon the Navy's been working on since Arnold played the Terminator, possibly longer. In all that time, they've never succeeded in building any power source small enough to be mobile."

"Up until now," Jordan said. She was convinced Zhen was telling the truth. "If we're to believe Zhen—and I do—that particular problem's been solved."

Davis stared at her for a moment. "You're serious, aren't you?"

Jordan nodded, then turned back to the kid. He was still a teenager. Eighteen years old, happy to make a boatload of money, proud of the work he'd accomplished, and convinced he'd been issued a license to hack by the U.S. government. How could someone as obviously smart as this kid be so dumb?

Davis was back nose-to-nose with Zhen. "Explain this weapon to me."

"You want the technical description?"

"I'll settle for layman's terms."

"Can I see your computer?"

Davis handed him Charlie's laptop. Zhen powered it up, typed a few keystrokes, then rotated the screen back around. A picture of a railgun mounted on the back of a large transport truck filled the monitor.

"Basically the gun has three parts. The armature, that's the part here that looks like a cannon." Zhen used the cursor to point. "It sits on a rail system mounted to the back of a transport truck. This thing that looks like a trunk-bed cargo box is called the compulsator. Basically it's a battery that stores up to a ten-megajoule charge."

"What's a megajoule?" Charlie's voice behind her startled Jordan. He'd gotten out of the desk chair and was squinting at the photo.

"It's a measure of energy that puts out a charge with a force equivalent to a one-ton truck traveling at 160 miles per hour hitting a brick wall." The more Zhen talked, the more animated he became. "When the electromagnetic pulse, or EMP, is released from the compulsator, it travels around the rails creating a magnetic field that slides the armature forward and launches the projectile."

Charlie looked impressed. "That must pack one hell of a punch."

"Hell, yeah," Zhen said. "This model fires at Mach 7.5. We're talking Star Trek. The actual speed depends on temperature and atmospheric conditions, but basically the bullet it shoots is moving at 5,300 miles per hour and hits the freakin' target at Mach 5. There's so much kinetic force behind it that the projectile starts to burn, coming apart on impact." To demonstrate, he slammed his right fist into his open left hand and then flung open his hands.

That would explain the shrapnel she'd found buried in the side of the plane. "How big are these bullets you're talking about?"

"Maybe seven pounds."

"That's all?" Charlie said.

Davis reached over and tapped the picture of the gun, causing the plasma screen to distort. "How far can it shoot?"

Jordan had read enough about railguns to know the answer, but she let Zhen field the question.

"According to the specs, two hundred nautical miles. It shoots up into the exo-atmosphere, like five hundred thousand feet into space, before gravity pulls it back to Earth. It's cutting-edge technology."

Davis sat back in his chair looking less than convinced. "I'll admit, it sounds great in theory, but how accurate can it be?"

"It's dead on, dude. The bullets use an internal guidance system. Once you lock in the preprogrammed GPS coordinates—"

"Wait a minute," Jordan said, cutting him off. "Are you saying that once the projectile's launched, you can't alter its course?"

"Not by a command system. They haven't made one yet that can take the heat. But that doesn't mean you can't take it over."

The food arrived before anyone could ask him to expound. Once it was doled out, Jordan steered things back to the subject of Eddie.

"Tell us about the people Eddie was looking to impress."

"I told you, the only guy I met was Ping."

"He never talked about anyone else?"

"I heard him refer to the dragon a few times."

"That's the name used for the head of the Triad," Charlie said. Jordan swiveled toward him. He was back sitting behind the desk with his plate of food in front of him. "Last year, the dragon was named one of the fifty most influential men in China by *China Digest*."

Jordan turned back to Zhen. "Are you sure Eddie didn't know who he was?"

"That was the whole point of the op. Eddie was supposed to find out who this dragon dude was. He said once he learned the dragon's identity, the CIA would have an inroad to the highest branches of the Chinese government."

"What did he mean by that?" Davis asked.

"How should I know? Eddie was pretty closed-mouth. All I know is this dragon was somebody powerful."

Charlie cleared his throat. "If Eddie was an NOC, his mark would have to be someone high up in the Central Military Commission or Communist Party government. Many Guangdong businessmen are also government officials."

"Ping?" Jordan asked.

Charlie shrugged. "Anyone making money in China has his hand around somebody's balls."

Since the inception of Chinese President Xi Jinping's anticorruption campaign, over nine hundred senior Communist Party officials had been accused of corruption. Jordan wondered if Eddie had tumbled upon someone not yet exposed.

"Are you thinking he got too close?" Davis asked, echoing her thoughts.

"It's possible." Charlie picked up his chopsticks. "In China, a little knowledge makes you both valuable and dangerous."

"It's a good reason to arrange an extraction," Davis said.

"What's a NOC?" asked Zhen.

"It's what they call a CIA agent with a *nonofficial cover*," Jordan said. "Basically, it means that if the agent gets caught spying, the United States government will disavow him and his actions."

Zhen sat bolt upright on the edge of the couch. "Hold on, dudette. That means they would disavow me, too."

"Unfortunately, Zhen," she said, "you were never protected."

The kid's face distorted in anger. "There's no frickin' way Eddie would just leave me here."

Jordan smiled sympathetically. "Unless he wasn't given a choice."

As the realization of his predicament sank in, the fear grew in Zhen's eyes. "You have to help me. I want to make a deal."

"That's not up to me. It's not up to any of us."

"Who is it up to, then?"

It was hard to say. With the U.S. government calling him a traitor and his cousin likely dead, things didn't look good for Zhen. Still Jordan went with the cliché. "All I can do is put in a good word for you, provided you've told us everything."

"I have. I swear. What else do you want to know?"

"Tell us what happened *after* you met Ping Mu."

The story he told fit.

"Once you doctored the plans, did Ping sell them?" she asked.

Zhen slumped back against the couch cushions. "He couldn't. No one wanted to buy them without proof the gun worked. He built two prototypes. Eddie said things were getting too dangerous after he sold one to some Russian dudes and arranged for me to get out. We were waiting for his contact in Guangzhou when the cops showed up."

"How did you end up back at REE?" Davis asked.

"The police asked me what I was doing in China. I told them I worked for Ping. Next thing I know, he's there picking me up. He wanted to know where Eddie was. I told him I didn't know."

Jordan mulled over what they heard. Letting her eyes wander, she took in the empty plates and the dirty glasses on the coffee table. She could hear Charlie's anime show chattering on the television, though she knew he'd absorbed every word of the conversation. Outside the windows, the sun was setting, coloring the sky above the Nanling Mountains blood red.

"Agent Jordan, I've told you everything I know," Zhen said. "Now I want to know where Eddie is."

She found it hard to look at him. There was no easy way to break this kind of news, and she hadn't had much practice doing it. "Kia, I think Eddie's dead."

"What?" The boy's voice broke.

Jordan told him about the plane and how it had gone down. How she had reason to assume it was him who had died.

"Then you don't know for sure that it's Eddie." Hope caused his voice to rise.

"They'll run his DNA or pull dental records. Then we'll know."

"Does this mean the Russians tried to kill me?" His voice rose to an even higher octave. "Did Eddie die because they thought he was me?"

"We don't know that. Maybe someone knew it was Eddie on board." Jordan wasn't sure her words were a comfort. She wished she could give him a minute to process his loss. Unfortunately, the clock was ticking. "Did you or your cousin get a good look at the Russians who bought that gun?"

"Yeah, we both did. I showed them how to program the weapon."

If the Russians wanted to keep the gun under wraps, eliminating both Zhen and Eddie made sense. Ping had to be the one who told them which flight to attack.

"Were they Russian military?" Davis asked.

"No, more like mafia dudes."

"Do you know what Ping plans to do with the other prototype?" Charlie asked.

"He's lined up a Chinese buyer. They're meeting tonight."

Jordan felt a surge of adrenalin but forced herself to stay calm. "Where? At the manufacturing plant?"

Zhen nodded.

Davis scrubbed a hand through his hair. "How do you know they're Chinese?"

"Because Ping made me create an interface to the Chinese GPS satellite system. I was just finishing when you guys showed up."

"What now?" Davis asked.

Jordan couldn't make this decision on her own. "I need to make a call."

* * *

It was midafternoon in Ukraine, and Lory picked up on the second ring.

"We found Kia Zhen." Without preamble, she filled him in on everything they'd learned, including the bit about the pending weapons sale.

"*Fuck.*" He banged his fist down on his desk hard enough to concuss the phone. "Hang on. I'll be right back."

When the line switched over to Muzak, Jordan started pacing the bedroom. She couldn't shake the feeling that somehow they were missing something in the bigger picture. Hopefully Lory would have some good news when he came back online—or at least some answers.

"Still there, Jordan?"

"Here."

"After we talked, I spoke with my CIA contact in D.C. He confirms there's been chatter about a weapons deal. Factions in Russia and China have been cozying up to each other for some time, but you just shed some new light on the situation. At least we know where the deal's going down. Well done, Agent Jordan."

"Thank you, sir," she said, but she didn't want praise. She wanted a plan of action. "What happens next?"

"I'll update the director and the ambassador and see if I can't fire up the Ukrainians to find these assholes. Zhen's word isn't much to go on, but it sounds like the Russians may be planning a coup d'etat. I'll also order a new DNA test on our dead fugitive. Another good lead."

"Any word on RSO Todd?" Jordan asked.

Lory hesitated. "She never made it out of surgery."

The news about Todd hit Jordan hard. The RSO died because Jordan had come looking for Zhen and then had left her lying on the restaurant floor in a puddle of blood.

"Jordan?"

She forced herself to refocus. "Still here, sir."

"You need to get back to Guangzhou with Zhen, and you better make damn sure your Reuters journalist doesn't print any of this. All we need is word getting out to spark a full-scale panic on the part of our Western allies. I don't know what the fuck you were thinking taking him along, but I'm holding you personally responsible for any leaks or negative repercussions."

"I understand, sir." She knew there was no point in arguing. She had her own reservations. "If it helps, he used to be Special Forces, and he claims to still be in the active reserves."

"It's worth checking out." Jordan heard him bark something at Mary. "Meanwhile, the PO is working on a way to bring you into the consulate and get you out of China. You need to go to the safe house and be ready to move."

"What about the gun?"

"What about it? The National Security Council has recommended to the president that she initiate a covert action to secure the prototype and the plans. My guy expects he'll get a green light within the next four hours. Unfortunately, the CIA doesn't have an operations officer in country. They're looking at fourteen to twenty-four hours to get someone on site."

"That's too much time. At best the agent would be looking at a recovery mission."

"Do you have any other ideas?"

He was being facetious, but she knew there had to be some way to stop China from acquiring a weapon with such long-range strike and defensive capabilities. Allowing the sale to happen would only increase the vulnerability of Western allies in the region and hamper the ability of the United States and Europe to defend them.

"What about Special Forces?" she asked.

"You know as well as I do that we can't send a strike team into China. It would be a suicide mission."

"Well there has to be something we can do. We know the Chinese and Russians are working together. There has to be an end game we're not seeing. But knowing as much as we do, you can't seriously expect me to stand by and do nothing."

"You and what backup, Jordan? A consulate driver, a Reuters journalist, and the traitor who stole the secrets to begin with?"

"I'm fairly certain the consulate driver is a CIA asset."

"We can check that out, too."

"My instincts are telling me they can be trusted. Both Charlie and Davis put themselves in harm's way today helping me do my job, and Davis saved my life yesterday."

"Admirable. Are you going to defend Zhen, too?"

"Truthfully, I don't believe he's a traitor. I think he honestly thought he was helping his cousin, who he believed to be a CIA undercover operative."

"Sounds a little naïve."

"Maybe, but it doesn't change my assessment."

He was quiet for a moment. "Just what is it you think the four of you can do?"

She hadn't really formulated a plan, but he was listening. That was a start. "The security at REE isn't that sophisticated. It's possible we could get in, retrieve the plans, and sabotage the meeting. At the very least, we could stake out the plant and document who comes and goes for later follow up."

Lory laughed. "Your RSO in Tel Aviv told me you'd be trouble."

"You talked to Daugherty again?" Jordan was sure he'd filled Lory in on her exploits. She may have earned a medal for efforts on behalf of Israel, but she'd still gone rogue in a profession where following orders was considered rudimentary. "What did he have to say?"

"He suggested I ask my CIA contact if he would consider you for the *hostage exchange program*."

The program had existed for years, designed to enable the CIA and FBI to temporarily swap personnel depending on need. She wondered if it really extended to other federal agencies or if it was just Daugherty's wishful thinking. "He wants to get rid of me, ey?"

"More likely he wants to absolve himself of any responsibility for your future actions."

"What did you tell him?"

"That it wasn't a bad idea."

Chapter 25

Sounds from the outside woke Kozachenko. Disoriented, it took him a moment to get his bearings. They were on the train car.

Clicking a button on his watch, he lit up the face. 1:00 PM.

Glancing across at Yolkin still sleeping in the truck's passenger seat, Kozachenko wondered how Barkov and the others were doing. He sent Barkov a text, fearing any verbal communication would lead to detection. Until they were under way, their phones and lips would need to remain silent.

It had grown warm inside the car. Kozachenko stripped to his T-shirt, though he knew he should relish the heat. It would be cold for the next few days. Still, somehow the temperature made his anger rise.

The noise outside increased, and Kozachenko strained to hear. Was it Dudyk?

He and the men with him had not returned. Kozachenko had texted Dudyk hours ago, but he'd heard nothing in return. The only thing convincing him they hadn't been captured was that no soldiers or police had come looking for them. Maybe their luck had returned. Time would tell.

A jolt rocked the train, and the voice sounded louder.

Railroad workers! They were coupling the cars. So far it had worked the way Stas had told him it would. Another good sign.

In a few more minutes, the refrigeration cranked on, and the air began to cool. Then came a jolt. The quick movement caused Yolkin to wake and sit bolt upright in the passenger seat.

"What's going on?"

Kozachenko signaled Yolkin to be silent.

The voices outside the car paused.

Yolkin's eyes widened. He clamped his mouth shut and sat stock-still. Kozachenko froze. It took several moments for the chatter outside to resume, then Kozachenko let out his breath.

A few minutes later, there came another jolt, but this time the train picked up speed.

"Okay, Yolkin, now it's safe to talk for a while."

"Sorry."

Kozachenko shrugged off the apology. As long as they hadn't been caught.

"How far is it to where we're going?"

Being just the two of them in the truck, Kozachenko hoped Yolkin wasn't the type who liked to talk all the time. "About an hour."

"Have you heard from Dudyk?"

"No, but we must hope he made his way back to the west and connected up with the Russian soldiers at the front. The window for rejoining us here has passed."

The two men rode in silence from then on. The temperature inside continued dropping, and Kozachenko briefly considered starting the truck and running the heater. The problem was the container was solid, and carbon dioxide buildup might kill them. It wouldn't pay to be warm and dead. Instead, he slipped his shirt back on, and a few minutes later he added a jacket. Finally, he pulled out his sleep sack.

True to the timetable Stas had presented, the train traveled for little more than an hour before it slowed to a stop. It jerked forward once or twice as the cars were positioned along the track, and then outside, he could hear a number of voices—Ukrainian soldiers and first responders, perhaps some volunteers.

He heard the doors of the railroad car slide open and shallowed his breathing.

"Fill this one with debris," someone yelled out. It sounded like Stas. "Put any bodies in the first two cars."

Kozachenko heard a tractor fire up and then, in a matter of minutes, felt the vibration of debris hitting the floor of the railroad car, rocking it on the track. His stomach turned at the smell. Even with the refrigeration, the stench was bound to permeate. He wondered how much Stas was enjoying their dilemma.

"Where are they taking us from here?" Yolkin whispered.

Kozachenko glared, pulling a finger across his throat. Was Yolkin trying to get them caught?

"Poland," he mouthed, then made the motion of zipping his lips.

Most of the passengers on Flight 91 were from Krakow. They would ship the bodies home to where an army of soldiers and volunteers waited to sift through the bits of refuse—separating body parts from artifacts, items of value from trash—with one exception. If all went according to plan, after they crossed the border the train would be missing one car full of rubbish and men.

Chapter 26

Jordan stood at the window and watched the lights of the city wink on. Lory had sent her a text. His directive to stay put until morning and then return to Guangzhou had changed. She'd texted him back, and he'd confirmed that Davis had told her the truth about his reserve status, and she'd been right about Charlie's being a CIA asset. Then he gave her carte blanche on dealing with Zhen.

Stepping back to where the others were sitting, she sized up the group. "Davis, how much money do you have?"

He narrowed his eyes. "Why?"

"The presidential mandate came through. As agents of the American government, we've been instructed to sit on the manufacturing plant, monitor all activity, and do whatever is necessary to prevent the sale of the weapon."

Charlie clicked off the anime. "Aren't they sending a team?"

"ETA is twelve to twenty-four hours."

Davis shook his head. "They'll never make it."

"Which is why we need to be prepared. We're going to need some equipment." Jordan hoped Davis had enough cash to cover the cost. She looked at Charlie. "We'll need you to pick up supplies."

"Tell me what to buy."

She outlined the items for him. They needed communication devices, four-way and hands free. Dark clothing, pants and T-shirts, and dark caps.

"What about weapons?" Davis asked.

"No way," Charlie said. "The only people who carry guns in China are the Triad and the military. Even the police rarely carry firearms. Under the circumstances, we can't use the black market. I can get some knives, and maybe some antistab vests, though those might raise a few eyebrows."

"Then forget the vests," Jordan said. "We need to stay under the radar."

"Anything else?"

"We need to figure out how to hack into REE's IT system."

"I'm all over it," Zhen said, scooping up the laptop on the table. Davis reached forward and plucked it out of his hands.

"Hands off."

"Hey, dude! I'm just trying to help."

"Don't you think you've done enough?"

Jordan saw the stricken look on Zhen's face and put her hand on Davis's shoulder. Her gut told her the kid was sincere. "Why do you want to help, Kia?"

"Why wouldn't I? Those assholes tried to kill me. They maybe killed my cousin, and they for sure had something to do with all those people dying in the crash. They wouldn't have the weapon if it wasn't for me." His voice cracked, and he swiped his fingers across his eyes. "I just want to make it right."

Jordan wished she could tell him it would be okay, but what was the point in lying? Unless he knew how to turn back time, it would never be right. The best he could do was keep it from getting worse. "Let's let him show us what he can do."

"Why not?" Charlie said.

Davis's muscle twitched under Jordan's hand, then he handed over the computer. She squeezed his shoulder, then slipped past him and sat on the couch beside Zhen. Fascinated, she watched as he played the keyboard like a piano, gaining access to the alarm system, cameras, and warehouse specs in under five minutes.

"Any chance you can get to the weapons plans?" Jordan figured that would be too easy, but she had to ask.

Zhen shook his head. "Ping is careful. His office is on a separate alarm system, and he keeps the plans in two places. One set on a computer in his office that's not connected to the Internet, and a backup on a portable solid-state drive in his office safe."

Jordan froze. "A safe?"

"What kind?" Charlie asked.

"Digital is all I know. It takes a code to open it."

Jordan flopped back against the couch cushions. "That's it. We're screwed."

"Not so fast," Davis said. "When I was on assignment for a big fire in Canada, one of the human interest stories was on digital fire safes. Ironically, most are made in China. It turns out they aren't all that secure."

Jordan felt a spark of hope and sat up. "Can you open it?"

"A Canadian locksmith did. He used a magnet. Digital safes have a solenoid—simple coils with a pin that moves through its center allowing the bolts to be locked or unlocked by the coil's motion." Davis used his hands to demonstrate, and then picking up a magazine, he circled a spot on the cover. "If this is where the digital keypad sits, you put the magnet here." He pointed to a spot up and to the left of the circle. "The magnet moves the pin, and the safe opens."

"That easy?" Jordan said.

"He cracked it in under ten seconds."

"What type of magnet?" asked Charlie.

"One with a 125-pound pull, though I doubt we'd need one that big."

"I put it on the list."

"What about the railgun?" Zhen asked.

Jordan pointed to the warehouse blueprint. "Can you show us where he keeps the prototype?"

He enlarged the diagram on the screen. "Here's the warehouse layout. This is the front office, the storage area. Over here is Ping's office, and down here, in this corner, this is where they keep the gun."

Jordan studied the screen from a distance. "We might be able to reach it."

"But what then?" Charlie said, pulling up a chair and sitting down.

"What about using a drone?" Kia pulled up some information on the computer. "We did some tests using drones while I was at Berkeley. You can buy and fly much larger drones in China. I think the weight limit here without having to register them for flight is up to 7.5 pounds. A drone that size could easily carry a payload of five pounds."

"A block of C-4 would do the trick," Davis said. "It weighs about 1.25 lbs."

"Where are you going to get it?" Jordan said. "Plus you'd need a detonator."

Charlie leaned in. "Any of the mines around here would have explosives."

Kia's face lit up with excitement. "All we'd have to do is rig the drone, fly it into the warehouse, and—*Kaboom*!"

"Provided the Triad doesn't shoot it out of the sky first," Jordan struggled with getting on board. "A drone that big will make noise."

Zhen shrugged. "It's noisy there to begin with."

"But what if they see the drone coming? We can't afford to lose the element of surprise. We have to get in there to retrieve the plans, anyway. Why not sabotage the warehouse from the inside?"

"That still requires us to obtain some explosives," Davis said.

"So give me a better idea," she said.

"If we can get to the gun, I think I know a way to neutralize it."

Jordan nodded for Davis to continue. "I'm listening."

Davis turned the computer. Pulling up an image of the gun, he pointed to a piece that looked like a cargo box. "The energy source, the compulsator, is just a glorified battery. All we have to do to is redirect the energy. When the charge is sent, the armature becomes the conduit. It should be enough to fry any computer or computer parts, not to mention pieces of the gun."

"How much time would you need?"

"A couple of minutes, depending on how easy it is to get to the wires and whether I have the right tools."

"Like what?" Charlie asked.

"A screwdriver, wire cutters, and electrical tape."

"Give me some money, and let me see what I can do."

* * *

Two hours later, parked in a small pullout to the north of the plant, Jordan looked at the others.

"Everybody ready?"

Her eyes lit on Zhen. He was the variable in all this. Realizing they needed his computer skills and his knowledge of the weapons plans, she'd made the decision to include him. Her other option was to duct tape his mouth, tie him up, and lock him in the trunk. Both options carried pluses and minuses.

Across the road, the REE Manufacturing plant's main warehouse slumbered in the moonless night like a dragon curled against the base of the mountain. Peaceful except for the occasional growl of a generator rising up like a snore, a long row of wide loading doors spanned the lower section of the massive warehouse like a large maw open and waiting for food. A string of smaller windows inset above formed a row of beady eyes, now shut against the night. The only sign that anyone was present on the property was the warm glow of light spilling out at the back of the building and lighting up a small section of the rock-cut.

A few hundred yards to the north, the main production facility was lit up like a football stadium. The place bustled with activity. Smokestacks in the roof belched steam, smoke, and chemicals into the air. The noise outside was deafening. So far there had been no apparent activity at the main plant, though the lights in the back remained on.

"Does everyone have their comms in?" She heard a chorus of yeses. "Then let's do this."

Zhen opened the laptop, lighting the dark interior of the car. He made a few keystrokes, then shut the laptop. "The alarms and motion sensors have been disabled, and I've frozen the camera images for the front door and main office areas."

Crossing the highway and the gravel parking lot went without a hitch. There was no one stationed in front, and no one appeared to be upstairs in the administrative offices.

Jordan stepped up to the door and jiggled the handle. "How about unlocking the door?"

Zhen flipped open the laptop, tapped a key, and the door latch clicked. He repeated the process at the top of the stairs.

Jordan took point entering the main office. Rounding the corner, she checked the bank of monitors. The office where the four of them stood appeared empty on the screen, dark except for a glow from the monitors. The remainder of the images detailed the warehouse floor, a couple of shots of the perimeter, and Ping's office. The latter appeared dark. The only people visible in the images were four men standing inside, in a back garage area of the building, around a truck with the mounted weapon.

Zhen pointed to the smallest man. "That's Ping Mu."

Jordan identified the others as Triad by the tattoos on their fore-arms. Big and tough looking, two of the men carried QBZ-95s, a standard issue Chinese bullpup rifle.

"There aren't as many guards as I thought there would be," Jordan said. Maybe it was a good omen.

Zhen punctured her bubble of optimism. "There're more. Ping insists they smoke outside. They're just off camera." He reached over and hit a button, unfreezing the camera at the front entrance. "Now we can see if anyone decides to come in that way."

"Are there more banks of these monitors?"

"A couple. There are some in Ping's office and some on the ware-house floor."

"Okay, then we'll go with the original plan. Charlie, you stay here and keep your eye on the monitors. Give us a heads up if you see any of the guards coming. Davis, Zhen, and I will head to Ping's office. Once we're done there, Zhen comes back here, and Davis and I head for the garage. If things go south, Charlie, you and Zhen are to leave and head back to Guangzhou. Get Zhen to the consulate and have the PO notify Lory. Understood?"

"Got it. But don't worry, everything is going to be fine."

"Because you know kung fu?" she asked.

"That's right."

Chapter 27

Zhen showed Charlie how to operate the camera feeds, then froze the images in the warehouse cameras. On Jordan's mark, she, Davis, and Zhen headed for the office on the other side of the warehouse. Large pallets of stored steel sheets and racks of pipe were laid out in grid patterns on the stone tile floor, leaving aisles between the stacks wide enough to maneuver a forklift. Overhead, a crane system was attached to metal beams that spanned the ceiling.

"So far you're in the clear," Charlie said. His voice sounded loud in Jordan's ear, and she reached up and turned down the sound. Taking the stairs from the warehouse floor to the second-floor office, she signaled to Davis and Zhen to hold up at the bottom. When Zhen used the laptop to unlock the door, she opened it, simultaneously turning on the radio jammer Charlie had given her. If it worked, the alarm system would pick up the electromagnetic frequency and block the central unit from sending out a distress signal. If it didn't, they would soon have company.

After a few moments, she heard Charlie's voice. "It looks like it's working."

Jordan shot him a thumbs-up, then entered and swept the office suite. It consisted of a main room with a secretary's desk and a tall credenza; a second room, which was clearly Ping's office; a bathroom; and a door that led into a large, empty conference room and the back way out.

"All clear."

Davis and Zhen sprinted up the steps to join her. The ambient light from the warehouse floor was enough to see by, so she left the lights off. While Davis secured the door, Zhen headed for Ping's office.

In the largest room, Ping's desk was at the far end opposite an outsized built-in wall unit. Both ornately carved and made out of Hong Suanzhi wood. A thick carpet covered the floor, and two tall-backed chairs faced the desk.

"I need to boot up his computer." Zhen tapped a key or two, then pointed. "The safe is inside the cabinet."

Jordan crossed to the built-in wall unit and opened the center double doors. Inside was a large safe with a digital keypad. "Do you have the magnet?"

"The big thing I remember was his warning not to get your fingers between the magnet and the safe." Freeing the magnet from its wrapping, Davis gripped it gingerly around the edges, positioned it just above and to the left of the keypad, and let it thunk into place. "Now for the test." Davis turned the handle.

Nothing.

"Try moving it," Jordan said.

Davis forced the magnet half an inch to the right. Still nothing.

"We need a bigger magnet, don't we?"

"It looks that way."

They'd known it was a possibility. When Charlie had returned from the store, he'd brought back a ten-pound magnet—the largest he could find.

Jordan headed back toward Zhen. "How are you doing on the files?"

"It's still frickin' booting up."

"Let it load and help me find the REE Manufacturing products list. Do they manufacture magnets?"

Zhen pulled up the list and skimmed his finger down the face of the laptop. The blue color of the screen cast his face in an eerie glow. "Yeah, they're listed."

"I need a product location."

"Near the northwest corner of the warehouse."

Jordan headed for the door. "Davis, you stay with Zhen. If he gets in, make sure the computer files are destroyed. Charlie, I'm going downstairs."

"So far, you're all clear."

Jordan reached the warehouse floor in seconds and started walking the shelves along the outside walls toward the northwest corner. Most of the boxes were products intended for export and labeled in both Chinese and English.

"Jordan, you've got company," Charlie said. "One armed guard coming from the back garage."

Jordan didn't respond for fear of attracting attention.

"Which way is he headed?" Davis asked, saving her from having to speak.

"Toward the office."

Jordan was about to turn back when she spotted the pallet of magnets. Each were individually wrapped in cardboard boxes. Checking the sizes, she found one labeled "one hundred pounds." Grabbing it off the shelf, she ducked between the pallets and moved quietly and quickly back toward the office. She rounded the corner near the stairs just as he opened the office door.

"Hey!" he shouted.

Bounding up the steps, Jordan pushed through the door. She found the scene inside contained. The guard lay sprawled on the floor, with Davis standing over him holding his gun.

"Charlie, are we good?" Jordan asked, shutting the door.

"So far."

"Keep an eye out. They may not have heard him, but they're eventually bound to miss him." Jordan handed Davis the boxed magnet. "Look what I found."

"Perfect."

While he unwrapped the magnet, she pulled a zip tie from her pocket and trussed up the guard. Then she started opening drawers. "There has to be something here that we can use to gag this guy."

Davis whipped out the roll of electrical tape.

"You are a regular MacGyver."

"I'll take it. As I recall, he was good with the ladies."

She laughed, then rolled the guard over and wrapped a couple of pieces of tape over his mouth.

"That should hold him for a while. Let's just hope no one comes looking for him." Jordan straightened up. "How's it going, Zhen?"

"I'm done."

"You're sure they're erased."

"The best way is to overwrite them. Turns out Ping's computer is full of porn. Nasty stuff. I used them to overwrite the Quinn Industry's files and then deleted them for good measure."

"How're we doing on the safe?" Jordan stepped up behind Davis.

"We're about to find out."

This time the bolt action clicked, and the handle turned. Jordan reached in, pulled out the solid state drive, and walked it over to Zhen.

"Check it."

He plugged it into the computer and pulled up the schematics.

"You have two guards headed your way."

"Hook into the Internet and send them to Lory, then wipe the drive clean. Hurry."

"You better get moving."

It took Zhen a matter of seconds. He handed her back the SSD, and she handed it to Davis. "Put it back in the safe and lock it up. Get rid of the magnets. Zhen, turn off the computer, then help me drag the guard into the conference room. We need to buy ourselves some time by making it look like no one's been in here."

Jordan and Zhen each tucked an arm under the guard's armpits and pulled him forward. The guard's head lolled to the side, and he moaned.

"What are we going to do?" Zhen said. "He's coming around."

"You need to pick up your pace," Charlie said. "They're at the bottom of the stairs."

Davis handed Jordan the guard's rifle, pushed Zhen out of the way, and dragged the guard into the conference room. Jordan shut the door about the time she heard the approaching guards at the top of the stairs. Zhen stepped forward and together, he and Davis lifted the guard off his feet and sprinted for the exit on the far side of the room.

"Get out. Now," Charlie said.

Davis and Zhen pushed through onto the stairs just as the two guards entered Ping's office, Jordan tight on their heels. Closing the outer door, she didn't let it click shut all the way. Raising a closed fist, she signaled Davis and Zhen to get down and hold at the top of the stairs. If they'd done the cleanup correctly, the guards would never know anyone had been inside Ping's office.

Charlie's voice cracked over the comm. "Good call, Jordan. On my mark, go back inside. Zhen and Davis, be ready to move."

Jordan kept one hand on the door and one on the assault rifle she'd taken off the tied-up guard. She breathed lightly and waited for the signal. If they reentered too soon, they risked being spotted. If they reentered too late, they'd be seen on the stairs.

"Okay. Get ready," Charlie said. "Go!"

Jordan pushed open the door. Zhen and Davis dove through on her heels. The guard between them bucked and kicked, his foot catching the door and banging it sharply in place. The two guards on the stairs pulled up short.

Throwing herself across the guard's legs, she and Davis pinned him to the floor while Zhen poked his head up to look.

"Wait," he whispered.

Jordan prepared to fire the bullpup rifle, then she heard boots on the stairs.

"Okay, you're clear for now. It's time to move."

Jordan rolled free of the writhing guard. "Want to hand me another zip tie?"

Davis did the honors. "What do you want to do with him?"

Jordan scanned the room and spotted another door. "Let's put him in there. They'll be back looking for him. Let's not make him easy to find."

Once the guard was secured in the closet, Jordan held up at the conference room door.

"We still need to take care of the gun. Zhen is coming back across the warehouse to you, Charlie."

"I want to stick with you."

"That wasn't the plan," she said. "We stick with the plan."

"But I know the gun. What if you need my help?"

"I do. I need you up there with Charlie to do a job only you can do."

"Yeah, what's that?"

"When I tell you to, I need you to set off the fire alarms in the production plant. Our best chance of making this work is to draw off some of their manpower. Can you do it?"

Zhen glared at her, and then finally he nodded. "How big a fire do you want?"

Jordan grinned. "Charlie, Zhen's coming your way. Davis and I are heading for the garage. On your go."

"You're all clear."

Jordan opened the door, and they made their way down to the warehouse floor. Zhen made speed toward the main office, while Jordan and Davis moved in the opposite direction.

"Davis, are you ready for this?"

"It's the most fun I've had all week."

Chapter 28

At the far end of the warehouse, the garage area was walled off by giant sheets of plastic that created a bay for the truck. Jordan worked her way into position at the edge of the opening. Behind her, the warehouse was dark and full of shadows from the muted light emanating from the production plant. Davis had taken up a position on the other side. She could see his tall, lean frame leaning against a rack of steel piping.

"How many are there?" she asked Charlie, speaking in low, hushed tones.

"I only count three guards and Ping."

That fit with the fourth guard being locked in the closet in Ping's office. Jordan crossed to where Davis stood. "What do you think?"

"It looks pretty sophisticated."

"Like you said earlier, it's just a battery." She hoped her pep talk worked. They were only going to get one shot at this.

Davis moved his head so his lips were close to Jordan's ear. His breath was warm and smelled faintly of mint. "Let's do this."

Jordan pulled back, their eyes met and locked for a moment, then she spoke quietly into the comm. "Charlie, Zhen, we're ready whenever you are."

"We're set on our end," Charlie replied. "Just say the word."

Jordan waited for Davis to nod and then issued the go order. Within five seconds, the wail of emergency sirens pierced the air. Ping and most of his men bolted outside to see what was happening. She could hear Ping yelling.

Davis didn't hesitate. He headed for the railgun, wire cutters in hand. Jordan moved forward to provide cover if needed.

"I need updates, Charlie." Without putting herself in the open, Jordan had no way of knowing where the danger might come from. The compact bullpup rifle felt odd pressed against her shoulder in ready mode.

"Most are running to the production plant. Ping left one guard. The two of them are standing outside watching the action."

"How long do you think we have before they figure out it's a false alarm?"

"Not long."

"How're you doing, Davis?"

"I'm almost done."

Jordan backed toward the gun.

"You're out of time." It was Zhen's voice, and it held a note of trepidation. "They're coming back."

Davis tore off a piece of tape with his teeth and fastened the wires to the contacts on the back of the armature.

"Davis, we need to go." Jordan started pulling back.

"One more piece."

She watched as he slapped the tape in place, his handiwork visible if anyone looked too closely.

"It's good enough," she said. "Let's go!"

Jordan covered him to the doorway, turning around at the last moment. Behind them she could hear Ping berating his men.

"It was a false alarm," someone said.

Agitated, Ping demanded to know where the missing guard went. He must have sensed something was wrong. Jordan knew that little voice, at least the one that lived in her own head. It was telling her that she and Davis needed to get out of there quickly. "Let's go."

"What if it doesn't work?"

"It will," she assured him. It had to.

"Get out of there, now!" Charlie said.

Jordan and Davis pulled back into the warehouse just as Ping strode toward the doorway. He stopped and sniffed, like a bloodhound on the scent. Pressing her back to the inside wall, she reached for Davis's hand to stop him from moving. She held her breath, felt his fingers grip hers, and they waited in the sharp silence.

A burst of Chinese released the tension. Ping had turned back.

Letting go of Davis's hand, she gestured for him to head for the main office while she brought up the rear. He was halfway up the stairs with her standing ready on the warehouse floor when Charlie spoke.

"We have incoming. A car is pulling around to the back."

She stopped moving. "The dragon?"

Davis turned on the stairs, and she waved him on. Zhen opened the door. Davis looked back, then disappeared inside.

"The car bears the flags of a government vehicle."

Jordan crept back through the warehouse toward the cordoned-off truck bay.

"What the hell are you doing?" Davis said over the comm.

She ignored the three men in her head and hunkered down just a few feet back from the opening slit in the plastic. Camouflaged by deep shadow, she watched two bodyguards and a middle-aged Chinese man in a suit climb out of a black Maserati. Jordan took in the red power tie and Ping's deference to the man. This had to be the dragon.

Pulling out her cell phone, she snapped several pictures. Then before she could retreat, Ping ordered his men to move the gun into position for a demonstration and insisted someone go check on the missing guard.

Jordan tucked herself between two pallets and held still. The gangster sent on the mission moved past her, and she edged back out.

"What's all the excitement?" The man in the suit asked. "Perhaps we should do this another time?"

"No, no," Ping said. "It was nothing, just a false alarm. There's no need for concern."

The suited man hesitated then signaled his men, who took up protective positions. "You indicated I could see a demonstration of the weapon."

"Of course, we're moving the gun into position now."

Jordan's heart started to beat faster. Would they notice the crude reconfiguration of wires? It was darker outside, and they were working to impress their potential buyer. How close would they check?

"How does this work?" the man asked, stepping into the garage, allowing the truck to pass.

Ping rattled off statistics of distance and velocity as the gun was repositioned outside. "From here, we must shoot on the horizon with reduced capacity. We have a range of only three miles. We've also placed several targets along the bullet's path to slow it down. The final target is a block of steel over eight feet thick. You will see that the bullet will nearly punch through and take under a minute to hit the target. When fired using the GPS guided system, the time to target can vary." Ping gestured that they should go outside. "We'll stand on the other side, where you can best see the action of the gun."

"Jordan, get out of there," Davis said over the comm. He sounded strained.

Not knowing where the guard had disappeared to, Jordan didn't respond and held her position.

"Watch your six," Charlie said. "It looks like he found your man in the closet. They're headed back your way."

Jordan heard them on the stairs simultaneous to the warning. She could see Ping on the far side of the weapon, his arm raised to signal the discharge.

"There she is," shouted one of the guards.

Jordan stepped into the open, fired the bullpup, and dropped one of the men on the stairs. The other man ducked for cover. Hiding behind the pallet, Jordan pressed her back to the steel and waited.

Ping dropped his hand. A bright flash lit the area. The air tingled, then everything went dark.

Chaos erupted around her. Men shouted. A large humming filled the room. After a few minutes, the generators kicked on. The electromagnetic pulse had knocked her down, and she pushed herself up off the floor. The guard who had ducked for cover appeared dazed. Through the doorway, she could see several men on the ground. The armature appeared warped, the metal twisted and melted by the charge.

"Mission accomplished," she said and then realized her comm was blown.

Chapter 29

In the chaos, Jordan made it back to the main office, and the four of them had slipped out in time to see the black Maserati pull away. Now safely back in the suite in Shaoguan, they faced another problem. They needed a way out of China.

"Word has leaked out that you have Zhen," Lory said. Jordan had him on speaker phone. "The police have issued an all-points bulletin on both of you. The good news is, it appears Davis and Charlie are both in the clear."

"What are the charges against Zhen and me?"

"You're being accused of spying. Ping Mu leveled the accusation. One of his men identified you. Of course, no specifics were given, but let's not forget that the Chinese have been known to execute spies. Even if you could make it back to the consulate, the counsel general will be forced to detain you for your own security."

"What do you suggest we do?"

Lory hedged. "You did a good job, Jordan. All of you. Exactly what was needed. I received the encrypted files, proof that REE was involved. It's a shame we didn't get the dragon ID'd. We may have been able to use that as leverage with President Xi Jinping."

"I have photos, provided Henry can pull them off the microSD card." Her cell had been fried when the pulse was unleashed.

"It doesn't change the present situation. Right now our priority is getting you out of the country."

"What about the embassy in Beijing?"

"The situation's the same there."

"How about a private jet?" Davis asked.

"We're actually working that angle, but we need someone we can trust."

"How about someone with a vested interest?"

Jordan frowned. "It sounds like you have someone in mind."

"Who do we know who is currently in Kyiv and has a vested interest in keeping details of your detention from going public?"

His words acted like a light switch. "Ellis Quinn," she said.

"What about her?" Lory asked.

"She's attending the leadership conference at the Intercontinental with Mrs. Linwood."

"Sit tight," Lory said. "Let me make a few calls."

* * *

It had taken him an hour to make the arrangements. Ellis Quinn would land at Ganzhou Huangjin Airport, approximately two and half hours north of Shaoguan. The region was known for its large reserves of tungsten, and Quinn Industries had a supplier there. She wasn't exactly happy with the situation, but she'd set up a meeting and been granted permission to fly into Chinese airspace. It was on them to figure out how to get on board the plane before she took off. She would arrive around 2:00 PM, and they'd been given a two-hour window to be on board.

"It's a private plane. They park them in a different area of the airports," Charlie said. "She'll need a car to pick her up and return her."

"How does that help us?" Jordan asked.

"I am a driver from her consulate. I'll go in to pick her up. Security will be thorough going in the first time, but not so thorough on the return. They will recognize me then and not be so concerned. I can take you through in the trunk. Trust me."

* * *

That night, Jordan spent a fitful night on the couch in the suite while Charlie and Zhen sacked out on the bed and Davis slept in the chair. In the morning, news of the explosion and fire at the manufacturing plant headlined the news. There were casualties, but no specifics were released of what exactly had happened.

They didn't talk much on the trip to Ganzhou, but Charlie broke the silence as they parked in a lot near the airport.

"Travel by private jet is a new phenomenon in China. Only the very affluent buy planes, and the government likes to make it difficult for them to fly. That is to our benefit."

Jordan bit. "Why is that?"

"It means the areas designated for private planes are small, usually off to one side and not heavily guarded. Observe." He pointed to a gate with only two guards.

It didn't take long before one of the guards disappeared.

"He's gone on break," Charlie said.

Jordan grinned. "And then there was one."

"One we can handle."

The Quinn Industry plane arrived early. While Jordan, Davis, and Zhen waited in the parking lot, Charlie drove to the gate. True to his prediction, the guards searched his car from top to bottom, even pulling out the spare tire in the back. Then they waved him through.

Davis put into words what Jordan was thinking. "You realize, even if they don't search the car when he comes back through, there isn't room for three of us in the trunk."

"Which means you're flying commercial," she said. He pouted and made her laugh. "Tell me you're disappointed."

"A little. Hey, it's a Gulfstream G-650."

"At least no one is looking for you."

"What about the gang members? They saw both Charlie and me."

"I doubt any of them could pick you out in a lineup. Me, on the other hand, I'm on everyone's no-fly list."

Their eyes met and caught.

"Will you be in Kyiv when I get there?" he asked.

"Why?"

"Because it's going to take Charlie and me a while to get back to Guangzhou and for me to schedule a flight, and you promised me a story, remember?"

Of course, the story. For a moment, she'd let herself think he wanted to see her again. She turned her head and stepped back, putting a little distance between them.

"I'll be there. Unless, of course, my job requires I be somewhere else. For all I know, they'll put me on the first plane to Tel Aviv."

Chapter 30

Landing in Kyiv in the early hours on Sunday, the Gulfstream had been met by an armed escort from the embassy. Zhen was taken into custody and booked into a holding area. Jordan was sent to see Lory.

Shown into his office, her first question was about the Russians. "Have they been located?"

"No. The general consensus seems to be that they're safely behind their front lines by now. The Ukrainians are eager to put this behind them. They've worked fast, and the first of the crash remains are on their way by train to Krakow now."

"They've completed the investigation?"

"As far as the IIC is concerned, the crash was due to a mechanical failure of the left engine." Lory leaned back in his desk chair and smiled. "Your work here is done, Jordan. RSO Daugherty has arranged for another agent to accompany the ambassador's wife home. He suggested you take a few days off."

"You're joking, right?"

"No, Agent Jordan, consider it a thank you for a job well done."

"Sir, the Russians still have a prototype of the railgun Quinn Industries has in development. They didn't bring it this far into Ukraine just to turn tail and run. They have a plan."

Picking up a pencil, he bounced the eraser off the desk. "In this business, there are times you have to sit back and let things play out.

This weekend, the prime minister and the ambassador are attending a summit. The minister is signing an alliance agreement that was nearly derailed by Russia's incursion into Ukraine. Meanwhile, they continue to make headway toward a peaceful end to Russia's take-over of the Crimean Peninsula. Bottom line, right now is not a good time to go accusing the Russians of illegal weapons trading, especially without solid evidence."

"But we know who the manufacturer is, and we have a witness to the arms trade."

"Do you really expect anyone to take us seriously? The only witness is a fugitive, wanted for treason."

"I saw the second prototype, so did Davis."

"Again, your word against the Chinese. There's just no tangible proof."

"What about the files we e-mailed back?"

"It's not enough."

She suddenly felt defensive. "We did what we had to when we destroyed the gun."

He was quick to allay her guilt. "I know that. You know that. In reality, everybody knows that. It's just that no one is going to take action unless we have a lot more evidence to back up the claims."

She still had her fried phone. If Henry could pull the files, she'd have pictures. "What if I can produce photos?"

"Give it up, Jordan. At this point, we gain nothing, and we stand to lose a helluva lot if we start leveling accusations we can't substantiate."

"But sir, I'm telling you, the Russians—"

Mary banged open the door. Walking past them to the credenza, she picked up the remote and clicked on the TV. "You're going to want to see this. A reporter, claiming to have been at the crash site, has just gone live with the information that Kia Zhen was not killed aboard PR Flight 91."

"Damn, if it isn't our guy Davis," Lory said.

When the television picture came up, it showed a split screen with the in-studio reporter on one side and Nye Davis on the other.

Stunned, Jordan watched him say he had an unidentified source who had confirmed that the man being transported by the DSS was not the fugitive wanted for espionage as suspected, but a man with a similar last name thought to be affiliated with the Triad. A surge of adrenalin hit Jordan's system, a buzzing in her ears overpowering his voice. He'd given his word he wouldn't say anything, not until she'd given him the green light.

When the picture cut away to another act of violence in the Middle East, Lory clicked off the TV. "Actually, he might have done us a favor. He just took the wind out of everyone else's sails."

Jordan stared at the blank screen. "He promised to sit on the information."

"He lied."

Funny, that's what she'd said to Zhen about Eddie. The only positive spin was that Davis hadn't filled in the details. He hadn't given any specifics about Eddie or his alleged connections with the CIA. He'd said nothing about the hacking of a U.S. defense contractor.

Jordan suddenly felt drained. "You know," she said, pushing up from her chair, "I think I will take a few days."

"Good idea." Lory got to his feet and shook her hand. "And next time"—he jerked his head toward the TV—"you might want to pick better friends."

She didn't bother to remind him that Davis had put his life on the line for her and to stop the Chinese. She doubted he'd care.

Mary wasn't at her desk, but Jordan helped herself to a lab request form on her way out. She still had the pictures to follow up on. Lory may have told her to walk away, but she had a nagging suspicion that they were all missing the bigger picture. She didn't believe the Russians had turned back. They were headed somewhere, and the clock was ticking.

Henry was in the lab when she pushed through the door and seemed genuinely glad to see her. "Whatcha got there? I thought maybe you'd left without a good-bye."

"Not yet. I need a favor." She pulled out the phone she'd been using when the electromagnetic pulse had misfired. "This phone was fried, but there were some pictures on the microSD card. Any chance you can pull them off? I really need an ID on the man in the photos."

He looked skeptical. "I'll give it a try, but I can't promise anything."

"What more can I ask? Any idea how long it'll take?"

"We're buried, but since it's for you, I'll fit it in. Do you have a new number?" He waggled the phone.

"It's on the form." She smiled and started to leave, then hesitated near the door. "Oh, and Henry?"

"Yeah?" He looked expectant, hopeful, like a puppy waiting for a treat.

"I'd appreciate it if you didn't tell anybody about the photos. Could you just give me a call when you have some answers? I'd like to keep this on the down low, just for now."

"Not even Lory's office?"

Especially not Lory's office. "I wouldn't ask if it wasn't important."

Chapter 31

The night train to L'viv departed at 11:00 PM. With no leads to follow, she decided to take a few days to research her family history. It gave her a reason to stay in Ukraine, plus L'viv was the birthplace of her father. It was as good a place as any to start looking into his past.

She purchased the last first-class ticket and found she was sharing the sleeping wagon with an elderly woman who snored. Jordan climbed into the top bunk and now lay in the dark, letting her mind churn over the details of the past week. With the rhythm of the wheels on the track lulling her toward sleep, she found herself grasping for the thread she knew still dangled somewhere out there.

One of the first things she'd done after leaving the lab was to call her RSO in Tel Aviv. Daugherty confirmed that she could take a few days. She considered calling Davis to confront him but figured his response would never blunt the edge of his betrayal. It was better to walk away.

In L'viv, she disembarked with her overnight bag and headed straight for the Hotel Leopolis. After unpacking, she pulled on a loose cotton shirt to cover her shoulder holster and gun and headed out to get something to eat.

The contrast between Kyiv and L'viv was like the difference between sunset and dawn. In Kyiv, a shroud had fallen over the city. The people were edgy, worried about the war, and stressed for money.

She'd been told L'viv was called "the little Paris of Ukraine," the lover's city, and the number of wedding parties and brides hurrying along the streets lent a festive atmosphere. Here the people seemed carefree, happy, and the mood was contagious. The aromas of chocolate and coffee prompted her to stop at a small café. Sipping the dark roast and munching on a bowl of buckwheat groats and *kovbasa*, she felt the knot in her stomach relax for the first time in days.

Jordan had made an appointment to meet Professor Fedorov at 2:00 PM. He lived in the Jewish quarter, an older section of town. Here, the buildings were painted in shades of yellow and tan, with cobblestone streets in need of repair. The driver seemed genuinely alarmed to be dropping her off here. She assured him she would be fine.

Professor Fedorov lived in a second-floor walk-up. A stooped man in his seventies, he had a shock of white hair and piercing eyes from which nothing could hide. He ushered her in to a large sitting room off the entryway filled with books on built-in bookshelves along every wall. In the middle of the room, two chairs sat on a rug flanking a small round table where a pot of tea graced a tray along with two cups and saucers, a creamer, and a small bowl of sugar cubes.

"May I offer you some tea?" he said in English, gesturing to the spread. "My wife is making *rugelach*. You know this?"

A Jewish pastry filled with chocolate, cinnamon, or fruit preserves. Jordan's grandmother had made it. "Of course. Thank you."

Jordan found herself happy to fuss with her tea. She didn't really know what to say to this man, though she had more questions than she had time to ask.

"You look like your father," he said.

She glanced up, surprised. "Most people tell me I look like my mother."

Fedorov tapped his spoon on the rim of his cup and shrugged. "She was beautiful, but you have your father's eyes. As Jesus said, the eye is the lamp of the body. Translated, the eyes are the windows to the soul."

As a Jew, his pull from the Bible caught her off guard. "You know the New Testament?"

"I am an educated man."

She rested her own spoon in the saucer. "What can you tell me about my father?"

"What is it you want to know?"

Jordan swallowed a lump that had formed in her throat. "Alena Petrenko said he was Jew, a teacher who later became a Russian spy."

"If it were only that simple." Fedorov sipped his tea and looked up when a woman about his age came in with a small plate of pastries. He introduced her to Jordan and waited for her to leave before he continued. "Olek Ivanova was one of the most gifted men I ever knew. He had the power to heal and the power to know what was in a man's mind. It was that power that brought the attention of Ilya Kravchenko."

Dyadya Ilya? "I've never heard the name Kravchenko." An image of the man she knew as Ilya Brodsky flashed in her mind.

Fedorov offered a sad smile. "Yes, I believe you called him dyadya. He was a Russian KGB agent, a major general in the army. He resided over the PSI program. You know of it?"

Jordan nodded. The program he referred to was Russia's "psychic faculty" program. Started back in the 1920s, the studies were quickly banned by Stalin. Then in the 1950s, the taboo was lifted, and the KGB got involved. It was hard for her to believe anyone took it seriously. But spurred on by Cold War articles alluding to the U.S. Navy's telepathic tests on atomic submarines, the Soviets launched a full-scale scientific exploration into the weapons potential of psychic energy. Terrified by reports that the Soviets were developing a psychotronic-warfare platform, the United States countered by creating its own, Star Gate. The difference in scope was substantial. The U.S. program was small and met with lots of skepticism. But the Soviets had gone with the adage *go big or go home.*

The knot in her stomach that she'd lost at lunch had returned. "It was a spy program specializing in remote viewing."

"Among other things." Fedorov picked up a rugelach and pointed to the plate for her to help herself. "Back then a person didn't have a choice in matters of state. Your father was selected by the major general to participate. Ironic considering his mother was Jewish."

Jordan snapped her head up.

"You didn't know." It was a statement, not a question.

"You must be mistaken," she said. Knowing what she did about the area, she found it hard to believe. During World War II, the Jews living in L'viv were murdered and the Poles forced out by Stalin, leaving only the Ukrainian nationalists here. Her father had been born here after the war.

He smiled sadly. "I'm sorry I was the one to tell you. Your grandmother chose to hide it. Your father only learned of it the year before he died."

"My mother knew?" If so, why had she never been told?

"Don't be too quick to judge decisions made in the past. People do the best they can. Sometimes their choices are misguided, but seldom are they made with malice." He reached over and patted her hand. "Anyway, your father grew up a Soviet, and as such, he did what he was ordered to do. They sent him to college, where he worked for me to make extra money, and he played hockey."

Her mouth felt dry. She sipped her tea and shoved aside thoughts of her hidden heritage. There would be time to explore those later. Now was the opportunity for her to gather details of her father's past. "How did he meet Ilya?"

"As I said, your father was a man of many talents. Some of which I think you share."

"What talents?"

"For one, he could read anybody. He had an inner voice that spoke to him. It was usually right, and he learned to listen well. For another, he had a knack for protecting the goal. They sent him to play for the Soviet hockey team. His athletic prowess along with his subsequent marriage to your mother afforded him access to the international community, and his psychic abilities made him an invaluable asset. Then shortly before your mother became pregnant with your brother, something changed. Your father grew angry, more distant. He claimed his inner voice had lost some of its luster. Then after your brother was born, your father started speaking of emigrating to America. The reins of the Communist Party were loosening, and your mother wanted to go home."

"Because she didn't like it here?" The question popped out. Her mother had rarely spoken of Russia, or her father, for that matter.

"I think she didn't like the direction things were going in her marriage. Over the years, Ilya had showered her with unwanted attention, and Olek had grown more distant. She had told your father how unhappy it made her, but he told her she was reading too much into the situation. By going home, she would kill two hares with one shot, removing Ilya from their lives and perhaps rekindling her marriage. But Ilya wasn't about to let your father go."

Here was the moment of truth. The information she'd been seeking. "Are you saying he killed my father?"

"More likely, had him killed." Fedorov looked down at his cup. "Rumor was Ilya Kravchenko asked your mother to stay after your father was buried. She was gone in less than a month."

"But why murder him?"

Fedorov set down his cup. "One must presume to protect the secret."

Jordan frowned. "What secret?"

"After World War II, the Soviets had constructed a massive research facility in Siberia."

Jordan had read about the facility. Known as "Science City," it was made up of approximately forty scientific centers and housed tens of thousands of scientists.

"The PSI program operated there, out of the Center of Automation and Electrometry, Special Department Number Eight. It was an exciting time. As many as sixty scientists working to uncover the secrets of PSI particles, the elusive elements thought to be essential to psychic techniques, such as biocommunications and bioenergy."

199

Fedorov sipped his tea. "But when Ilya was promoted to major general, he had other ideas. He formed a splinter group, hand-picking a few of the greatest scientists and researchers to work out of the Basmanny District in Moscow. It was a small bunch but well-connected. They called themselves the *Futuristy*, the Futurists."

"How do you know all this?" Jordan asked, reaching for a rugelach heavily laced with cinnamon. Maybe it would settle her stomach.

"I learned it from Olek. He came to me. He felt things were progressing out of hand. He refused to elaborate, perhaps fearing for my safety. All he would say is the Futuristy had very big plans, global plans. He was meeting with the U.S. ambassador that night to discuss his defection to America, but he never made it to the embassy."

They sat in silence, Jordan holding the untouched rugelach between her fingers. After a few moments, Professor Fedorov pushed himself out of his chair.

"You know, I have a book that you might find interesting. It lists many of the names of the international scientists recruited to come to the Soviet Union. Your grandfather was one of those men." He walked to the bookcase and searched the spines of the books. "It was a Soviet operation following World War II, one very similar to your U.S. Operation Paperclip, called *Operation Osoaviakhim*."

Jordan watched him struggle to see on the top shelf. "Can I help you find it?"

"No, it's here somewhere. The book was written by a member of the People's Commissariat for Internal Affairs, the NKVD. It tells how The NKVD and the Soviet Army units recruited more than two thousand specialists for employment following the fighting."

"How did they even get that many people to come out of the West?"

"That was the easy part. Many of the men, like your grandfather, had ties to the Soviet Union. His family and your grandmother's family were from Ukraine. They wanted to come. No, it was crossing the borders with the specialized equipment they needed to do their jobs that presented the biggest challenge. The Soviets had to specially modify ninety-two train cars with secret compartments in order to accommodate the families and all their belongings."

Jordan tried to imagine her grandma and grandpa packed onto the trains. Then when his words finally sank in, she surged into action. Jumping to her feet, she bumped the table, causing the cups and saucers to rattle. "Professor Fedorov, I have to go."

"But you haven't eaten your pastry."

"I'm sorry," she said, setting the rugelach down. "You've been a huge help. I really do appreciate the time you've taken, and the insights into my father and my family." She walked over and shook the man's hand. "I hope you'll have me back sometime, but right now there's something I have to do."

"Please, take this with you." He pressed a thin leather-bound volume into her hands. "If you like, you can bring it back next time you come for a visit."

"I will." She smiled, then clutching the small book moved swiftly for the door. She waved as she made her exit, and then midway down the stairs, she started to run. She needed to call Lory. She knew how the Russians were moving the gun.

Chapter 32

Jordan caught up to Lory when he was on his way out the door to play golf.

"I thought I told you to leave it alone," he said.

"I did. I came to L'viv to take some time off and research my family connections. That's how I learned about Operation Osoaviakhim. It doesn't hurt us to check it out. What if the Russians are using one from their own playbook?"

"I hear your concerns. Believe me, the Ukrainians haven't concluded their investigation yet. Until they do, all we can do is monitor the situation. The belief is that the Russians have pulled back behind the lines into separatist territory. If we uncover actionable intel or perceive an imminent threat, we'll take action. Until then, we can do nothing but wait."

"Is there a chance we missed something in the police report regarding the contact outside of Shyshaky?"

"Hold on, let me pull up a copy." She heard Lory typing and then mumbling, spitting out an occasional word. "Okay, it says here the vehicles split up near Yares'ky. The reporting officer followed the last vehicle when it headed south. Several officers converged on the other two from the west. Then the vehicles vanished."

"What's in Yares'ky?"

"Not much. It's a very small village with a grain silo or two."

"And a train yard?"

"The officers claim to have searched the area and concluded they'd turned around."

Jordan drew a deep breath. Her gut was telling her they were wrong. "Is there any reason I can't revisit the satellite images on my own?"

"We've gone over them ad nauseam."

"Maybe, but did you look at the train?" She heard Lory sigh.

"You really are a pain in the ass."

"So I've been told."

"Look, if it'll get you off my back, I'll forward you copies of the satellite images."

"And maybe some that are current."

"There's a limit to what I can pull. We're keeping most of our eyes on the Middle East. To achieve complete coverage in other areas, we have to rely on other countries to share their images. Obviously, in this case, we have to be cautious about asking." He cut away, speaking to someone behind him. "Look, I've got to go. I'll be in touch as soon as I have something. Meanwhile, will you do me a favor?"

"What's that?"

"Try to enjoy your vacation."

He wasn't giving her much choice. It was late Sunday afternoon, and without the satellite photos, all she had was speculation.

When her phone rang a few minutes later, she reacted quickly, only to be disappointed. She'd hoped it was Lory calling back. Instead the number showing belonged to Davis.

Dumping the call, Jordan hailed a cab and told the driver to drop her at the gates of the Lychakiv Cemetery, officially a state history and culture preserve. She hadn't been there since she was six years old.

The main gate looked like she remembered—a neo-Gothic, grand, white triple-arch with a wrought iron gate. Inside, the mausoleums, statuary, and ornate grave markers stood as a testament to those who were buried there. Among them were some of Ukraine's most famous writers, artists, scientists, and community leaders. There were also Austrians, Poles, Armenians, and Russians. There were fields of soldiers who had died in battle. And there was her father.

If what Professor Fedorov had told her was true, her family didn't belong here. Lychakiv was for Christians only. The Jews had their own burial grounds at Yanivs'ke Cemetery.

Jordan needed a map to find the graves. They were interred in an older section of the cemetery where the foliage grew thick and the birch trees tall. The wind rustled the leaves overhead, diffusing the sounds of the crowds. She liked the peacefulness.

She found her grandparents' simple markers first and stood staring down for a moment, trying to remember. The last she saw of them was when she left Russia, and her memory was dim. Near to them, her father's grave looked almost gauche. The marker was a towering sculpture of a winged Adonis, his head resting against a granite slab that bore the name Olek Ivanova. Tears flooded her eyes at memories of her dad, and she found herself sniffling.

"Here." It was Davis's voice. He held out a tissue.

She was surprised to see him. What was he doing there? Instead of asking, she took the tissue and said nothing.

"Look, I'm sorry." He touched her back, a gesture she would have appreciated a few days ago. Now his touch scalded, and she moved away.

"Why are you here?" It didn't escape her that this was a question she'd asked him before.

"I get it. You're angry. I should have warned you about the broadcast. I thought Lory would have told you."

"Told me what? Are you saying he knew?"

"I just assumed. When I got back to Guangzhou, the PO asked me to go live with the piece on Eddie. I was happy to oblige. I'm a staff reporter, and Reuters doesn't pay me to sit on a story. Besides, Claire Vance of the BBC was about to go live with a report on Kia Zhen, and it gave me a chance to scoop her."

Jordan dabbed at her eyes with the tissue and wiped her nose. "Claire Vance. Is she the leggy blonde who's always reporting from exotic locales?"

"Yes."

She clutched the tissue in her hands, hating her display of weakness, particularly at this moment. "You broke your promise."

"At the request of my government. Claire was all set to bring up the espionage charges and speculate about a weapons deal. I'm not sure where she was getting her information, but she had more right than wrong."

"How do you know?"

"I've got good sources. If it's any consolation, besting her wasn't as much fun as I thought it would be, especially when you refused to answer my calls." He stepped closer, and she caught the familiar scent of mint. "Jordan, you have to believe me."

She really wanted to. "You should have called."

He took her by the shoulders and turned her toward him. "If I could do it over."

"But you can't." *Trust was something you earned.* Davis had broken her trust, and he was going to have to earn it back. She lifted her chin until their eyes met. "There is one thing you can do."

"Name it."

"Does your source have access to satellite images?"

"Some."

She explained that she wanted images of the train being loaded at Hoholeve, leaving out the part about Operation Osoaviakhim. Davis wasn't fooled.

"Are you thinking the Russians might be on the train?"

"Call it a hunch."

"I'll put in a request. It could take a day or two."

"Thank you." Her eyes held his for a moment or two, and then she turned away toward her father's grave.

Davis stepped up beside her and looped an arm around her shoulders. "Do we know this guy?"

"He's my dad." But then, she figured he already knew.

Chapter 33

For the past day and a half, Kozachenko had suffered flashbacks of Siberia. Only living there had been worse than his current situation, with temperatures averaging minus twenty-five degrees Celsius in the wintertime. This car set around two degrees was balmy by comparison. Cold by refrigeration standards, but not freezing. Hunched down like he was inside his sleep sack with a bottle of vodka, it was tolerable.

He and Yolkin had talked for a while once the train had begun moving, but now Yolkin snored softly in the seat beside him. There were no cell connections out here, so he'd turned off his phone to conserve the battery. Lulled by the rocking rhythm of the train, he tried to sleep, but it eluded him. Their days were running short.

Reluctantly, he gave Stas credit. The plan seemed to be working, and they were back on schedule. He was sure the pakhan was pleased, but it irritated Kozachenko to be beholden to Stas. Not to mention it made Stas look good.

Kozachenko took another swig of vodka, and the train lurched, spilling it down his shirt.

"What a waste," he mumbled.

When the train lurched again, he realized they were stopping. He pressed the button on his watch and noted the time. It was 11:00 PM, which put them at the Polish border crossing.

His heart rate quickened, and he kicked Yolkin's leg. "Wake up!"

The last thing he needed was for Yolkin to wake with a start again while the border guards searched the train.

"What? What is going on?" Yolkin asked. "Why did you kick me?"

"We're at the border. It will take some time for the train to pass, and we must stay alert. First, the wagon wheels will be adjusted. The track is wider in the west than in Ukraine. Then there will be border guards."

Yolkin's expression showed concern. "Will they come inside?"

"I doubt if they can," he said. Imagining what was stacked inside the car behind the false walls, he assumed it would be hard to search. "It's possible they will open the doors."

The Ukrainian border was heavily policed. It was the most traveled border between the Eastern bloc countries and Poland and served as a smuggling route for goods and illegal immigrants to the EU. It was easy to get into Ukraine, but difficult to leave.

He could hear the guards outside now and signaled to Yolkin to stay very still. No light seeped into the metal car, so he could only imagine that they were shining flashlights along the undercarriage. He heard a shout, and then the train crept forward.

"We're through," Yolkin cried. "We've made it across."

"Ssshhh," Kozachenko said. "We are not through yet."

There was a series of false stops and starts as the wheels on each car were adjusted, then the train pulled forward a distance before stopping again. There came more voices, still in Ukrainian.

"The first guards were customs," Kozachenko said softly. "These are Ukrainian border control."

Again, it seemed as though they conducted only a cursory check before the train lurched forward. This time it traveled twice the distance before grinding to a halt.

Kozachenko listened carefully. Now the guards were speaking Polish, and from the commands, he could tell they had dogs. Would they pick up the scent of the live men among the dead?

He strained to listen, trying to figure out what they were saying, but the language was just a jumble in his ears. Had they noticed the difference in the size of the car?

Two men began arguing, then the latch on the door was popped open. The guards were coming inside. The door slid back, and Kozachenko sucked in his breath. He could hear the disgust in the voices of the guards. Even the dog whimpered. Then the door was slammed shut, and the train moved on.

Kozachenko took another swig of vodka and shared the bottle with Yolkin, who was now wide awake. They drank in companionable silence. Then about the time the bottle was finished, the train stopped again.

"What now?" Yolkin asked, his voice full of alarm.

His fear was a bad sign, thought Kozachenko. There were too many hurdles to jump before this mission was done. It was no time to be dragging along a coward.

Chapter 34

Jordan woke up in Davis's arms. It wasn't what she'd planned or expected, but she hadn't resisted. In her line of work, relationships were hard to maintain. She didn't much go for casual sex, but she had to admit it—last night was nice.

Slipping out of bed, she cinched on a cotton bathrobe and made coffee.

"Sleep well?" Davis asked as she stirred in some creamer.

Jordan smiled. There hadn't been much sleep. "How do you like yours?"

"Black."

She poured him a cup, thinking back on the previous night. The two of them had eaten dinner at Restauracja Baczewski, a Galician restaurant dedicated to a famous family of nineteenth-century philanthropists who also happened to own the spirits factory. The food was a delightful mix of Jewish, Polish, Ukrainian, and Hungarian dishes, each course paired with a recommended shot of vodka. They'd both had too much to drink, and now her head felt fuzzy.

She jumped in the shower first. Then while Davis showered, she checked in with Lory about the satellite images. He told her he was still working on it. After that, she called the lab about the cell phone pictures. Henry wasn't in yet.

The hotel concierge recommended a place for breakfast. Finding it proved difficult, the entrance unmarked except for a small easel propped on the ground next to the door. Davis knocked, and a peep-hole slid open.

"We're looking for *Kryjivka*," he said to the eyeball staring out.

The door opened, and a guard in military uniform holding a bullpup rifle shouted, "*Slava Ukraini!*" Glory to Ukraine. "*Moskal'ee ye?*" Are there any Russians among you?

At least that's the closest translation she could pull.

"No," Jordan answered in English. "Breakfast?"

The guard grinned, clapped an arm around Davis's shoulders, and pulled them inside. It was a small room, with floor-to-ceiling bookshelves and a table with a bottle of vodka and numerous glasses. He poured both of them a shot and insisted they drink.

Hair of the dog, thought Jordan. Davis must have been think-ing the same because he didn't hesitate before clinking glasses with her, both of them slamming back the sweet-tasting vodka. Then the guard opened a panel behind the bookcase, revealing a hidden stairway. At the bottom was the restaurant, a hidden bunker filled with weapons, war memorabilia, and a well-stocked bar. They both ordered a potato with cheese and sausage skillet.

About the time their food arrived, so did a band of guerillas. They came inside and fired off a pistol, which made Jordan reach for her weapon. Her ears ringing, she watched as they dragged away one of the customers. All part of the tourist show. She imagined it was much different during actual times of resistance.

"Interesting place," Davis said.

"Hmmm."

Davis set down his fork. "What gives?" He'd been watching her all morning. "Regrets?"

"About last night?" She smiled and shook her head. "Not at all."

"Then what's bothering you?"

Last night they'd talked about nonessential things, like child-hood memories, their families, their ambitions. She'd told him a few things about her father, but not the secrets, and not about her conver-sation with Professor Fedorov.

"I think we're missing something, some connection, some thread that ties all this together."

Before she could tell him what the elderly man had told her about the Futurists and Operation Osoaviakhim, her phone beeped. It was an incoming e-mail from Henry. He'd managed to pull the photos off the mini SD card, run facial recognition, and gotten a hit.

Jordan opened the attached document. It was a dossier with a picture attached.

"Check this out." She held the up the phone so Davis could see. "It's a picture of the Chinese buyer."

Sitting shoulder to shoulder, she held the phone so they could both read. His name was Deng Xue, a party committee secretary of the Hainan Province, commonly called the party chief. A rising star in the Communist Party, at forty-five he'd been named to the politburo. As party chief, he oversaw two hundred plus islands off the southern coast of China, including the disputed territory in the Spratly and Paracel Islands.

"He's a bigwig." Davis sounded surprised. "The politburo is the chief political decision-making body in China."

"More importantly, the Chinese have a military base on the south end of Hainan," she said, scrolling up the page to read on. "I'll bet that's where he was taking the gun."

Davis picked up his tablet, tapped on the screen, and pulled up a map and some information on the Hainan Province.

"If China puts a railgun here, it would be able to intimidate anyone trying to stop their expansion into the South China Sea." She reached across and pointed to the islands involved in the land-grabbing dispute.

"Meaning the U.S.?"

Jordan didn't want to discuss the role she felt the United States had been forced to take in policing international policies and turned back to scrolling the dossier. Davis, to his credit, dropped his line of questioning.

"It looks like Hainan is a booming place," he said.

"It's the home of GhostNet."

"The cyberspying operation?"

Jordan nodded. They'd been infiltrating high-value targets around the world for almost a decade. "Of course the Chinese government vehemently denies in it. In fact, some of the research shows it might actually be a for-profit operation run by some unknown patriotic hacker."

"Deng Xue?"

"It's an idea."

"If Deng's an entrepreneur, it's possible he's looking for some state-of-the-art weapons technology to help him build his assets."

"An arms dealer?" Jordan considered it.

"That might be the connection to the Russians."

"Except there's one hitch . . .if his intention is to mass produce and export weapons, why not hack the specs himself and build them in Hainan? It would make more sense."

"Unless Ping outmaneuvered him." Davis tapped a few more times on the tablet. "It says here Hainan Province is designated one of the special economic zones."

That didn't surprise her. The former Communist Party leader Deng Xiaoping had allowed free-market economy policies and instituted more flexible government control in several areas. It encouraged exports and drew in foreigners interested in doing business with China.

"Hainan would be a natural choice."

Davis looked up from the tablet. "It seems like the policy worked."

"Just maybe not the way Deng planned."

"How so?"

"Deng gets credited for being the architect of modern Chinese politics and expanding trade while trying to maintain the Communist Party's socialist ideology, but it didn't work. While the zones grew the wealth, when it came time to share and transfer the assets inland, the provincial governments fought to hold onto the money."

"Money corrupts," Davis said. "Any chance the two Dengs are related?"

Jordan picked up her phone again and scrolled down the buyer's dossier to the section about family. "It says here that Deng Xue likes to think so, but he's never been able to prove common lineage."

What she read next tugged at the elusive thread.

"Wait a minute," she said.

"What?" Davis draped an arm over her shoulders and leaned in to see what had caught her attention. Jordan repositioned her phone so he could see.

"It says here that back in the 1950s, the elder Deng helped establish a think tank system. He modeled it after the Soviet's Science City."

"I don't see how that fits in."

Of course he didn't. She hadn't told him about her talk with Professor Fedorov. The professor had indicated there were other groups scattered across the continents. If Deng Xue considered himself the inheritor of Deng Xiaoping's legacy, the Futurists might be his tie to the Russians.

She felt Davis squeeze her shoulders. "Are you going to tell me what you're thinking?"

"It's a crazy idea."

"You seem to have a lot of those." When she glared at him, Davis pulled his arm back, feigning fear of reprisal. "I'm just saying."

"You really want to know?"

"I asked, didn't I?"

She didn't often have the desire to confide in people. But despite the fact he'd betrayed her before, she wanted to trust him. "I was thinking that maybe Deng and the Russians are working together."

Chapter 35

Glancing over Davis's shoulder, Jordan caught sight of their waiter over by the bar. He glowered in their direction.

"I think we've overstayed our welcome," she said. "We should go."

Paying the bill, they'd moved outside. Finding a bench in the square, Jordan bathed in the sun, while Davis pulled out his tablet, logged in, and checked his messages. "Good, the images are here. They're not spy quality, but they should do the job."

Jordan scooted across the bench to look at the tablet.

"I asked him for everything that was taken in the last eight days within a fifty-mile radius of the crash site."

"You do realize how many images that is, don't you?" Jordan asked.

He gave her a look. "It can't be that many. They throw out the bad ones, the ones with cloud cover or where it's too dark to see anything. The software also filters out about forty percent because there's been no change in the photo from the previous shot. He told me the quickest way to find what we're after is to look through the thumbnails."

"We're talking about ten thousand images."

"You're kidding, right?"

"No," Jordan said. "If it takes a satellite roughly ninety minutes to complete an orbit of the earth, it will shoot about one million photos. Multiply that by eight days."

Davis whistled. "No wonder there are people whose entire job is analyzing these photos."

Jordan scanned through the first twenty-five images on the screen and decided if that was her job, she'd go crazy. She got faster as she flipped through the pages, and then something caught her eye. "Check this out."

She pointed to an image that showed a truck and two SUVs parked in a clearing in the woods to the east of Dykanka. The truck was covered in camo, and it was difficult to see the make or model of any of the vehicles.

"You think it's our guys?" Davis asked.

"Can you zoom in closer?"

"Like I said, these aren't spy satellite images. If we accessed those, we'd be in jail. The government restricts the output on these images to fifty centimeters per pixel and requires my source to blur faces."

"Are the files time and date stamped?" Jordan flipped forward through the screens. "We need to find photos that show the train being loaded at the crash site, those taken in the last three days."

Davis checked the source code. The images she sought were near the end, and Jordan immediately spotted the anomaly.

"There, that's it. That's the car." She pointed at one in the middle that was longer than the others.

Davis measured the difference in car length with his fingers. "It's clearly bigger, but is it big enough to hide two or three vehicles and still leave loading space?"

"I think so." Pulling up Lory's e-mail address on her phone, she held it up for Davis. "Can you send the photo here? Type 'imminent threat' in the subject line."

After he'd sent the e-mail, she dialed the RSO's number. "Check your in-box."

"What am I looking for?"

"An e-mail from Nye Davis. It's a satellite image of the train in Hoholeve."

"What the hell are you doing with Davis, Jordan?"

"Just look at the picture."

It didn't take Lory but a second to see what she was seeing. "I'll be damned!"

"Do we know where that train is now?"

"They finished loading it yesterday. It's headed for Krakow."

"Can you find out on what track it was routed? Did it go through Kyiv, or is it still en route somewhere? We need to locate that car."

Instead of saying he'd call her back, this time Lory put her on hold. He didn't keep her waiting long.

"Okay, I've got people checking. According to the Ukrainians, the train traveled a southern route through L'viv. It crossed the border into Poland last night at Mostyska II, just outside of Przemśl. They're pulling the camera footage at the border crossing now. If you're right about the Russians being on that train, we may have a *big* problem."

His tone opened a small fissure of fear in her. She looked at Davis, who shrugged. What hadn't Lory told her? "I'm listening."

"Remember the summit I mentioned? The one the Ukrainian prime minister and the ambassador are attending."

The fissure expanded. "Yes."

"It's the EaP Summit. The Eastern Partnership is an initiative of the European Union composed of leaders from the post-Soviet states."

"I know about the EaP."

"The purpose of the summit is to open up trade, develop economics strategies, and revisit travel policies with the EU. If the two entities reached an agreement, it will derail the Russians' plan of reunifying the Soviet bloc as the Eurasian Union."

"Where is it being held?"

"Gdánsk."

Poland. And there you have it. "How many other leaders will be there?"

"The six foreign ministers in the EaP, and twenty-eight representatives from the EU countries. There will also be other top politicians there, like the ambassador. And since its Gdánsk in the summer, I'll bet most of them brought their families."

Thirty-four European and East European leaders. "This is all about the who, though."

"It's a big deal," Lory said. "A yes vote cements a relationship between the EaP and the EU. Everyone expects it to pass. The signing is scheduled for sixteen hundred hours tomorrow afternoon."

Jordan sat for a moment, contemplating the magnitude of damage the Russians could do. Someone needed to act.

"The first thing we need to do is find the long car and ascertain if the Russians are on that train," she said. "Once we do that, we'll have a better idea if Gdánsk is their target. It's possible they're headed to Kaliningrad."

She was grasping at alternatives and knew it, but it made sense for them to take the weapon there. Kaliningrad sat smack dab in the center of the small Russian enclave wedged between Poland and Lithuania and served as a Russian naval air base and manufacturing city for trade between Russia and the EU. It was only two hundred kilometers from Gdánsk.

"We should be so lucky," Lory said.

"Can we at least raise a red flag?"

"The ambassador has made it clear. He isn't going to change his agenda or do anything to disrupt the signing without substantiated threats. Especially not one that involves the Russians. We need to find them, Jordan."

"Then we need to get eyes on that train, sir."

"I'll pull the spy satellite images and forward them to you. Meanwhile I'll send someone out to question the personnel at the train yard in Yares'ky and to reinterview the police officers involved in the chase. Somebody has to know something."

"Someone on the ground had to be helping them," she said. "What about alerting Krakow?"

"I'll put in a call to my counterpart and have him send someone over to see if the train arrived with the long car still attached. You need to be ready to move on my orders." Lory cleared his throat.

"Our job is protecting the ambassador, Jordan. And now that means finding that weapon."

Davis had been quiet, listening to the one-sided conversation. When she hung up, he waited for her to speak.

"Can your source pull photos of the area east of L'viv? We need to go as far east as Krakow."

Jordan hadn't given him all the details, and Davis hadn't bought into her conspiracy theory. Not until they'd gone back to the hotel and spent the next few hours waiting for the images of the train to come in and digging up research on relations between China and Russia. What they'd pieced together was a frightening scenario that amounted to a geopolitical coup and cemented the theory that the Russians planned to attack the EaP Summit.

Proving the Russians and Deng Xue were working together was another story. The two countries were certainly friendly. The thaw began with President Xi Jinping's visit to Moscow in 2013, and since then the relationship had only strengthened. Xi was a popular president, pushing for what he coined the "Chinese Dream," not unlike the "American Dream." But the Chinese Dream wasn't about the individual, but about the collective lifestyle.

China and Russia needed each other. Trade was the cornerstone of Xi's plan. Putin fantasized about opening a trade route to Germany. A Russia–China collaboration would allow for a network of new trade routes Xi called the "New Silk Roads," but it all hinged on whether Putin succeeded in developing the Eurasian Union.

Seated cross-legged on the bed beside Davis, who was propped against the headboard, Jordan grabbed him by the arm to get his attention and pointed to the tablet. "Here's the tie-in. You were right, it's all about money."

Davis scooted up to listen.

"If Putin had succeeded in pulling together the former Soviet bloc countries, the EU would be signing an agreement to open trade with the Eurasian Union, not the EaP."

Davis closed the tablet and set it aside. "Or all this could be a coincidence, and the Russians could be headed for Kaliningrad. You said it yourself."

"We both know that's where they plan to end up, with a railgun strategically positioned near the mouth of the Baltic Sea. But they won't go there before putting an end to an EaP and EU agreement."

"Either way, it means the train went north."

"Or possibly just the truck."

Chapter 36

Davis's source never called back, but Lory came through with the spy satellite images late in the afternoon. Cameras showed the long car crossing the border, so Jordan and Davis scoured the photos between there and Krakow. Every now and then, they caught glimpses of things hidden below the tree cover, things that might be a train but could just as easily be rooftops. The first time the train was clearly visible put it just outside Tarnow, Poland. By then, the long car was already gone.

Within the hour, Jordan and Davis were in a rental car headed to Poland. She had intended to leave him behind. Lory would have insisted on it. But Davis had been a big help, enough to earn his stripes. Plus she figured she might need the backup. They'd struck a new deal. If he did anything to compromise this mission, she would charge him with obstruction and throw him jail with Zhen.

The route was easy, straight down the M10 to the border. Lory had his people checking visuals on all trains headed north from Rzeszow and Prezeworsk, the only two places where the train car could have been diverted. She hoped he found the information they needed by the time they reached the border.

The road proved a challenge. If the roads in Poltava were pitted, the road to Poland was full of divots. The map indicated seventy-one kilometers to their destination, a trip that should take a little over an hour. Hitting another pothole, Jordan doubled the time in her head.

They would get there by 10:00 PM—provided they made it with all four tires.

Davis braced himself as she swerved. "What happens if we get there?"

Jordan laughed. "We're meeting a JW GROM unit at the customs crossing."

"In English, please."

"It's short for *Jednostika Wojskowa Grupa Reagowania Operacyjno-Manewrowego*, translation: the Military Unit Group for Operational Maneuvering. Basically it's a Polish Special Forces unit, or GROM for short. We're supposed to connect with Captain Adamski, who heads up one of the best teams in the world. GROM ranks right up there with the SAS and Navy SEALs. I don't imagine the captain will be happy to follow my lead on this."

"He'll come around. Wait until I tell him how you thrashed the Triad."

"I did sort of kick their asses." She glanced over at Davis.

They rode in companionable silence. With previous lovers, she'd felt pressure to carry on conversation the next day, but not with Davis. He made it easy.

He dozed off as Jordan wove the car through the Ukrainian countryside, taking in the lush farm fields, the well-kept houses, the children playing in the yards. Here was a world removed from the turmoil in the east. It was almost as if she could divide the country in half.

Rounding the next corner, a large brightly lit building loomed into sight. Two flags flapped in the wind—one Ukrainian, one Polish. She gently nudged Davis.

"We're here."

The border guard waved them in and asked to see their passports. Next there came a customs guard, then a Polish guard and a Polish customs guard. At the last stop, a large dog came out and circled their car. Communication was difficult. The guards didn't speak English. Jordan didn't speak Polish. They settled on French. In all, it took them thirty minutes to cross the border, and by the time Jordan pulled into the well-lit parking lot on the west side of the building, they were running late.

This fact was not lost on the military captain sitting in front of an air-conditioning unit waiting impatiently. "Agent Jordan?"

He stood, towering over them. She introduced herself and Davis.

"I wasn't informed that you'd have someone with you." His accent was thick, and she had to listen carefully. "We've extended you the courtesy of carrying your weapon, but arrangements have not been made for this man."

"He doesn't carry a gun."

Davis kept his mouth shut, and the captain let the matter drop, to Jordan's relief. If he'd chosen to contact Lory, there would've been hell to pay.

"Have you talked with the train crew yet?" she asked.

"No. I've been waiting for you." The captain headed for the door, leading the way to a large black Land Rover Defender. Davis climbed into the back, Jordan into the front passenger seat.

"Where's your team?" Davis asked.

Jordan wondered the same thing. Based on her past experience with the Russians, she knew they were going to need one.

"Let's first see what we learn." He merged onto the M10 and drove west. "It's about half an hour to the train yard in Rzeszow. You want to tell me what this is about?"

Jordan wasn't sure how much he already knew, so she started at the beginning and told him only what he needed to know. The plane had crashed, a Ukrainian medical transport carrying two dead Americans was attacked, and a country doctor and his wife were murdered. "We believe the men responsible are Russian. It appears they may have escaped into Poland by hiding on a railroad car."

"I'm assuming these men are heavily armed."

"Yes, they have weapons."

"Any big enough to shoot down a plane?"

The captain was sharp. Either that or he'd seen Davis's report. Jordan went with the truth. "Yes."

Their arrival at the train yard saved her from having to answer more questions. After a consult with the trainmaster, they were escorted to a small break room in the back of the main building. It was cramped, with yellow lighting and plastic and metal furniture. A good decor choice if the intent was to discourage loitering. Before they had time to sit, a team of four men and one woman came in.

"I'm the yardmaster. The trainmaster says you wanted to talk to us," the woman said, taking an alpha role. She clearly wanted the GROM officer and his colleagues to know whose turf they were on.

Jordan countered. "We have reason to believe that a long refrigeration car was taken off a train that came through here sometime last night. It was part of the train carrying the remains of PR Flight 91."

"I remember it."

"That long car never arrived in Krakow. We need to know where it's gone."

The yardmaster walked over, picked up a clipboard, and flipped back through the pages. "It was rerouted north, headed to Elblag."

Jordan looked toward the captain.

"It's up near the Baltic Sea, close to Gdánsk," he said.

"It's also close to the Russian border," Davis reminded her.

"Do your records indicate who issued the order to reroute the car?"

The yardmaster scanned down the sheet. "It was signed by a Ukrainian sergeant in Hoholeve."

What were the odds? "His name wasn't Hycha by any chance?"

The yardmaster looked up. "Yes. It says right here. Sergeant Stas Hycha."

Hycha's involvement answered the question of how the Russians knew where to ambush the transport. It also explained why he wasn't there to provide backup. He'd manipulated the situation from the start, but it still didn't answer the question of who had ordered the Russians to shoot down the plane or whether Poland was part of their original plan. She doubted Hycha or even the Russians on the ground were orchestrating this plot. They were answering to someone, but who?

"Can you stop the train?"

"No, it's already left Elblag and is headed toward Gdánsk."

"May I have a copy of that?" Jordan asked. The yardmaster sent one of the men to make a copy. After he came back, the crew filed out, and Jordan turned to Adamski.

"Captain, your team needs to meet the train."

"I can issue the order, but first I want to know what's really going on."

Jordan went with the truth again. Better they all be on the same page going forward. She told him about the gun and what they believed was the next target.

The captain stood ramrod straight while she talked, then took a moment, digesting the information. "Have the summit leaders been informed of the danger?"

"A few of them know."

"Then why haven't they taken precautions?"

She glanced at Davis, who leaned against the wall, watching quietly.

"For two reasons," she said. "One is that we don't want to alert them to the fact that we're onto their end game."

"Alleged end game," Davis threw in. "For all we know, they could be headed straight for Kaliningrad."

Jordan shot him a look. "We don't know who is behind the attack. It could be the Russian mafia looking out for their own interests, or it could be someone else issuing the orders. Either way, if they think we're close to stopping them, they might decide to act sooner."

"And the second reason?"

This is where it got dicey, thought Jordan.

"We don't have any proof to back up our claim. It's hard to convince anyone to take action when you have no tangible evidence."

Now she sounded like Lory. In truth, she hoped Adamski would ignore their reasoning and alert someone to the danger.

"None?"

She thought back. Between the three of them, they'd destroyed everything. She had a picture of Deng Xue and an e-mailed file the government didn't want exposed. She had fragments taken from the crash scene that showed high levels of rare-earth metals tracing back to a Chinese manufacturer that was one of the leading exporters of Chinese steel. They had a witness who was wanted for treason, and they had a boatload of conjecture.

"None. We can only substantiate the attack on the ambulance. We can't prove the Russians' capabilities or intent."

"You have nothing, and yet here you are." He looked down on her, forcing her to take a step back to meet his eyes.

"You have my word, Captain. Please believe me when I tell you there *is* a credible threat."

Adamski rubbed his chin, searched her eyes again, and then jerked his head toward the door. "Then we better get going."

Chapter 37

Lory choked on whatever he was drinking when she told him about Hycha. "I'll have the Ukrainians detain him for questioning. Maybe they can break him and get us something actionable."

"Do you know where the signing is taking place?"

"In the old town hall at the end of Dluga Street. It's a popular tourist area."

She repeated the information for the captain and Davis, who pulled up a picture on his tablet and turned it so she could see. A wide stone street lined with tightly packed two-story houses ended at a large brick building with a clock tower topped by a belfry. All along the street were signs for shops and outdoor eateries, and the picture showed people, lots of people, strolling.

"A direct hit will annihilate that building."

"That's why you're going to find the weapon and destroy it. You have fourteen hours, Jordan."

No pressure there.

"I appreciate your vote of confidence, sir, but I need you to do something for me. I need you to bring Kia Zhen to Gdánsk."

The silence that followed was so complete, Jordan thought for a moment the call had dropped. Then Lory's voice erupted in her ear. "Why in hell would I do that?"

"In case we don't find the gun. He's met the Russians. He can identify them. Consider him our plan B."

* * *

Adamski and Davis were leaning against the fender of the Land Rover when she hung up the phone. The captain's team was headed to the train station in Elblag.

"How much have you told them?" Jordan asked.

"Only that we're helping the Americans look for some Russians who are wanted for murdering one of their agents. I'm hoping they'll have some answers for us by the time we get to Elblag."

"How far away is it?"

"Seven and one-half hours by car. It won't take us that long."

A Special Forces' tactical transport helicopter picked them up in Rzeszow, and the flight took just over two hours. It reminded Jordan of her old training missions, only this was for real, with real lives at stake. Their flight path crossed acre after acre of wooded land broken by small villages. Darker areas dotted the ground, most likely lakes. Unfortunately, there was plenty of wooded territory to hide in.

The GROM team radioed from Elblag. They'd interviewed the ground crew and let them go home. According to the crew, the long car had passed through the station. It showed on paper but couldn't be confirmed by camera feeds.

Adamski sent them on to Gdánsk to check on the train and told them to wait there for further instructions.

On the ground in Elblag, Jordan and Davis walked across to the train station while Adamski refueled the chopper at the helipad. Jordan found it hard to believe that there were no visuals of the trains passing through. Nearing the building, she spotted two cameras up in the eaves.

"Check it out," she said to Davis. "Why would the yardmen lie to GROM?"

"Maybe they didn't. Maybe the cameras aren't hooked up. Or it could be the system's down." He rattled the door, but it was locked up tight.

Jordan peered through the windows. The station was empty and locked for the night.

Davis rattled the door again. "What now? Do we call in the train crew?"

"And have them tell us the same thing they told Adamski's team? I'd rather see for myself."

"You're not going to break in, are you?" When she pulled out the lock pick she kept tucked in her holster, he stepped back from the door. "Of course you are. Do we know what the punishment is for breaking and entering in Poland?"

She worked the pick in the door until she felt the latch give. "What are you talking about, Davis?" she said, turning the handle. "The door was unlocked."

It didn't take them long to find what they were looking for. The security camera feed was on the second shelf of the bookcase. Jordan rewound the tape and played it forward. The image was blurred, like the tape was old and had been recorded over a number of times, and the angle made it next to impossible to get a clear enough look at the train to tell anything about the length of the cars. Still something was off.

Jordan ran the tape again. "How many cars were on the train that left the station in Rzeszow?"

"Where would that be listed?"

"It's on the top of the operations paperwork."

Davis rifled through the papers stacked on the trainmaster's desk and pulled out a sheet. "It says here the engine was hauling twenty-four cars."

"Which is the number of cars I count on this tape." Jordan stuck her hand in her back pants pocket and pulled out the sheet the yard-master in Rzeszow had copied for her. Flattening it on the desk, she found the notation she was looking for and stabbed at it with her finger. "Right here it indicates the train left Rzeszow with twenty-five cars. The long car never made it this far."

* * *

Back aboard the helicopter, the radio crackled. Adamski picked up the mic. A deep voice came over the static. "We checked the camera feeds in Gdánsk. The long car wasn't part of the train when it pulled in."

More confirmation that it hadn't passed through Elblag. Jordan signaled for Davis to hand her the tablet. "Soldier, do you know what time the sun sets?"

"Around nine fifteen PM," the voice came back.

Jordan pulled up the last satellite images of the area. "These would be the last pictures taken. They would have been shot around eight ten PM."

She scanned the thumbnails with Davis looking over her shoulder. *There was the train!*

Tapping the tablet screen, she enlarged the picture. The shadows had been long, but the train slithered along the track, a white snake in a sea of green trees. Near the middle, the long car was clearly visible.

"I found it," Jordan said. "Where was this picture taken?"

Davis tapped the coordinates from the picture into the GPS app on his phone. "Just coming into Ostroda."

"That's south of here," the captain said.

She skimmed through the rest of the images just to be sure. "The satellite moved out of range before the train left Ostroda. We have no way of knowing if the car was cut from service, switched to another track, or headed on toward Elblag."

The captain's face tightened.

"What?" she asked.

"There are some heavily wooded areas near there. If they jumped the train car near Ostroda and went into the trees, we may not be able to find them."

"Except they couldn't stay there," Jordan countered. "Even if this is where they jumped off, it's too far south. It's at the edges of the gun's firing limit. In order to hit their target, the Russians would have to move north."

"Unless they headed northeast for the border," Davis said. Jordan looked over at him, and he shrugged. "I'm just saying you have to consider the possibility they're headed for Kaliningrad."

Jordan shook her head. "I don't buy it. There are easier ways to transport a weapon to the Russian enclave. But that's not the point. The point is, we know they left the train somewhere between Ostroda and Elblag."

"That's a lot of ground to cover," the captain said.

"The train car has to be on the tracks somewhere. Let's find it first and go from there."

While the captain readied for takeoff, he pointed to a cargo box near Davis. "Take out two Kevlar vests and put them on."

Davis dug into the box, producing one vest that fit him and one that came close to fitting Jordan. She strapped it as tightly as she could, overlapping the sides under her arms.

"That's still a lot of spurs and sidelines to cover," he said through the mic. "This is farming country. Many of the towns have silos with train car access." He pointed to a duffle lying near Davis's feet. "There are some night vision goggles in there. The two of you should put them on."

He flew south along the tracks, skimming close to the trees, while she and Davis searched the ground. Even with the night vision goggles, it was difficult to see.

"What about thermal imaging?"

He pointed to a screen mounted near the control panel. "There have been some hot spots, but they could be houses just as easily as anything else. I haven't seen any unusual activity."

From Ostroda, they flew west to east over heavily wooded areas that provided ample cover. Jordan stowed her night vision goggles and watched the thermal imaging screen.

They searched for over an hour and came up with nothing.

"I need to refuel again soon," Adamski said, turning back after their last pass. "Once dawn breaks, we can take a small railcar and drive along the tracks. If they're under cover of the trees, that's the best way to find a sidelined train car. We'll have better luck in the daylight."

Jordan hated the idea of turning back, but she agreed with Adamski. They were getting nowhere like this.

"Have your men talked to the train's driver?" she asked. "He should be able to tell us where a car was removed from the train."

"Unless it happened at a stop where cars were to be added or removed. In that case, he might not have realized anything was out of the ordinary." Adamski radioed his team. The news that came back wasn't good. They had detained the driver in Gdánsk, but he'd come on in Elblag.

Jordan thought it a little too coincidental. "Is that a normal place to exchange drivers?"

She could hear the soldier asking the questions, the driver's muffled response, and then the soldier's voice came on again. "He says no, but sometimes it happens. In this case, it was prearranged."

"Why didn't the crew in Elblag say anything about it?" Jordan said.

"The change had to be done. The original driver had outlawed, meaning he'd been driving too long without any sleep. When we go back to pick up the handcar, we will question them again."

"If they're even around." Jordan figured they were long gone by now.

Chapter 38

The refrigeration was turned off when the train turned north, and in the past eight hours, the rotting debris in the car had heated. The smell of death choked the air, triggering Kozachenko's gag reflex. He dry heaved. They were out of food, out of vodka, and the car had stopped hours ago.

Kozachenko had insisted Yolkin remain quiet in case of listeners outside, but the time had come to break his own rule. He turned on his phone, dialed, and hoped Anatoliy picked up. "Are you okay?"

"Yes, unless I'm dead, and this is what hell smells like," Barkov answered. "How do we get out of here?"

"Stas said it was arranged. That someone would come."

"They better come quickly. We've searched the barrier wall, and there's no way out, Vasyl."

"In another hour, I'll place a call to the pakhan."

* * *

As his self-imposed deadline approached, finally there was a noise outside. Two men talking in Russian.

"Hey!" Kozachenko yelled. "Get us out of here."

It seemed an eternity before the walls came down. Kozachenko didn't wait for the wall to be entirely removed, but climbed out over the debris. The piles of detritus smelled like burning trash and rotting flesh, and Kozachenko found himself gagging again.

Even distancing himself from the train car didn't help. The smell had permeated his clothes and his senses. He would be smelling death for days.

"What took you so long?" he demanded of the men. "It's well after midnight."

"We had to wait. Polish Special Forces came to the station asking questions. They looked at everything. They checked the camera feeds and the work orders. The paperwork showed the long car headed to Gdánsk. The soldiers finally left, but we must assume they'll be back. We need to hurry."

While the men worked to free the vehicles, Kozachenko signaled Barkov to follow him over to one of the trainmen's trucks. Opening a map on the hood, he pointed to Elblag. "We are here, correct?"

Barkov shook his head and pointed to the town of Piławki. "They know we are getting close."

A helicopter flew low over the trees above them, close enough to set the leaves overhead quaking.

Kozachenko closed his eyes and drew a breath. "I'm thinking that once the vehicles are free, we get on the road and beat a path toward the border. When the sun rises, we take cover until the time comes to fire the weapon. Then in the chaos that ensues after the weapon is fired, we'll make our run for the border."

"They will have eyes on the main roads, Vasyl. We'll have to go a back way. We don't have much time."

"They'll expect us to go east, so we'll go north," Kozachenko said.

"Agreed."

"Good. We will take this road toward Pagórki and Elblag Upland Landscape Park." He pointed to a small winding road that went north, one without too many towns to navigate. "By the time the sun rises, we will have over one hundred square kilometers of forest in which to hide."

Barkov nodded his approval. "It's a good plan, Vasyl. It leaves only one more problem."

Kozachenko bristled. "And what would that be, Anatoliy?"

"The compulsator isn't charged enough to fire the weapon."

"What are you talking about?"

"The compulsator charges when we drive the trucks. We drained the power when we fired the weapon. Now because we haven't been driving enough, there is not enough charge."

"I don't see the problem. As soon as they free the trucks from the debris, we can charge the battery."

"It's not that easy."

Kozachenko rubbed his temples and wished for a vodka. "Explain to me again how this works."

Barkov leaned against the truck. "The gun works off an electromagnetic pulse driven by the compensated pulse alternator. It's small and must be recharged either by running the diesel engine or by hooking it up to another electrical source."

"How long does it take to recharge?"

Barkov took his time doing the math. "Using the truck engine, it would take five hours, possibly more."

Kozachenko slammed his hands down on the truck's fender. They couldn't afford to run the truck engine that long for fear of running out of fuel. "What if we hook the machine up to more than one engine?"

"We don't have enough horsepower available to cut the time by much. Bundling the truck and the GAZ, it would still take several hours to charge."

Kozachenko threw back his head and stared up at the branches of the tree above him. The leaves rustled in a light breeze, allowing glimpses of clear sky and stars. The night was clear, and the stars winked overhead as if taunting him, reminding him that with the rising of the sun came the chance of detection. "Can we use another type of power?"

"To charge it instantly would take something big. If we hook up to a large enough electrical source, we can fire the gun all day. What we need is a big generator."

He'd been the one to nix hauling the extra equipment. The plan called for the weapon to only be fired once, so he had erred on the side of mobility. None of them knew they would be forced to fire the gun multiple times.

"What do you mean by *large* power source, Anatoliy?"

"The compulsator needs twenty to thirty megawatts to create a pulse strong enough to launch the projectile. Only a small substation or large transformer could instantly provide that kind of power."

Kozachenko gestured to the overhead power lines. "What about those?"

"Maybe, *if* we had an insulated bucket and hot sticks. We don't. And I don't feel like getting fried today."

Kozachenko didn't appreciate Barkov's flippancy. "There are worse ways to die, Anatoliy."

Barkov nodded. "A substation would be better, Vasyl."

"Why is that?"

"We can throw breakers and use a t-tap. Even a small base would allow us to bundle enough power to instantly charge the compulsator."

"Then we have a plan."

Chapter 39

While Adamski went to bring his team up to speed, Jordan and Davis took a cab to the Gdánsk Grand Hotel. At this hour of the morning, the only people around were a desk clerk and a janitor. The clerk stopped them on the way in.

"Boardroom II?" Jordan said.

The clerk nodded and pointed them past. "Fourth floor."

Standing in front of the elevators, she grabbed Davis's hand. "You might want to wait for me down here. Lory won't be happy to see you."

"I have a thick skin." He narrowed his eyes. "You're not benching me now—"

She wasn't sure if he was asking a question or making a statement. "From here on out, it's not going to be up to me."

"I'll take my chances."

Jordan let go of his hand before stepping off the elevator. Two agents stood in the hall. One opened the door of the boardroom.

"Nice place," she said, stepping into the room. A bank of windows faced the sea, while the other three walls were painted a tasteful beige. At the far end of the room was a large flat screen mounted over a credenza. Lory and Zhen sat at a burnished wood table in overstuffed leather chairs. They both looked up. Then Davis entered behind her, and Lory came out of his seat.

"What the hell is he doing here? Get him out, now! The last thing we need is for this to leak to the press."

The two agents in the hall came through the door. One of them grabbed Davis by the arm.

"Wait!" Jordan said. She'd known this was coming, but she wasn't going to alter her alliances now. "He's with me."

Lory stared at her like she'd lost her mind. The two agents stepped back.

"You can trust him," she said, as if that decided the matter.

"Have you forgotten he leaked information about Zhen?"

She hadn't, and maybe she didn't trust him completely. She hadn't confided any of the secrets surrounding her father, world-changing secrets that jeopardized her job. "What's the old adage, *keep your friends close, your enemies closer?*"

Lory remained on his feet. "I'm still in the *with friends like* that, *who needs enemies* camp."

Jordan pled her case. "Without Davis and his resources, we wouldn't be as close as we are to catching the Russians, not to mention one of the prototypes would be sitting at Yulin Naval Base in Hainan, China. He understands he's been privy to classified information he can never reveal." She glanced up at the man standing beside her. "Right?"

"I just want a story I can tell at the end."

"He's earned a second chance, sir."

"Plus, I can be useful," Davis said. "I have great sources I'm not afraid to use."

"He did help us obtain those satellite images."

Lory flopped back down in his chair, and Jordan knew they had won the battle. Now they just needed to win the war.

Chapter 40

It took them an hour to get on the road. Kozachenko drove while Barkov navigated. Much to his relief, Yolkin joined the others in the GAZ. In addition, they'd picked up four new men, two who were part of the train crew and two from Kaliningrad.

"We should charge the compulsator soon," Barkov said.

The moon had set, leaving the night dark. Only the hum of the tires marred the stillness. They had encountered no traffic, but potholes scarred the surface of the road, making the driving slow.

Barkov lowered his phone with the GPS. "There's a road coming up on the right. You need to turn there. There is a substation six hundred meters up on the left. We should let the men go in first and make sure it's secure."

Kozachenko geared down and braked, alarmed by the loud growl of the engine. Barkov stuck his hand out the window and signaled the tailing vehicle to pass. The GAZ shot past, then braked hard and turned sharply in front of them.

"*Yebat*'!" Kozachenko cursed, stepping on the floor pedals, the screech of tires rolling across the farm fields.

"They're hot shots," Barkov said, coming up off the seat, palms flat against the dashboard. "Not unlike you and I in our day, huh? In a few minutes, you will appreciate their youth."

Kozachenko glanced sideways at the major and wondered how much this man actually knew about him. Kozachenko had at least ten years on him, and he'd worked hard to keep knowledge of his past private. When they were done here, he planned to ask. For now, he let the comment pass, pulled the truck to the side of the road, and doused the headlights.

"What's the next move?" he asked.

Barkov keyed the radio. "Yolkin, have the men check for security and report back."

As they waited, a car appeared in the distance. Kozachenko restarted the truck, but left the headlights off. Slipping the rig into gear, he pulled forward and turned off onto the gravel road taken by the men.

Startled, Barkov twisted toward him. "We haven't gotten the all clear."

"It's more important that we not be noticed sitting by the side of the road."

Parking the truck in the deep shadows, Kozachenko waited for the car to speed past. Weak headlights hugged the road, and metallic rock blared from open windows. As the car's taillights disappeared into the distance, the truck radio crackled. It was Yolkin.

"There are no watchmen, just cameras."

Finally, some good news, thought Kozachenko. "Can you disable them?"

"Can a cat eat fish?"

"Do it, then," Barkov said.

"Wait!" Kozachenko ordered. "Is it possible to position the truck without it being seen by the cameras?"

"Da," Yolkin said. "If you pull forward to the far side of the transformers, you can back it in next to the fence without being picked up by the lens."

Kozachenko was pleased. Even though they'd have to cut the camera feeds when the men went over the fence, by positioning the truck beforehand, they bought more time to slip in and out undetected.

Barkov pointed at the substation. "Do you see the enclosed metal structure in the center between the incoming lines and coils?"

Kozachenko nodded.

"That's the target. Back the truck along the chain link fence and stop when the tailgate is even with the panel box." Barkov opened the passenger-side door and swung down to the ground. "I'll signal you from the back."

Once Barkov was clear of the truck, Kozachenko pulled forward. Then, cranking the steering column hard to the left, he backed up on the narrow road. The front end of the rig swung wide as he maneuvered into position, the right front tire creasing the edge of the ditch. When he finally straightened out the wheels, he saw Barkov dead center in his passenger mirror waving him back.

Kozachenko popped the clutch and slowly reversed.

"Keep coming," Barkov shouted. "Just a little more." When he raised his fist, Kozachenko stopped, put the truck into park, and climbed out of the cab to watch the men work.

The men swarmed the truck, unfastening the tarp and exposing the gun. Spreading four long electrical lines on the ground, they bundled one end together and attached it to the compulsator.

Barkov turned to Kozachenko. "Are we ready? Once we cut the camera feeds, we are on the clock. This station supplies power to the north, so everything between here and Elblag will go dark."

"How long will this take?"

Barkov grinned. "If we used standard precautions, forty minutes. Doing it our way, we should be in and out in fewer than twenty."

Kozachenko hesitated. He wasn't much concerned about triggering a power outage. A short disruption of power shouldn't draw undue attention. Power outages were common in Poland, especially away from the cities. And even if someone were dispatched from the power company, their headquarters was fifty kilometers away. It would take an hour or more for anyone to get out here. No, his concern was that once the power company realized their cameras had been tampered with, they would dispatch the local police.

But they needed the weapon ready to fire, so what choice did they have? He nodded at Barkov. "Go."

Barkov cut the wires to the camera feeds while the men scrambled over the chain link fence. Two men dragged the ends of the lines to the panel box, while a third jimmied open the panel doors with a knife.

"Ready to rock and roll?"

Kozachenko recognized the speaker as Yolkin. He stood on this side of the fence. "Do exactly what I tell you."

Following Yolkin's directions, one man threw the first breaker, killing all the lights in town, then he cranked out the lug to the stationary line, repeating the process three more times. As each lug was detached, another man came behind and secured the taps to the temporary lines. Once the lines were all attached, Yolkin instructed them to move back down the panel box, flipping on the breakers.

Barkov switched on the compulsator. In what seemed like no time, the charge light turned from red to green.

"Done," he shouted.

At Barkov's signal, Yolkin signaled the men to move back down the row and reverse the process. This time, when they flipped the breakers open, the lights in town flared back on. Before the last man was over the fence, the gear was stowed and the tarp refastened.

"Eighteen minutes," Barkov said. "It must be a record."

Kozachenko scrambled up into the truck. "Celebrate later. We have to go!"

Chapter 41

Zhen refused to cooperate, insisting that if they wanted his help, they would have to grant him immunity from prosecution on the espionage charge. The one thing none of them could facilitate. Jordan understood his motivation, but they didn't have time for it.

"Listen to me," Jordan said. "Do you remember when you said that just because there wasn't a command guidance system in the projectiles didn't mean they couldn't be controlled? I need you to explain what you meant."

"Do I have a deal?"

"How many times do I have to say it?" Lory asked. "No one here can negotiate terms of an agreement. It's out of our hands."

"Then you're shit out of luck. My memory is a little fogged up."

Jordan made another plea, appealing to his conscience. "Zhen, what's about to happen will be on you. Step up and I'm sure the government will take it into consideration."

Zhen feigned boredom. The kid showed a stubborn streak wider than her own.

Having exhausted his repertoire of diplomatic skills, Lory resorted to threats. "Kid, do you want to spend the rest of your life in Gitmo? You've been charged with hacking military secrets. If you don't—"

"Can you prove that I stole them?"

"We know you did."

"But can you prove it?"

"We don't have to prove it to detain you."

Lory was right. They could hold Zhen on the espionage charge under the Patriot Act, but that wouldn't help them in the moment. Jordan cut in. "Guys, we don't have time for this."

The two withdrew to their respective corners, but not without Zhen landing a parting shot. "You can't prove anything. I know it for a fact."

He knew because he'd helped Jordan destroy the evidence, the government didn't want to admit that the plans to their new billion-dollar weapon had been compromised, and Ellis Quinn was standing by Quinn Industries' hack-free record. Who could blame her? She was one of the Navy's top defense contractors. It would be bad for business to admit that an eighteen-year-old kid fresh out of high school had cracked their firewall.

Davis slid his chair around to face Zhen. "Forget all of them."

"Stay out of this, Davis." Lory's face was red. Jordan poured him some water.

Davis ignored the RSO and leaned forward conspiratorially. "You can't really hack the guidance system and take control of the projectile, can you? It's all theory, isn't it? I mean, you're smart, but are you smart enough to figure out something like that?"

"It's not rocket science."

Close enough, thought Jordan, stifling a laugh. Davis shot her a look suggesting she tread lightly, then turned back to Zhen.

"If you could, and I'm not saying I believe you can, what kind of stuff would you need in order to build a gizmo that can capture the signal?"

"It would help to see a copy of the specs." Zhen was talking directly to Davis now. Jordan was holding her breath.

"We don't have a copy," Lory blurted, shattering the connection.

Jordan stood up and leaned with her hands on the table, trying to help diffuse the tense situation. "Maybe we can arrange to get a set?"

Lory nodded and pushed himself up from his chair. "Let me see what I can do."

He left the room, and while they waited for the verdict to come in, the three of them ordered room service. Neither Jordan nor Davis had slept in twenty-four hours, and they hadn't eaten since lunch the day before. They were scarfing down cheeseburgers when Lory came back.

"I'm gone ten minutes and you throw a party?"

Jordan decided not to point out he'd been gone for twenty and pushed a burger in his direction. "We ordered you one, too."

Lory sat down and pulled the plate toward him. "It's been arranged. Someone from Quinn Industries is going to Skype in on a secure server so we can pull the plans up on the monitor. Anyone know how to operate the system?"

Zhen grabbed the remote off the table. A few clicks, two bites of burger, a six-thousand-mile bounce off of a U.S. spy satellite, and the specs for the guidance system came up on display.

Zhen zoomed in. "First I had to alter the basic hardware design of the guidance system in order to make it work."

"Is he for real?" Lory asked.

"Keep going, Zhen," Jordan said.

"Just for the record, I started taking college IT classes when I was eleven." Zhen directed his speech toward Lory. "The Navy design definitely needs some tweaking, and the software program sucks. If the Navy ever wants to control these projectiles with a command guidance system similar to the one in the Patriot missiles, they're going to have to build something with the same specs as the railgun's self-guided system."

"What makes it so different?" Lory asked.

"There's a whole punch list. First it's smaller and lighter, otherwise it would throw off the projectile's center of gravity. It's able to withstand higher temperatures and strong enough to withstand higher speeds. And it's radiation hardened to withstand the exo-atmospheric flight."

Lory swiveled his chair to look at Zhen. "Are you saying this gun can shoot things up through the atmosphere?"

"Come on, dude."

Jordan pulled a slide up on Davis's tablet showing the trajectory of a railgun projectile and set it in front of Lory.

"Last, its power consumption is under eight watts, and its battery is designed to last a minimum of five minutes from the time of launch." Zhen leaned back in his chair and put his shoes up on the conference table. "So far they haven't come close to a command GS design, but what they don't realize is that they don't have to make it internal. All they have to do is design a back door."

"Get your feet off the table," Lory said.

"I don't understand," Jordan interjected. Not that it was important. The important thing was that he could actually do what he said.

Zhen pulled his feet back and spoke in a tone that indicated he thought he was speaking to morons. "Basically all we need to know are the approximate GPS coordinates of where the gun is fired and where it's headed. I can create a device that allows me to locate the signal. You just have to understand how GPS works. Anyone have a piece of paper and a pencil?"

Davis found some in the conference room credenza.

Zhen set the paper on the table in front of him and drew a large circle in the middle. "Our GPS system works off of Navstar, the global positioning system run by the U.S. Department of Defense. While we have the Global Navigation Satellite System, or GNSS, the Russians have a system called GLONASS, China has COMPASS, the EU has GALILEO, and so on."

"Which means the Russians will be using GLONASS," Jordan said. "Can your device access their system?"

Zhen looked up and grinned. "It can access any system in a matter of seconds." Looking back down, he started making dots around the circle, which Jordan figured stood for the earth. Then he drew a crude map inside the surface, with four lines from four of the dots to a point she assumed was Gdánsk.

"It takes twenty-four satellites to have a fully operational system. Your receiver sends out a signal, and then, based on the time it takes four of the satellites to receive the signal, the system locks in your location. After that, you program in the coordinates of where you want to go and the system will calculate time and distance based on your current position."

"How does that help us?" Jordan asked.

"Basically my device filters the incoming signals." Zhen kicked back in his chair. "If we know the approximate location of the weapon when the gun discharges, I can read the coordinates of where they're sending the projectile off the satellite. Once we have the exact end destination, then all I have to do is set my device and boost my signal so the projectile locks onto it."

"How does that help us neutralize the damn thing?" Lory asked.

"Once it's locked on, I can throw that signal wherever I want."

"You can send the projectile anywhere?" Jordan asked.

"Well, anywhere we have time to send it. We have to stay within the projectile's range and within the window of time it will stay in the air."

Lory frowned. "I thought you said you'd be in control."

"Dude!" Zhen pointed to the tablet and the drawing of the railgun trajectory. "There's only so much I can do. A railgun sends a projectile up through the atmosphere at Mach 7 and it comes back to Earth at Mach 5. You point the gun toward a target on the horizon and it takes about six seconds to impact. You shoot it through the exoatmosphere and you have maybe six minutes."

Lory stared at Jordan. "This is our plan B?"

"It's better than having no plan."

"Are you sure we can't make a final appeal to the ambassador?" Davis asked.

"I tried, then I tried going over his head. The director, the secretary of state, the president, they're all in agreement. Not one of them is willing to pull the plug on the signing of this agreement. They fear the repercussions. They've been watching the intel. There's been no chatter. China's been dark, Russia's been dark, and the IIC is moving closer to publicly declaring that PR Flight 91 went down as the result of engine failure. Ellis Quinn denies any breach. It would appear that the cover-up is complete."

Jordan studied Lory for a moment. She wondered what he would say if she shared her conspiracy theory with him. Better to leave that for another day.

"Then we're counting on you, Zhen," she said. "Tell us what you need to build the diverter."

"A gaming device and a drone so I can test the thing. Oh, and I'll need a couple more things." He rattled off a short list that included needle nose pliers and a soldering gun. Agents were dispatched to collect the items.

"Let me ask you another question, young man. How do you know you're hacking the right system? For all you know, you could be commandeering Grandma's new Audi."

"The software handles it. The algorithms will run through every known operating system to choose the correct one and then search out the exact coordinates. We can have control in four minutes. In this case maybe faster, since we know they're bouncing it off Russian satellites." Zhen looked around the table. "I'm telling you, it'll work."

"Have you done this before?" Davis asked.

"I wrote the program for my honor's thesis. To prove it worked, I hijacked a drone from the Berkeley parking lot."

"Works for me," Jordan said. "How long will it take you to build it?"

"A few hours. First I have to get into my mother's computer to snag my old software program. Once I modify it, I can install it into the gaming device."

"I've got a question," Davis said. "How are we going to know when and from where the weapon is fired? Six minutes isn't much time."

Everyone looked to Jordan. She closed her eyes and thought for a moment. "Okay, let's start with what we do know. We know the signing is scheduled for sixteen hundred hours. Striking at that precise moment will be a symbolic gesture."

Zhen bounced in his chair. "We know they'll use a Russian satellite, and we know the GPS coordinates for the town hall. I can start scanning for a signal a few minutes ahead of time. It's possible I can snag it."

"Let's not forget one thing," Jordan said. "We haven't given up on finding the Russians."

* * *

Two hours later, the four of them made their way to the beach with what *still* looked to Jordan like a gaming console with a wireless controller and a sophisticated camera drone.

"You really think this will work?" Lory asked. Standing in his bare feet with his pant legs rolled up, he placed the drone on the sand.

"Positive. Tell me where you're sending it."

Jordan stared out at the Baltic Sea. Night still blended the water and the horizon, but she could see a cruise ship bobbing on the water in the far distance. "How about somewhere in the middle of the Gulf of Danzig?"

"Have you got the coordinates?"

Before she could answer, Davis whipped out his cell phone, opened the GPS app, and rattled off some numbers.

Zhen typed them into the device. "Okay, all set. Now give me the coordinates of where you placed the drone, and I'll show you how this baby works." Zhen gripped his gaming device in both hands.

Lory fired up the drone and input the destination. Using the drone's control device, he lifted it into the air and flew it on a straight trajectory down the beach and out over the water.

"Here we go." Zhen flipped on his own device, and Jordan clicked the stopwatch on her phone. As he worked, the drone got harder and harder to see, until it suddenly banked to the right and started heading back.

Jordan looked at Lory. He held the drone's controls flat in his hand.

Zhen had taken control.

She clicked the stopwatch. "Two minutes."

There still might be a chance.

* * *

Dawn broke as they stood on the beach. It was almost time to meet Captain Adamski. The light brightening the sky meant their time was running out, and she couldn't get Davis's question about knowing when and from where the danger was coming out of her mind. As the sun broke the horizon, the streetlamps flickered on and off like warning signals against the day.

On and off. "That's it!"

"What are you yelling about, Jordan?" Lory perched on the sea wall, unrolling his pant legs.

"I think I may know how to find the Russians, at least to find out where they've been."

"How?" Davis asked.

"When the gun is fired, it uses a lot of power, right?"

"So?" Zhen said.

"They need power to fire the weapon. If they already fired the weapon once, they'll need to recharge the battery."

"The compulsator recharges as they drive."

"But they haven't been driving, Zhen. Not enough. Which means they're going to have to find an alternate power source."

"I see where you're going with this. A large drawdown on the grid would signal the Russians were charging the gun." Lory grinned and gripped Zhen on the back of the neck. "Einstein and I will go back to the boardroom and see what we can find out. We'll look for unexplained power draws, blackouts, any anomalies in usage for a hundred mile radius."

Jordan nodded. "In the meantime, I'll go meet Adamski. If you find something, call me on my cell."

"Let's do it," Davis said, following Jordan toward the parking lot.

"Maybe you should stay here this time?"

"No way. You're not getting rid of me that easy." He smiled down at her. "Consider me 'in bedded.'"

Jordan laughed, and then put both her hands on his chest. "Seriously, it could get dicey if we catch up to these guys."

"More dicey than China?"

"It's different now. Here I have Polish Special Forces backing me up."

"I'm a trained warrior, Rae. Don't bench me now."

She could feel his heart beating. *Damn*, he knew how to play her.

"This is an unsanctioned mission, Nye. You could be risking your active reserve status."

"I know."

"Most importantly, you need to remember one thing." Jordan held up a finger.

"I know. If we get jammed up, I have to do what you say."

Chapter 42

Kozachenko had cranked the engine and ground the truck into gear when the radio crackled.

"Brigadier?"

He recognized the voice of one of the new men, the one who had been monitoring local dispatch. His heart banged against his rib cage. "Is there a problem?"

"A call just went out about the power outage. There are two police cars headed our way."

Kozachenko slammed his hand against the wheel. "Derr'mo."

Now he could hear the sirens in the distance. He needed to keep them away somehow. Turning off the truck, he jumped to the ground and gathered the men. "Which of you speak Polish?"

The two trainmen raised their hands.

"You two come with me. The rest of you stay here with Major Barkov and the truck."

Barkov saluted. "What are you going to do, Vasyl?"

"I'm going to try to save the mission." Kozachenko climbed into the back of the trainmen's vehicle. "You must beat the police to the turn off. Move." As the driver accelerated toward the main road, Kozachenko radioed Barkov. "Can you reattach the cameras?"

"It's possible, but there are no guarantees. The wires for video can be tricky."

251

"Make it happen," Kozachenko said and then turned to the men. "What are your names?"

"I'm Celek," the driver said. "He's Janko."

Kozachenko held up the radio mic. "I am going to keep the mic open so the men can hear what's happening. We need to keep the police from going to the substation, or we'll have no choice but to kill them. Understood?"

"Yes, sir," Celek said.

Janko turned in his seat. "I have a question."

"What is it?"

"What is wrong with just killing them now?"

"Think about it. What do you think happens if the officers fail to report in?"

"They send more officers," Celek said.

"That and they put out an alert. It would be like standing up and waving to the Polish Special Forces. You need to do your best to make them go away."

"Who are we supposed to be?" Janko asked.

"Tell them you are military out on maneuvers. You heard the call and stopped to check. Tell them whatever you need to. Just make them go away."

Celek shifted into third gear and floored the SUV. Kozachenko watched from the back seat as they neared the highway intersection. If the policemen were able to turn in on the service road, the game was over.

The SUV and first police car reached the intersection at the same time. Kozachenko dropped to the seat while Celek slammed on the brakes, maneuvering the vehicle sideways across the road and forcing the police car into the ditch. Jumping out, he took the offense.

"You stupid imbecile," he shouted. "What the hell are you doing? Trying to kill us?"

Kozachenko peered over the back seat and watched the other police car skid to a stop. An officer jumped out, his weapon drawn. "Put your hands up. Who are you?"

"We were sent out here to check on the substation," Celek said. He ignored the officer, and Kozachenko hoped he didn't get shot in the back. Celek quickly moved toward the car in the ditch and yanked open the driver's-side door. "Are you okay?"

The officer climbed out and supported himself by leaning against the car. "I'm fine."

"I told you to put your hands up!" the officer yelled from the road. He stood in a shooting stance, weapon leveled at Celek's chest. "Why would they send soldiers?"

Celek played along, halfheartedly raising his hands in surrender. "We were on maneuvers when the call came over the radio. We thought we could help. Why don't you put your gun away so we can discuss this?"

The policemen looked at each other, and then the one on the road gestured toward the substation with the barrel of his gun. "What did you find there?"

Celek shrugged and shook his head. "Nothing. Everything was in order."

The officer maintained a one-handed grip on his gun and shined his flashlight down the road. The beam dissipated after a few feet, so he turned the light on Janko in the front seat of the SUV. Kozachenko ducked. The light remained on Janko for a few moments, and then the officer shined the light back on Celek's face. "I don't believe you. The electricity was out from here to Elblag, and dispatch informed us the cameras were down."

Celek shielded his eyes from the light, squinting at the officer. "The electricity is on now, isn't it? And the cameras all seemed to be working. Call the power company in Ostroda and ask for yourself."

The officer looked at his colleague, who nodded. "Go ahead and do it, Vann."

"Don't move until I get back." Officer Vann holstered his weapon and headed back to his car. A tactical error, thought Kozachenko. If he and his men wanted to, they could easily kill these men now.

"Are you sure you're okay?" Celek asked the policeman beside him. He sat against the car fender and twisted to look at the man's name badge. "You look a little green, Officer Soskin."

"I bumped my head. It's nothing."

Celek was doing a great job of feigning concern. "That's not good. You may need medical attention."

"I told you, I'm fine."

Officer Vann climbed back out of his patrol car and walked toward them. "The power company says everything is working again. They claim it must have been a malfunction or something."

Officer Soskin jerked his head toward Celek. "Did you check with dispatch? Did they say anything about soldiers reporting to the scene?"

Kozachenko tensed, ready to spring into action if necessary. Janko reached for the door handle.

"The man I spoke to said he didn't talk to anyone. But he admitted there were three dispatchers fielding calls. It's possible one of the others handled the communication."

"What did I tell you?" Celek said, pushing himself off the fender. Janko settled back in his seat. Kozachenko remained on guard. "Now I think you need to get your man to a doctor."

"Are you hurt, Soskin?" Vann looked concerned.

"I'm fine." Soskin glared at Celek, who had climbed up on the road and now stood beside Vann.

Celek leaned in. "He admitted smacking his head in the crash. Haven't you ever heard of Talk-and-Die Syndrome?"

Vann frowned. "No."

"It's terrible. Sometimes when someone hits their head, they claim they are fine, and then within hours, they're dead." Celek tapped his skull. "Traumatic bleeding inside the brain. Even a minor head injury can be serious."

"I'm telling you, I am perfectly okay." As if to prove it, Soskin pushed himself to his feet and started forward, stumbling over a rock in the ditch.

Kozachenko buried his laugh.

Celek pounced on the opportunity. "See?" he said to Vann, flicking a finger toward Soskin. "The sooner he sees a doctor the better. I've seen too many head injuries in my day. I say take him, now."

"I'm telling you, it isn't necessary," Soskin insisted.

"I don't know, Soskin. You may have hit your head harder than you think," Vann said.

"Where is the nearest hospital?" Celek said. "My buddy and I can follow you there with his car."

"No, just leave it," Vann said. "I'll have someone come out in the morning."

"You're sure?" Celek asked.

"Positive," Vann said, depositing Soskin into the passenger seat of his car. After shutting the door, he reached out his hand. "Thanks for your help, Private."

It was clear the officer expected a name.

"Sergeant," Celek corrected, removing his glove and reaching to shake. "Good luck, Officer Vann. I hope your colleague is all right."

"Thanks."

"No problem. We're here to serve."

Chapter 43

Two railcars waited for them on the tracks in Czerwona Karczma, just north of Ostroda. Jordan had been expecting a handcart with a hand pump, the ones usually seen in old movies. She was pleasantly surprised to find they would be driving what appeared to be modified truck cabs on train wheels.

"What about other trains on the track?"

"The Polish State Railways has agreed to an engineering possession for the next two hours. It means they will close the track in both directions, indicating a maintenance issue. Once the time is up, trains will be allowed to pass."

They were on the clock in more ways than one. "Let's get on with it, then."

Adamski gestured to the lead vehicle. "You're with me, Agent. You and I will take the first spur we can find," he said. "You, go with him." He pointed Davis toward a soldier sitting in the second railcar.

"What about the rest of the team?" Jordan asked.

"They will continue the helicopter search. From here to Małdyty, the train passes through forest, and there are a number of abandoned spurs. North from there to Elblag is all farmland. The team should be able to easily spot any sidelined train cars from the air. If and when we find something, we'll reconnoiter." Adamski produced an earbud and a transmitter and held them out to Jordan. "We need to get you linked in on the comm."

The devices he produced were top of the line—a small earbud that fit out of sight and a transmitter that hooked at the waist.

"Anything special about these?" Jordan asked, slipping the device into her ear.

"These are set on VOX, voice operated exchange, so the teams can hear each other at all times." He handed her the transmitter. "We are the white team, the duo behind us is the green team, and the crew in the chopper is the black team. If you need to talk privately, say the word *koala* and switch to channel three."

"Koala?"

"My wife's favorite animal."

She hadn't known he was married.

"Keep the chatter to a minimum. Got it?"

"Got it."

Adamski activated the comms. "Let's take roll call."

Each member of the team sounded off in alphabetical order, each one using a code name starting with the first letter of their last name. Davis sounded off as Deadline.

Adamski signaled it was her turn next.

"Jumper." It was the first thing that came to mind, the closest thing she could think of to floater, which in spy talk meant a person used one time, occasionally, or even unknowingly for an intelligence operation.

"Avatar," Adamski said. "Ready, Jumper?"

Jordan nodded and climbed up into the cab, wishing she had a cooler name.

Both sides of the old Unimog were open, and the breeze felt nice. It was a warm day, clear for a change, with no chance of rain until late afternoon. The trees grew tall on both sides of them, forming a deciduous tunnel over the tracks. They were moving fast enough that it was difficult to scan the woods. Not that it mattered. She was convinced the Russians had already headed north.

"Okay, we're approaching our first spur," Adamski said. "You need to jump off and manually throw the switch."

Jordan looked down. The ground rushed past at approximately thirty-five miles an hour. "Seriously?"

"I'll slow down."

Jordan listened closely while he explained the process. She would manually throw a lever and wait for the tracks to change. Once the Unimog cleared the switch, she would throw the lever back.

"That allows green team to continue on to the next spur," Adamski explained. "They check that one, we check the one after that, and so on. The best anyone could tell me, there are eight or nine sidelines between here and Małdyty. Spurs four and six are heavily used. We're on the clock, so we'll skip them. Are you ready for the first switch?"

"Let's do it."

Adamski braked the vehicle. Jordan waited until they were moving at the speed of a moving walkway before stepping off. Then, running ahead, she flipped the switch. The track rotated, and Adamski and the cart diverted. Once he cleared the switch, she reversed the lever. The track had barely locked into place when the green team cruised past. They repeated the process six times. Each diversion required driving the Unimog forward and then reversing to the main track and proceeding on. Adamski and Jordan were coming up on number seven.

"This is the last one," Adamski said.

She'd been listening to the chatter on VOX, not understanding the language, but by the sense of urgency, she realize that the GROM crew in the helicopter, the black team, had found nothing so far.

"It looks like we're at the end."

"Right," Jordan said.

Adamski checked his watch. "Our two hours are up. Green team, vacate the track."

"Copy that."

Jordan jumped out, flipped the switch, and flipped it back. The trees weren't as dense here. Tipping her head back, she looked up at the sky. That's when she spotted the vultures. They were circling about a mile down the tracks.

"I think we might have found it," she said, pointing out the birds.

"Don't get too excited. This is the country. It could just be a dead deer." She heard the words, but took note of his carriage. He seemed more attentive, leaning into the wheel with a sense of anticipation.

The smell reached them before they rounded the corner. An odor of burned and rotting flesh permeated the air, making it hard to breathe. The refrigerator car gaped open. On the ground in front of it were two large mounds of remains from PR Flight 91. Inside, the two false walls lay haphazardly on top of more piles scraped to the side to make way for two vehicles.

Jordan could see the tire tracks of the trucks marked by pieces of flesh and bone mixed with tattered clothing on the ramps they used for unloading. They had driven over and through the remains of somebody's mother or father or wife or child. Jordan felt her anger swell. What type of men could be so callous, so irreverent? Were they men who believed in a cause? Were they men influenced by greed? Or were they men who blindly followed orders? It didn't matter. She intended to make them all pay.

While Adamski called in the other teams, Jordan took her transmitter off VOX and checked in with Lory and Zhen.

"Let me put you on speaker," Lory said.

"Any luck finding a spike in energy usage?"

"According to the power company, the only oddity was a power outage early this morning that knocked out electricity from Pasłęk to Elblag and towns to the northeast. According to the person I spoke with, the power was out for eighteen minutes thirty-seven seconds, and then it just came back on. They sent two officers out to check on things, but they radioed in that everything was fine. The video was working. There were no cut fences."

"What time was that?"

"Sometime before dawn."

It had to be their guys, thought Jordan. She wrote down the number for the power company and took directions to the substation, though a part of her knew both would be dead ends and they shouldn't waste time. The Russians were moving and would be long gone from the area by now. "Where are the two officers stationed?"

"Pasłęk."

North.

A quick call to the police station confirmed what they'd already pieced together. Then Jordan walked back over to where Captain Adamski stood staring at the piles of remains. His eyes were wet, and she wondered if it was because of the weight of their find or the stench exacerbated by the heat of the day.

He recovered quickly when the green team arrived. Shortly after that, the black team swooped in with the chopper.

Davis walked over and gave her shoulders a squeeze. "Are you okay?"

"Fine." She leaned against him for a moment before pulling away. "Captain . . . I can call you that again, right?"

"We only use code names when we have teams separated in the field."

She told him about the power outage in Pasłęk. "The Russians headed north from here, stopping long enough to charge up the power source for the gun. My best guess is they kept moving in the same direction. Once the sun came up, they would have needed a place to hide. Any ideas?"

"The best place to disappear would be Elblag Upland Landscape Park. It's a protected area—trees, reservoirs, and 134.6 square kilometers of land. We can't cover that much ground in the time we have left. Unless we get lucky, we'll never find them in there."

Chapter 44

Hearing the chopper in the distance, Kozachenko knew time was running out. GROM had been searching all day. He and his men had played a cat-and-mouse game, but now their enemies were getting closer, and time was running short.

They were outside of Nowinka, approximately thirty-one kilometers west of the Russian border. In one hour's time, this would all be done and they would safely be home, provided they weren't discovered.

"Is the gun ready?" He'd asked the question before, and he got the same answer.

"It's ready, Vasyl." Barkov slapped a hand on Kozachenko's shoulder. "Maybe it's time for a shot of vodka."

"We can toast once the job is done," Kozachenko said, shaking off Barkov's hand. "We are not home free yet. We need to keep our wits about us."

"You worry too much, Vasyl."

Kozachenko ignored him and gathered the men. "Up to this point you have done an admirable job. We have one more task, and then we go home to Russia. It is most important that we get the gun back to Kaliningrad, and we all know that the Polish Special Forces will try to stop us." His thought went to the DSS agent responsible for the manhunt. The pakhan indicated she was in Poland, no doubt leading the chase. "Many of you have military training, but these

261

men are like our own *Spetsnaz*. They have better training than you, better weapons. Once we fire the gun, we must move quickly for the border."

Kozachenko outlined the route they would take on the map, then asked if anyone had any questions.

"Won't they already have patrols set up on the major roads?" Yolkin asked.

"I'm sure they will have the guards on alert at the checkpoints, but I know of a crossing place to the north. It's here." He showed the men on the map.

"And what if they catch us?" Celek asked.

"Then Barkov and Yolkin will keep driving toward the border, and the rest of us will stand and fight."

"You want me driving the truck?" Barkov said.

Kozachenko wanted nothing more than to drive the truck himself, but a leader stood with his men. "Yolkin is injured and, next to me, you stand the best chance of reaching the homeland."

* * *

The team dropped Jordan and Adamski at Łęcze, where an armored Range Rover waited for them. Davis stayed with the team on the chopper while they continued their aerial search. They'd switched back to their code names. Avatar (Adamski) and Ratchet, the name of the chopper team leader, were both on VOX. The others could listen but not speak without pushing their transmit buttons.

Jordan tapped the captain on the shoulder. "Avatar, tell your men to keep the thermal imaging camera lens open to its widest aperture. When the gun is fired, it's going to get hot, so hot that it should light up the truck, at least long enough for us to spot it."

"What then?"

"First we get the GPS coordinates of the location for Zhen, and then we go for the Russians. They'll make a run for it. If the team can get eyes on and guide us in, we may be able to stop them before they can cross the border."

At five minutes to 4:00 PM, Jordan got Lory on the line. "It's almost time, sir. Are you ready on your end?"

"As ready as we'll ever be."

She kept the line open as she listened to the voices through the comm. She could occasionally pick up Davis's voice and pictured him happily snapping photographs of GROM in action. Then the urgency of the voices changed. She heard a shout, then Ratchet confirming what she already knew: the Russians had fired the weapon.

"Lory, it's coming," she said. "Tell Zhen! Lory?"

"He's already working on it."

"Stay on the line." Jordan could hear him urging Zhen to hurry.

Ratchet's voice came through the comm. "Avatar, the Russians are somewhere near Nowinka. We're headed there now."

"Roger that." The captain turned to Jordan, throwing the SUV into gear. "Buckle up, Jumper. We're sixteen minutes away, and I plan on making better than average time."

Jordan tightened her seat belt, still hanging on the phone. "Lory, tell me he's found it."

"Not yet, he's still working."

They were two minutes in.

Adamski drove at breakneck speed along the winding country road, sirens blaring. Birch and oak trees whipped past the window, and Jordan found herself hanging on.

"Avatar, we've lost the signal," Ratchet said.

"That's impossible," the captain said. "The heat couldn't have dissipated that quickly."

Jordan shook her head. "Unless they covered the gun. Maybe the tarp has a heat shield? Tell them to keep looking, to look for a cluster of people, several vehicles."

"Lory?" The line was dead. *Shit*!

Redialing his number, she checked the time. They were four minutes in and counting.

"He's still working on it," Lory said when he answered. Jordan's fear climbed into her chest, making her skin tingle.

"We're at four minutes, twenty seconds."

"I know where we are. We're fu—Wait! I think he's got it. Yes, it's locked on!" Lory celebrated, then stopped short. "He says there isn't enough time. It's not going to go far enough out in the gulf. *Fuck.* No!"

"Lory, what's happening?"

Jordan heard the explosion, then the phone went dead. Twisting, she looked out the back window of the Land Rover and saw a plume of smoke rising into the air along the coastline.

"We need to turn back," Adamski said.

"No! We need to stop the Russians from taking the gun across the border." Jordan didn't like not knowing what had happened in Gdánsk. But she knew with no uncertainty that if the Russians managed to get away with the gun, they could back engineer the latest in U.S. weaponry, and the world would be screwed.

The captain pressed harder on the accelerator. The Land Rover picked up speed. "Ratchet, keep eyes on the main road. Use extreme measures."

Jordan felt him brake as they came to a small town, and then he accelerated through a series of S-curves that followed. Time was quickly running out.

* * *

The Russians had gotten out ahead of GROM and made their way north along the Pasłęka River. The road across the border that Kozachenko knew was an old abandoned farm road north of Rusy. From where they were stopped now, getting there posed a problem.

Kozachenko leaned against one tree, Barkov against another, both staring out at the farm fields.

"We'll be out in the open for over three kilometers, then visible along the trees for another one and a half, Vasyl."

Kozachenko looked at Barkov and shrugged. "It's the only way. It's simple. We wait for the air patrol to fly south along the border, and we make our run."

"And if they see us?"

"We shoot them down with an RPG." Kozachenko could see the distaste on Barkov's face. "What? You don't have the stomach to kill a few Poles?"

"I don't have the stomach for going to jail for committing terrorist acts. You can't believe for one second that pakhan can save us if we're caught."

Kozachenko swallowed the sour taste in his mouth. He wasn't used to having his orders challenged; something Barkov had been doing for days. If he were any other man, Kozachenko would have put a bullet through his head by now.

"No more discussion," he said. "We go at dusk."

Chapter 45

Other than the hit on the thermal imaging camera near Tolkmicko, they'd come up with nothing. There was no trace of the Russians. They had moved on, and all available emergency units were being called to Gdánsk. They'd diverted the missile, but it had struck the fuel tanks at the port, setting off an explosion and starting a chain reaction fire. The northern port and inner port were both in flames. Two tankers had been at the docks, along with a ferry and a cruise ship. The tankers had exploded, and the passenger ships were on fire. The number of casualties was still unknown, and the flames were spreading toward the city.

"We've been ordered to return to Gdánsk," Adamski said.

"We can't go back. Not yet. What we have to do is find the Russians." They were parked on the side of the road just outside of town. They were so close. "We need to get the people who did this, so we can stop them from doing it again. If they get across the border with that weapon, this is only the start."

"How do you propose we stop them? We can't even find them."

"There has to be a way." Jordan pulled up a map of Poland on her phone. "What if we map the border? How many roads cross into Russia from Poland?"

"Three."

"What about old crossings?"

"I don't know what you're getting at."

"During World War II, all this land belonged to Prussia. They must have had roads interconnecting the towns with Königsberg, now Kaliningrad."

"Sure, but they haven't been used since the war."

"Are there any parts of the border that are less protected?"

"What are you implying? Our border is secure. We have been fortifying ever since Putin singled out Poland as an enemy." His contempt for the Russian president was palpable. "To protect ourselves, we installed CCTV towers along the entire 232 kilometers, and we fly regular air patrols."

"That's good," she said. "It keeps the Russians out, but does it stop them from crossing the other way?"

That silenced him.

"Heading east puts them north of the Gronowo border check. Have we had Ratchet and the team fly the border from Gronowo to the Lagoon?"

Adamski shrugged. "Ratchet, check the border to the north. Look for old crossings."

While they waited for the team to report, Adamski monitored the activity in Gdánsk via the radio, and Jordan tried calling Lory again. Still no casualty reports. Still no answer.

"There's one," Davis said, his voice clear through the comm. "It looks like an old service or logging road."

Jordan perked up and depressed her transmitter. "Where?"

"Just north of Rusy," Ratchet said. He gave them the coordinates, and Adamski plugged them into the GPS. The monitor showed a thirty-two-kilometer drive, about forty-three minutes away. That would put them there just before dusk.

"We're going to head your way," said Avatar.

"Copy that, but we're running low on fuel."

"Gas up at the border crossing, then rendezvous with us in the north."

Forty minutes later, they pulled into the small town of Rusy, a cluster of seven or eight red-roofed houses with barns. Adamski pulled over to talk to a farmer walking on the side of the road. The conversation was animated, then Adamski thanked the man and rolled up the window.

"They came through about two hours ago," he said. "They're probably across the border by now."

"I don't think so," Jordan said. "Look at the picture." It showed an aerial of Rusy, the forests and the road crossing the border. "The GROM helicopter was patrolling, and the Russians must know about the CCTV towers. They wouldn't want photos of themselves circulating, identifying them as terrorists. They would lay low and wait for dark. CCTV cameras are only good in daylight."

"Our CCTV cameras all have night vision capabilities."

"Even so, they require some light. Until the moon rises, if the Russians drive without headlights, it will be incredibly dark out here."

Adamski drove cautiously around the next curve. The trees were thick on each side, while ahead of them farm fields stretched to another copse of birch and oak. The light had faded. In the middle of the fields, two vehicles and a truck lumbered toward the forest on the opposite side.

Adamski slammed his hand on the steering wheel. "There's no way we can catch them. Ratchet, this is Avatar. How close are you to being fueled?"

"Another ten minutes."

"Hurry. We've found them, and they're making a break for the border."

Adamski started forward, but Jordan reached out and put her hand on his arm.

"Turn right."

Adamski braked to a stop. "The road crosses here and doubles back along the tree line on the other side."

"True, but there are access roads that run along the fields." She showed him the map. "I'll bet there's also a maintenance road that runs alongside the border."

Adamski sat at the intersection. "Why wouldn't they take the shorter route?"

"The longer they remain out of sight, the closer they can get to the homeland. Crossing the fields where they did, at dusk, no one but a farmer or two would have seen them. The good news is it forces them to double back along the tree line. That will take time. We can beat them to the crossing."

Adamski nodded and juiced the accelerator. Jordan felt a surge of excitement. She had no idea what was happening back in Gdánsk or whether Lory, Zhen, and the ambassador were safe, but they had a chance to stop the Russians.

"Go fast," she said.

Adamski wrestled the Land Rover down the path alongside the field. It bucked over rows left by combines, tracked into the ruts, and slid sideways when the tires gripped the road again. Turning left, he started down the eastern edge of the fields, and Jordan looked to see what progress the Russians were making. They were still in sight.

"What's our play?" Adamski asked.

Jordan looked across at him. "You don't have any ideas? I figured you've led missions like this before."

"We're two against a minimum of three, and we know they have weapons."

Jordan estimated the number of Russians higher. There were four men involved in the ambush and at least one person who had remained with the truck. Not to mention they'd had help. More likely they were talking about five to seven armed men. "Do we have any weapons?"

"There are two semiautomatic rifles in the back, and I have my Glock."

Jordan had her 9-mil.

They beat the Russians to the intersection. Adamski parked the truck sideways across the road, making it impossible for another vehicle to pass. He handed Jordan a rifle and took one for himself.

269

"Let's split up and move down the tree line on each side," Adamski said, stuffing ammo into his pockets. They came up with a makeshift plan, hoping that they wouldn't have to implement it before the helicopter came back. "Whatever you do, don't shoot me."

Jordan grabbed a couple of extra magazines and didn't bother to tell him about her sharpshooter medal. In a situation like this, it wasn't apt to matter.

"Ratchet, what is your ETA?"

"We're four minutes out."

Jordan peered down the road and saw the three vehicles moving toward them. They didn't have four minutes. They'd be lucky to have two. She waited for the truck to pull abreast of her hiding place in the woods. Then, executing the plan, she shot out the truck tires on her side and took out the tires on the trailing vehicle before one of the Russians opened fire.

They'd caught the Russians unprepared, but it didn't take them long to regroup. Jordan shot the first man out of the truck. He had a weapon in his hand, which meant he had the potential to kill her. Four men climbed out of each SUV.

"Barkov is down," a man yelled. "You two and you, with me. Flank the shooter. Take him out."

Jordan smiled grimly. This is where she had the advantage. She spoke Russian and had understood every word. Quietly she slipped back into the trees, far enough that one of the men circled around in front of her. She hit him hard on the back of his head between his ear and his spine with the butt of her weapon. He fell at her feet, and she took his rifle. That was two down.

She heard gunfire and wondered how Adamski was faring. Then she heard the whoop of the chopper blades. The reinforcements were here.

The chopper fired a rocket on the truck, exploding it into the air. Through the trees, she watched the gun come apart, then the flash of an RPG bathed the roadway in red. She could see Ratchet's face as he turned the chopper, but he wasn't quick enough. The RPG caught the tail rotor. He immediately powered forward and put the chopper in autorotation. Before he reached the ground, the man holding the RPG reloaded. Jordan took him out and in the process gave away her position.

Spinning toward the men coming in from both sides, she shot one before the other grabbed her gun and used it to throw her. She hit the tree hard. He raised his weapon to shoot, and she ducked sideways. The semiautomatic pummeled the bark near her head. She forced herself to stay completely still. She wanted to look and see if the helicopter had landed safely. She hadn't heard a crash or felt the earth shake. Maybe they were okay.

The shooter emptied his magazine, and she heard him reload and start forward. By the sound of his walk, she could tell he thought she was dead. Without a sound, she slipped her 9-mil out of its holster. Her only chance was to shoot him before he found her pressed up against the tree. She counted to three, spun into his path, and shot him in the chest.

She heard the staccato of his gun as he doubled over, and then he fell backward and hit the ground hard. The gun bounced out of his grasp, and she kicked it away, holding her gun on the man.

He looked up and laughed, blood staining his teeth. "DSS Agent Raisa Jordan, I should have known."

"How do you know who I am?"

"You're infamous. I told the pakhan you were trouble." It was a Russian term for the head of a bratva, mafia. That supported Zhen's account of Russian mafia at the gun sale in China. But the fact that he knew her name gave her the chills. She didn't recognize this man.

His head lolled to the side, and Jordan shook him with her foot. "Who is the pakhan?"

"Among other things, he sent me to retrieve the letter."

A light dawned. He was one of the men who had attacked the ambulance. She nudged him again with her foot. "Stay with me. What did you do with the letter?"

He laughed harder and then coughed, spitting more blood. "It's useless, you know. You haven't changed anything."

His eyes started to glaze.

"Changed what?" Jordan squatted near his head. "What are you talking about?"

But he was gone.

Looking up, she saw the men climbing out of the damaged helicopter. Davis was the last one out. She watched him unfold his tall thin frame from the doorway and scan the crowd. When his eyes landed on her, he smiled. *Thank God*, he was okay.

Before anyone came near her, she checked the pockets of the dead man for the envelope. She found it in his inside pocket, the same pocket where McClasky had carried it. It was open, and she pulled out the paper inside. All that was written on it was a jumble of letters, numbers, and characters. pUrpl3*para5oL.

Was it a password? Maybe a code? Had this man shared it with anyone?

Davis jogged toward her. Standing up, she folded the letter and stuffed it into her back pocket, and then his arms were around her and he was hugging her tightly. "Are you okay?"

"I'm fine." She pressed her cheek to his chest and listened to his heartbeat. "Better now."

Chapter 46

Jordan smiled as she set down the paper.

"You've outdone yourself," she said to Davis. His AP story on the bombing in Gdánsk had been picked up on the wire, landing on the front page of newspapers all over the globe. "Has Lory seen it?"

Davis nodded. "I let him vet it. He didn't want me linking the Russians' gun to a weapons sale in China, but other than that . . ."

The exposé had covered the events of the ten days spent tracking the Russians. He started with Ping's sale of the weapon to the Russian mafia and revealed that Zhen's cousin, Eddie, who facilitated the sale, had arranged to take Zhen's place on the doomed flight. He then detailed the downing of PR Flight 91, the chase through Ukraine and Poland, and the subsequent destruction of the gun. He hadn't mentioned the theft of the plans from Quinn Industries, the CIA's suspected involvement, or that the weapon used in the attacks was a state-of-the-art American-designed railgun. Lory should have been happy.

The rest of his article alluded to the possible motive for the bombing of Gdánsk and the damage. The port was a total loss, as were blocks of the adjacent commercial and residential properties. The explosions from the projectile striking the fuel tanks at the northern port had triggered a chain reaction, the explosions of the two tankers igniting a fire and triggering more explosions. The fires had spread to

273

the cruise ship and ferry docked at the inner port. In all, the attack had claimed 419 lives.

Even though the agreement was ratified and the Western leaders spared, it somehow felt wrong to consider it a victory. Though not everyone felt that way. Chalk one up for the free world.

Jordan looked out at the Mediterranean. She and Davis were in Tel Aviv, sitting on the balcony of her apartment, watching the waves roll in. It was a beautiful day, and a number of surfers and swimmers were out on Dolphinarium Beach. She wondered how long it would take before Gdánskers once more frolicked in the sea.

"I hear Lory took credit for uncovering the plot," Davis said, interrupting her thoughts.

Jordan smiled. That had been their deal. She cared more about the outcome than the glory. "He likes the attention."

"And you don't?"

"Not really." She still hadn't told him all the reasons—the biggest one being that, by all accounts, her father was a Russian spy. And according to Fedorov, he was complicit in creating a society where a few individuals felt they knew what was best for the world. Her fears of a second generation who saw it as their duty to affect some sort of coup would only make Davis laugh.

She looked over at the handsome man staring out at the sea and felt a surge of happiness that he had come to visit. He turned toward her, caught her gaze, and smiled. Jordan looked back at the view.

"Any idea what's going to happen with Zhen?" Davis asked.

"He'll likely walk. Lory's inside man told him that neither the NSA, FBI, CIA, nor Homeland Security have any evidence of the hack, and Ellis Quinn is still denying the security breach. Zhen answered all their questions and gave them enough ammo to question the PO about his involvement with Eddie and how much he did or didn't know about the weapons deals."

"Do you think he'll be fired?"

"More likely reassigned. He's a spy. That's what they do. But even though your article didn't say anything about the CIA and the Chinese likely knew, the PO's cover as chief of station has been publicly blown. He'll be moved stateside and assigned to a desk."

"And what about you?" he asked, moving back into her line of sight. "What are you planning to do?"

"Me? I'm back at work doing what I do."

"Which is . . . ?"

"Investigating a lot of passport fraud, looking for criminals and terrorist trying to forge documents to gain entry to the United States, hunting for fugitives who may have come into or out of Israel." She didn't mention her ongoing covert investigation into her father's past.

"No more law enforcement duties?"

"Not until the next time an American gets into trouble, or causes trouble, or an American politician comes to visit."

"Any free time to take a long weekend in Eilat?"

The invitation came out of nowhere and caught her off guard. This was a man who lived back in the States, while she lived in Israel. Theirs would be a long-distance relationship doomed to failure.

"This weekend?"

"Yeah, if you can take Monday off. Or you could always phone in sick."

She had never played hooky a day in her life, and she wasn't about to start now. But Daugherty had offered her a few days off, his way of rewarding her for a job well done.

"Yes, let's," she said, surprising herself. There were so many reasons to say no, and yet she found Davis hard to resist.

"Oh, before I forget." He reached into his camera bag and pulled out the book Professor Fedorov had given her. "You left this behind in the rental car. It must have fallen out of your bag in the trunk. I meant to give it to you sooner."

She took the small volume, remembering Alena's admonition to let the dead sleep. As she rubbed her hand over the leather cover, she knew her father had just turned in his grave.

Acknowledgments

Like most writers, I couldn't do what I do without my backup team!

My forever love and gratitude to my family, especially Wes, for his unflagging confidence and support, and our kids, Mike, Gin, Cherie, Mardee, Danielle, and Addie, for their continuous encouragement. You all make me feel pretty special, and a lot of times, it was your confidence in me that kept me going. Addie, thanks also for making the trip to Ukraine and Poland with me. Your voice of reason and your adventurous spirit made it a journey to remember.

A debt of gratitude goes to Laura Ware. Thank you for your support—and not just in book sales! I greatly appreciated your help brainstorming, being a sounding board for the good and the bad, and being my biggest cheerleader. It means the world to have you in my corner.

A giant thanks to my critique partners: Don Beckwith, Tom Farrell, Marlene Henderson, Tom Holliday, Chris Jorgensen, Jedeane Macdonald, Mike McClanahan, Bruce Most, Piers Peterson, Suzanne Proulx, and Laurie Walcott, who listened, advised, and dished out endless criticism of my work. You push me, and it's helped me become the writer I am today. And thanks to my Think Tank pals, Kay Bergstrom, Carol Caverly, Chris J., and Leslie O'Kane, for their sage advice and (mostly) good humor about the publishing world.

I would be remiss not to mention the experts who helped along the way: my brother-in-law, Ran, who was a fountain of information on all things trucks; Chris J., for her expertise on China; Russ Mogler and Stacy Santman, for their insider knowledge of all things electrical; and the people of Ukraine and Poland, for their generous hospitality.

I owe a special debt to Peter Rubie, who is as much my friend as my agent; to Matt Martz, Maddie Caldwell, and Sarah Poppe, who edited my manuscript with great care—as always, the book takes better shape under their expert guidance; and to Heather Boak and Dana Kaye, for their efforts in getting the books out to readers.

If I missed anyone, please know it wasn't on purpose. Which reminds me, thanks to my fellow Rogue Women Writers. Together we're making a splash.